THE GIRLS AND THE GOLDEN EGG

PENELOPE BANKS MURDER MYSTERIES
BOOK 10

COLETTE CLARK

DESCRIPTION

Two missing young women…and one discovered Fabergé egg.

New York, 1926

Jack Sweeney, the head of one of the most notorious gangs in New York City, has come to Penelope "Pen" Banks to call in a favor. His seventeen-year-old daughter has gone missing and he wants Penelope to find her.

The next day, Charles Easton, one of the wealthiest men in New York City comes to her with an identical case. His daughter, a flamboyant flapper of the same age, has also disappeared.

A golden egg, which Penelope suspects may be an authentic Fabergé, somehow lands in her possession soon after. It may be the clue that connects both cases.

At least until a dead body is found, one which only raises more alarming questions.

Now, the race is on to solve both cases before it leads to another murder, a gang war, or an international incident!

***The Girls and the Golden Egg* is the tenth book in the Penelope Banks Mystery series set in 1920s New York. The enjoyment of a historical mystery combined with the excitement, daring, and danger of New York during Prohibition and the Jazz Age.**

cially in those inconvenient times of Prohibition. Still, murder wasn't quite as rampant as the less clustered parts of the country would have liked to think. Even then, it was usually some domestic squabble that turned ugly or related to organized crime.

"They haven't released his name, but it says here that he worked for the U.S. Customs Office."

Well, that one was a stumper. Penelope had flirted with the idea that he'd been some highbender, taking bribes from bootleggers to ease the flow of their alcohol into the country. After learning his occupation, she quickly dismissed it. Pen was close enough to the underbelly of that illicit business to know that most didn't bother involving the Customs Department. Why, when it was so easy to simply drive across the border or drift in on a boat under the cover of darkness?

No, that Sorry Sam, had obviously gotten entangled in some nasty personal business. A jealous husband? A jealous wife? A jealous mistress?

But the bit about being roughed up was odd. In a fit of passion, one either threw a few punches or did the deed with a bullet. Why do both in this instance?

At any rate, the feds would probably take the case seriously enough. They typically did when it came to one of their own, poor guy.

Pen quickly scanned the headlines of the *New York Register* in her hands to see if they'd written about it. Her eyes danced across various eye-catching headlines she made a mental note to return to for her own curiosity or light amusement: Mayor Mickey Driver caught at a liquor-infused party with two Ziegfeld girls; A ship with two-hundred and fifty thousand dollars worth of liquor seized after a twenty-mile chase last week; A four-thousand-year-

CHAPTER ONE

NEW YORK 1926

"Any wickedness going on in New York these days, Jane?"

"A dead body!"

Penelope "Pen" Banks quickly lifted her head from her own newspaper to stare at her associate, Jane Pugley. It was morning and they were both in the inner office of Pen's private investigative business, drinking coffee and reading the morning newspapers, as usual.

"You don't say?" Pen remarked, her bright blue eyes wide with interest.

"I do," Jane said, her much softer cornflower blue eyes growing even wider. "They found him in the East River. Apparently, he was caught up on the pilings at Pier 6."

"A dockworker who fell in and drowned without anyone noticing?"

"Oh no, he was shot, and there were signs he'd been—" Jane lowered her voice before continuing. "—*roughed up.*"

"Zounds," Pen muttered, "this city is getting more dangerous by the moment."

New York was certainly a city filled with crime, espe-

old biblical artifact disappearing from an archeological site; A scandal involving a beauty contest winner who'd had to forfeit her hundred-dollar prize.

Her perusal was disrupted by the sound of the outer door opening, announcing they had a new client. Both Jane and Pen perked up and immediately disposed of their papers, putting on a professional facade. Jane leaped from her seat and headed toward the front office to greet their guest.

Penelope waited, wondering if this would be another missing pet, thieving maid, or cheating husband. By now, she was starting to become a name in the private investigation business. She still worked at a nominal rate for those who desperately needed help. Frankly, after her last serious case, she would welcome the respite of a fairly simple, non-violent investigation.

"Miss Banks," Jane announced, walking back in, the epitome of professionalism. "I have a Mr. Sweeney to see you."

"I'm sorry, who?" Pen asked, sitting up straighter in alarm.

"Jack Sweeney," the man himself repeated, walking in past Jane with a dark smile on his face. "I'm here to call in that favor you owe me, Miss Banks."

CHAPTER TWO

"Heads will roll, and I don't mean that figuratively, Miss Banks," Jack Sweeney said.

"Hopefully, we can find a solution to your problem before you have to resort to the guillotine," Penelope replied with a forced smile.

Mr. Sweeney did not return one, forced or otherwise.

Penelope had thought she would regret using the help of the head of one of New York's most notorious gangs in her last murder investigation. She'd already had a tenuous relationship with him prior to that, mostly from her days of illegally gambling with cards to earn money in the kinds of places that encouraged such illicit activities. She had helped him with a morally ambiguous case back then.

Oddly enough, it seemed he had a perfectly legal and legitimate case for her to handle. Even Detective Richard Prescott, the man she was involved with, couldn't find fault with her taking this one on. Well, he could, but he couldn't claim it was tied to any of Mr. Sweeney's illegal activities.

Penelope cast a quick look at Tommy Callahan standing behind him to the left. He was one of Mr. Sweeney's most infamous henchmen, even though he was probably only thirty. He was the one Pen was more familiar with, always at the Peacock Club, which was still a favorite haunt of hers.

Tommy's piercing eyes were as hard as the emeralds they resembled, and his sharp, dangerously handsome features were pulled so taut she felt herself go tense waiting for him to snap.

Which did nothing to settle her unease.

Jane sat at her desk behind them, staring in awe. She'd met Tommy before, but Mr. Sweeney was a rare vision, enough to inspire a sense of danger by his mere presence.

"Just to review, your oldest daughter, Kathleen Grace Sweeney, has disappeared and you would like me to find her?"

"That's the gist of it."

"How old is she?"

"Seventeen."

"I see."

Not *quite* old enough to strike out on her own. Still, certainly old enough to want out of the prison her father probably kept her in. Pen was twenty-five, older than his daughter but still young enough to remember what she was like at that age, especially with an overbearing father.

"Has it occurred to you that she might have run away?"

"Katie knows better."

"I remember my own father saying the same thing. That never stopped me from escaping his prison."

"Your father ain't me."

"You'd be surprised how much you two have in common, including a daughter you underestimate."

"As much as she would like to think it, my Katie ain't like these modern girls. Flappers they call 'em, the kind that disobey their parents. She's a good Catholic girl who knows better. Yes, she may act out every once in a while. That's to be expected at that age, but she always comes home. Seventeen may be old enough for girls down on Bowery Street to act older than their age. But we're talking about my daughter, not some cheap little—"

"Mr. Sweeney, I have to ask that you watch your language around Jane and me. This is a respectable business."

"Respectable business, huh?" He chuckled. "I seem to recall the days you weren't involved in such a *respectable* business."

"Even back then gentlemen knew how to watch their tongue around me, and if you hope to avail yourself of my services then you'll do the same."

He studied Penelope, not happy. "If I was you, I wouldn't mistake me for a gentleman, Miss Banks. Any other woman who talked to me that way would get a firm reminder of who I am. Besides, you owe me."

"We both know I'm well aware of who you are, Mr. Sweeney, and that I owe you a favor."

"Then you know when I want something, I get it."

"Did your daughter learn that same lesson?" Pen arched an eyebrow.

Mr. Sweeney's brow furrowed in anger. "I beg your pardon?"

"I have a sneaking suspicion that living with you might be fairly stifling, since you're so quick to remind women of who you are. Even those who, as you put it, know better."

He narrowed his eyes. Behind him, Tommy twisted his lips into a wry smile. Penelope wasn't sure if that was out of respect for her standing up to his boss, or at the punishment she'd get for standing up to his boss.

"You got a real smart mouth on you. I guess with five

million in the bank, you think you're safe from the likes of me, huh?"

It didn't surprise her that he knew exactly how much she'd been left last year by Agnes Sterling, a family friend of her dearly departed mother.

"Have I said anything that you haven't already suspected yourself?" Penelope said, trying to sound confident, even though she was well aware of the danger she was sinking further into. Still, if she was going to find this girl, she didn't want his pride masking important information.

Instead of answering, Mr. Sweeney reached into his pocket and pulled out a cigar case. He selected one, then gestured with it. "You mind?"

"I'd rather you didn't."

A low chuckle escaped his lips before he cut the end, planted it right between his lips, then lit it, despite her objection.

Penelope's mouth tightened, but she saw Tommy in her periphery just barely shake his head, telling her to leave it be. As if she was stupid enough to do anything else. Pen's eyes narrowed slightly as he exhaled a cloud of smoke.

Jack Sweeney's eyes were a much colder shade of blue than hers, a hue that could send a chill through the sun itself. They were set in a face that had once been handsome but a life of sin had taken its toll. The broken nose and scarring just above his right eyebrow and left cheek reinforced the rumors that he had started out as a boxer and literally fought his way to a top position in the criminal underworld. His ruddy complexion and fair, ginger-hued hair reflected the Irish heritage he liked to promote even though Penelope had it on good authority it was his grandfather who had originally traveled across the Atlantic from the Emerald Isle.

"Dare I ask if you've informed the police?" Penelope continued dryly.

"The people who need to know, know."

Pen wasn't sure what that meant, but she figured he had several members of the police department in his pocket who were working on this as well. They obviously hadn't gotten results so far, otherwise, he wouldn't be in her office.

"When did you last see Katie?"

"Yesterday, at Sunday dinner. She wasn't in her room this morning and didn't show up to school today."

So recent? It was rather surprising that he'd call on Penelope the very next day. Perhaps he didn't want his friends on the force to know about this. Or perhaps there was another reason?

Maybe he was just taking advantage of the favor she owed.

"Do you have a picture of her?"

Mr. Sweeney snapped his finger behind him and Tommy instantly produced a photo from the inside pocket of his suit. As he slid it across the desk a subtle smile touched his lips.

When Penelope's eyes landed on the girl, she understood why.

"*This* is your daughter?" Pen was almost daft enough to cough out a laugh.

In the photograph, Kathleen Sweeney smiled back angelically, a dimple in the left cheek. She wore a simple white dress with a modest, lace, sailor collar. A cross, presumably gold, with her Christian name inscribed on it rested innocently against her chest.

Penelope recalled a far different version of the girl. With her brain's ability to remember things like a photograph, that image was even clearer, in vibrant colors. That

Katie Sweeney had the same blonde wavy bob. She also had a blur of red lipstick, sharply heeled shoes, and a fringed red dress shimmering under the lights of the Peacock Club as she danced the Charleston—and minutes later when she was dragged out of the club by Tommy.

"Why is it you've come to *me* for this, Mr. Sweeney?" Penelope asked, studying him with a piercing look. She considered herself a good investigator by that point, but he had the money and resources to hire someone with far more experience and access. Penelope wasn't exactly persona grata with the NYPD, save one detective.

"You're a broad."

"I beg your pardon?"

"Sorry, a *lady*," Mr. Sweeney said with a half-cocked smile.

"I see," she said tersely, then paused to study him even more, weighing what she was going to say next.

Mr. Sweeney stared back, his cold blue eyes daring her to speak.

"Here's what I think. I think your oh-so-obedient Katie landed herself in trouble with you recently and you decided to lay down the law much more harshly than you ever have before. I think she figured she was already close to eighteen so why not escape while she could, if only to end the prison sentence?"

The lips surrounding the cigar curled up on one side as he stared back at her. Then, he pulled the cigar out and slowly exhaled a long white cloud of smoke.

"Her clothes, shoes, even what little makeup and jewelry I allow her to wear, are all still back in her room."

That was interesting, but Penelope had an idea that didn't mean much considering what she knew of Kathleen Sweeney.

"Besides, with what money would she have plotted this escape, Miss Banks?"

"You didn't give her an allowance?"

"Only enough to see a picture show, or buy a pretty dress at Neiman Marcus."

"And I assume she didn't have a job."

He just stared back, no comment, which told her enough.

"Perhaps she met an older man who—"

"Let me stop you right there, *Miss Banks*. Out of consideration for the, uh, *delicate sensibilities* of you and your assistant—"

"Associate."

"I won't go into detail as to what would happen to any man that got ideas about my Katie in that way. The last name Sweeney would have stopped them dead in their tracks. And I do mean dead."

"Right," Penelope said, casting a reassuring look toward Jane, who had just gone deathly white.

"You're friends with that girl who sings at the Peacock Club, ain't you? What's her name?" Mr. Sweeney snapped his fingers back toward Tommy.

Pen felt her breath stall and her gaze sharpen at the sudden detour.

Tommy was the one to answer, his voice void of any emotion. "Lucille Simmons."

"Ah yes, Lulu, right?" Mr. Sweeney cocked his mouth into a half-grin, his taunting eyes trained on Penelope. "I'm not dumb. I know, on occasion, my Katie broke out of her prison—a prison plenty of girls in this city would happily be stuck in, mind you—and escaped to the Peacock Club. She liked listenin' to Lulu sing. Katie had aspirations herself, not that I would ever let her get anywhere near the stage of some jazz club. Still, maybe Lulu knows something about what happened to her. What do you think, Miss Banks?"

Penelope considered Lulu a good friend. She'd been the one to help guide her through the world of illegal gambling when Penelope had first been cut off by her father over three years ago. Lulu had even helped out on a prior case or two. Pen was certainly closer to her than anyone in her own social set.

And Mr. Sweeney darn well knew all that.

"Is that a threat?" Penelope asked, sitting up straighter and glaring at him.

"Not at all," Mr. Sweeney replied in a deceptively placid tone. "I just think she could be helpful. Now that I think on it, I think she should *definitely* be a part of this case. In between her performances of course. I'd hate to do something to interfere with her career, something that made it so she never sang in this city again."

That was most definitely a threat. Mr. Sweeney knew he couldn't do much to Penelope because of her social status. Lulu, on the other hand, was an easy target, and not just because of her race.

All the same, now she'd have to take this case. Lulu had been there for her all those years ago. Pen wasn't about to abandon her when her livelihood—or worse?—was at stake.

"Fine, I'll take on your case," Pen said in a terse voice. "Just be forewarned, I will try my hardest to find your daughter, as much as I would for any other client, even without the threat. But I can't promise anything, Mr. Sweeney. I'm not a miracle worker."

He paused, taking a puff of his cigar, before nodding ever so slightly.

"I'm also *not* in the business of helping women get kidnapped, even by their own fathers. If I find her and she doesn't want to come back, the best I can do is let you know she's safe."

A slow grin spread his mouth. "She'll come back if she knows what's good for her."

"That's up to her."

"We'll see about that."

"Or I could just inform the police?"

He belted out a laugh. "You do that and see what happens."

Penelope swallowed, but made sure to keep the fear from showing on her face. Jane already looked like she was about to melt into a puddle at her desk.

"Then it's settled." Another humorless smile touched Mr. Sweeney's lips. "Anything you need to find her —*anything*—you got it. I'll leave Tommy here to work as an...advisor."

Penelope knew exactly what that meant. He'd be an enforcer more than anything else. Her eyes met Tommy's. What tiny inkling of goodwill there had ever been between them disappeared under his hard, green gaze. She knew where his loyalties would lie.

Mr. Sweeney stood up and tapped the ashes of his cigar into her wastebasket before walking toward the door. With his back still to her, he left one final warning. "I expect to have my daughter back before Friday at noon, Miss Banks."

It was late Monday morning, which gave her most of the week to work on the case. When he opened the door and left, the air in the room seemed to lift only slightly.

Tommy took the chair Mr. Sweeney had just vacated. Without asking, he took a cigarette pack from his pocket, pulled one out, and lit it.

Penelope gave him a studying look. "Now then, Tommy, why don't you tell me what's *really* going on?"

CHAPTER THREE

At first, Tommy's only response to Penelope's question was a cool look and a long drag on his cigarette. Then he spoke.

"You know everything you need to know about this case."

"I'd rather have *all* the facts at hand so I know exactly what I'm working with. Especially with so many threats being thrown around. I'm sure Lulu would appreciate it as well," she hinted.

Something in his eyes hardened only briefly before they cooled again. "If I was you, I would stop askin' questions you know I can't answer and start looking for Katie."

She considered him for a moment. She had one trump card in her hand and that was the time to use it.

"How long have Lulu and you been together?"

Behind Tommy, Penelope watched Jane's jaw drop open in surprise. Tommy was placid as ever, studying her with a glint in his eye.

"What makes you think I have anything to do with Lulu?"

"Oh for heaven's sake, it's been obvious for quite some time now. Honestly, I'm surprised it's taken me so long to finally put it together. The way you two bicker and banter, you're like an old married couple. Frankly, she's the only woman you let talk to you in a certain way. That sharp tongue of hers cracks your facade like an egg." Pen gave him a coy smirk. "You only ever offer a genuine smile when she's around."

There was something in his eyes that sent a ripple of concern through Pen, warning her that she might have overstepped. She realized it wasn't anger in his gaze but worry. She'd never seen Tommy worried. Which only proved her theory true.

"Mr. Sweeney knows as well," she warned him.

Tommy cursed under his breath and dropped his eyes to the cigarette in his hand, concentrating hard. Pen gave him a moment before she spoke up.

"Why do you think he brought you here and made you stay to help work on the case? That threat to Lulu wasn't just for my benefit. Now, do you want to tell me what Mr. Sweeney didn't want to?"

He focused on his cigarette, so long Penelope wasn't sure he had heard her. Just when she was about to repeat the question, he answered.

"I assume you know the Messina family?"

That question didn't bode well. Pen nodded.

"Tino Messina, the youngest, he's suddenly gone missing as well."

Pen coughed out a laugh of incredulity. "Is this some gang war you've got me in the middle of? Kidnapping each other's children?"

"No." Tommy was not a man of words, but that was enough an answer. Not that Pen necessarily believed it.

"Well, it's obviously related, don't you think?" Her tone was patronizing, but Tommy let it slide off him with an idle shrug.

"Is he the same age as Katie?"

"Eighteen, and I know where you're headed." He chuckled. "It ain't that either."

"Why? Because he's a Messina, and neither father would allow it? I assume you've heard of Romeo and Juliet?"

Tommy laughed again and shook his head. "Let's just say, there are certain rumors about Tino that tell me he ain't the marrying kind. Too flowery, if you catch my drift."

That did put a question mark on things. Still, it was too much of a coincidence for Penelope to ignore.

"Do they know each other?"

Tommy shrugged. "They've met over the years."

Penelope considered it in light of things. Perhaps Tino wanted to run away as well. She figured that a boy who "wasn't the marrying kind" would have had a tough existence growing up in the Messina family. She had yet to meet a gangster who was accepting of "flowery" boys or men.

"Is there any *other* relevant bit of information you can tell me?"

"Only that the clock is ticking, so I suggest you get started doing whatever it is you do."

Penelope stared at him, knowing there was more to this. She gave up, realizing he certainly wasn't going to tell her. She might as well work with what she had. She'd worked with far less before, and the answer might eventually present itself.

"Fine then, I suppose that means starting with the obvious. I need to inspect her bedroom."

"Her room? We already went through it with a magnifying glass. Nothing there."

Penelope gave him a sardonic smile. "Any girl wily enough to escape the confines of a man like Mr. Sweeney wouldn't be the kind of Dumb Dora to leave something blatantly incriminating in her own bedroom. Besides, I'm specifically looking for what *isn't* there as much as what is."

Tommy gave her a questioning look.

"You did tell me to focus on finding Katie, no? This is an important part of that. So, are we going or not?" Pen said with impatience.

"Yes, ma'am," he drawled before rising.

As Pen rose, she turned to address Jane. She was still recovering from such an unusual morning—which was saying something, considering the past year working for Penelope.

"Jane, I need you to check the newspapers over the last few days. Look for anything that might involve organized crime." Pen shot Tommy a sour look. "I have a feeling we haven't been told nearly everything that's going on."

───────

The Sweeneys lived in an impressive mansion on Riverside Drive. The stately appearance belied the dirty money that had been used to buy it.

The front door was opened by a man in a suit, too casual and gruff to be a butler. The two silently nodded at one another as Tommy breezed in ahead of her. He cast a more wary look at Pen, but said nothing as she followed Tommy inside.

Tommy led Penelope to the living room where a woman

sat in a chair looking out the window. She could see a mild resemblance to Katie in the light hair and rounded cheeks.

Somewhere in another part of the house, Pen heard the muted sound of children running and shouting, unconcerned about what may have happened to their older sister.

"Mrs. Sweeney," Tommy said in such a respectful and considerate manner, Penelope had to turn to make sure it had actually come from him.

"Oh hello, Tommy," the woman said in a distracted way as she turned to face them. There was a deep crease of worry on her pallid face. Penelope instantly felt a pang of sympathy for her. Despite whatever her husband was, she was still a mother with a missing seventeen-year-old daughter.

"This is Miss Penelope Banks, a private investigator. She was hoping to have a look-see to figure out where Katie's gone?"

Her eyes flitted to Penelope, a look of confusion on her face.

"Tommy's right, Mrs. Sweeney. I've worked on cases like this before." Pen only hoped this one didn't turn out as unfortunate as those had. "Could I see Katie's room? I think there may be clues there to help me find her."

Mrs. Sweeney breathed out an exasperated laugh. "I've torn that room apart already and found nothing."

"A second pair of eyes, maybe from someone not as close to Katie might see something you didn't?"

She sighed forlornly and nodded. She rose from the chair to guide them upstairs. Along the way, they passed several more men in suits. All of them were tense and on guard, as though they were soldiers preparing for battle.

Pen hoped, for the sake of New York, it wouldn't come

to that. She didn't particularly like the fact that the Messina family might be involved.

An older maid in uniform had just finished tidying up the room when they arrived. She reminded Pen of a schoolmarm or governess, which had probably given Katie all the more reason to want to leave. She silently nodded, a stern look on her face as it landed on Penelope, then slipped out of the room as they entered.

Pen was instantly struck by how girlish the room was. The walls were a soft baby pink. Too many pillows with too many ruffles covered the canopy bed, also in pink. The furniture was all white, matching the gauzy curtains on the windows. It certainly maintained Katie's good-girl image, no doubt for her parents' sake.

Penelope started with the closet. It was large enough to walk in, as befitted the princess of a wealthy gangster. It was also filled with the kinds of clothes that would have made the average overly sheltered young girl green with envy. The wardrobe was quite fashionable, lace and chiffon in pretty pinks and yellows and baby blues in a variety of styles, all of them appropriate for a good Catholic girl. Katie was obviously quite spoiled in this area. There was even an entire wall dedicated to shoes.

She turned to find Tommy and Mrs. Sweeney studying her with questioning looks.

"There isn't a missing suitcase, I presume?"

Mrs. Sweeney shook her head. "We would have noticed."

Pen nodded and left the closet to walk over to the dresser. She pulled open the top drawer to find it almost full of Katie's underthings. The white cotton intimates had been rifled through. That was understandable. Many girls kept their secrets hidden amid their most private things, knowing most people might be too embarrassed to explore. *Most people* were unaware of just how cunning the average overly sheltered girl could be. Still, as Pen opened the other drawers, containing long, cotton nightgowns and opaque stockings, she was gleaning a few clues.

She walked to the vanity in one corner near the window. Sitting atop were a variety of creams and lotions, bath water, hair barrettes, and even some baby pink lip color.

"I think I have a better picture," Penelope finally said.

"Of where she is?" Katie's mother asked, her voice filled with incredulity, but tinged with hope.

"No, I'm sorry." Pen turned to give her a sympathetic smile. "I need to explore a few more places first."

"Where? I can't think of any place or anyone we haven't already visited."

"Who is her closest friend?"

"Moira Mahoney. She claims to know nothing. My husband has already spoken with her."

I'm sure he has, Penelope ruefully thought to herself. He probably scared the poor girl half to death while he was at it. She cast a quick look to Tommy whose only confirmation was a slightly raised brow of acknowledgment.

"I may pick up on things your husband missed. Tommy, do you have her address?"

"I do."

"We should go. After all, time is of the essence."

Mrs. Sweeney's look of confusion was even more pronounced at this point. "That's it? One quick look through the room and you're done? Even Jack's own men did more than that."

Pen stared at her, realizing there *was* something more she could discover while she was here. "When was the last time you personally saw Katie?"

"Yesterday evening. I came in to wish her goodnight before bed."

"What would you say your relationship with your daughter was? Had she grown distant as many young people do? Was she likely to confide in you? Were you strict or permissive with her?"

A mild smile came to her face. "I was more indulgent with Katie than Jack was. I know what it's like to be that age, and keeping girls on a short leash only leads to trouble. If Jack had his way, she would have been in a convent until marriage. I at least allowed her to go out at night, supervised of course. To her friend's house, or the movies, or a play."

But certainly not to the Peacock Club. Again she glanced at Tommy who gave absolutely nothing away this time.

"Was something different or odd about last night? Did she say anything unusual, or look at you differently? Give you any clue something was wrong or had changed for her?"

Mrs. Sweeney fervently shook her head. "No, everything was fine last night. We had our usual Sunday dinner. She read a book in the library, then played some records in her room. When it was time for bed, I said goodnight and kissed her cheek as always. I don't understand it! She's still just a girl, she shouldn't be out there on her own!"

She broke out in tears, burying her face in her hands.

Tommy gently put his hand around her shoulder and whispered something to her. He turned his head and gestured to the maid. She hurried to gently escort Mrs. Sweeney away.

When she was gone, he turned back to Pen. "So, did you find anything?"

"As a matter of fact, I did." She walked past him down the stairs. "Let's go visit Moira."

Once outside, he pressed her again before opening the car door for her. "You going to tell me or not?"

"I should keep it to myself, see how you like being left in the dark."

"That wouldn't be very productive, Miss Banks."

Pen ignored the threat in his voice. "It's what I *didn't* find."

"What does that mean?"

They were far enough away from the house that she felt comfortable speaking frankly.

"That room up there was the bedroom of a good little Catholic girl. Pretty, demure dresses in soft colors. Innocent stockings and nightgowns."

"And?"

"We both know that isn't Kathleen Grace Sweeney."

"And?"

"I didn't see a low-cut red dress with fringe, no spiked heels, no red lipstick, no black silk stockings."

"Okay, okay, I get it. So she was obviously hiding them someplace else."

"Considering the number of goons lurking about, and a maid who probably doubles as her prison warden, it's definitely not anywhere in the house. Her best friend should know more."

"Mr. Sweeney already—"

"Please, Tommy," Penelope interrupted, giving him a scolding look. "We both know how Mr. Sweeney handled it, something akin to a bull in a china shop."

He exhaled and nodded. "Okay, yeah he may have been heavy with the girl."

"And probably terrified her into silence while he was at it. That's going to make it that much more difficult for me to get anything out of her," she snapped. "But if anyone knows what happened to Katie, it'll be her best friend. So let's go."

CHAPTER FOUR

MOIRA MAHONEY'S FAMILY LIVED IN A VERY NICE brownstone on a quaint street on the Upper West Side. Nothing so lavish as the Sweeney's mansion, but the Mahoney's were certainly more than comfortable.

It was late enough that Moira would be home from school. The door was opened by a man who immediately gave Tommy a hard look. He was large with muscle that had long ago softened into something that could probably still throw a decent punch. Tommy, taller and much leaner by comparison, simply stared on with a look that was almost bored with indifference.

"Now you listen here, Tommy, my Moira already answered all of Mr. Sweeney's questions before she left for school. I won't have any of you bullying her anymore."

Before Tommy could browbeat his way past the front door—though in his case, he'd be more likely to offer some quietly sinister threat—Pen stepped in.

"Mr. Mahoney, my name is Penelope Banks. I'm a private investigator," she said in her most appeasing tone. "I'm here to follow up with a few questions, no bullying involved. In fact, Tommy is going to wait outside the entire time."

She turned to give him a pointed look. She could see that he didn't like that, but he offered no protest. Instead, he leaned back against the stone railing abutting the steps.

"I don't know," the man said, giving Pen a wary look. "She's still in a state from earlier."

"I'm sure she is, but I imagine Mr. Sweeney only acted out of concern for his daughter. He's very sorry about over-stepping."

The man snorted and glared at her, as though wondering if Penelope thought he was stupid enough to actually believe that.

"However, his daughter is still missing. If your Moira disappeared, wouldn't you want to talk to her best friends?"

"You think he'd let me near his precious Katie? It ain't fair, I tell you."

"I realize that, but what about Moira?"

"What about her?" he asked, suddenly wary.

"Don't you think she wants us to find out where her best friend is? I'm sure she's in a state of worry just as Katie's parents are. Maybe there's something she forgot to tell Mr. Sweeney earlier. I can help her remember. I promise you, I'll go gently with her."

He worked his jaw, obviously still filled with resent-ment. One quick dart of the eyes to Tommy, and he knew he had no choice.

Pen gave Tommy a warning look to stay outside. He returned a cool, sardonic smile, but stayed put, pulling his pack of cigarettes out to smoke another.

Moira was in the parlor with her mother. The poor girl looked up with a terrified gaze. Pen noted that she was exceptionally pretty. She had the kind of sloe eyes starlets and models dreamed of, framed by thick lashes. Her brunette hair was long, gathered in back with a ribbon, leaving tendrils surrounding her heart-shaped face. Her parents probably hadn't let her cut it into the modern bob her friend had. It was a reminder to Pen that these girls weren't as mature as they probably thought they were.

"Hello Moira, my name is Penelope Banks. I'm a private investigator hired to find out where Katie is. Do you think I could ask you just a few questions?" Pen's eyes flitted to her mother, who placed a firm hand on her shoulder. Pen added, "Alone?"

"Absolutely not!" her mother said almost before Penelope could finish asking. Moira flinched, and Penelope was almost certain she would break out in tears.

"Mrs. Mahoney," Penelope said gently, offering an accommodating smile. "I don't work for Mr. Sweeney. I'm independent, and he doesn't pull any of my strings. I'm just trying to find a missing girl."

"Then you'll do it in front of me," she insisted.

Penelope sighed and tried to catch Moira's eyes. Something passed between them, a silent communication that only girls who knew how to sneak out of their bedrooms at night without getting caught could understand. For once, Penelope's meddlesome nature in her youth—and perhaps even in more recent years—was coming in handy.

"It's fine, Ma," Moira said, sagging underneath her mother's grip. Her mother wanted to protest further, but Moira wriggled from beneath her hand and stood up. "I'll be fine, really."

"I promise I won't do anything to cause her any more stress," Penelope assured her mother in a soothing voice.

"Let them go, Bess," Moira's father said in a resigned voice.

Her mother didn't look happy but she didn't argue further.

Moira led Penelope up to her bedroom and closed the door. She fell onto the bed with a heavy sigh. Penelope wasn't sure if it was out of relief or exhaustion. After a moment, she sat up and swung her legs over the side. Pen walked over to sit next to her. Now that she was this close, she could see a spray of freckles across her nose that she hadn't noticed before. It made her look even more young and vulnerable, and yet even lovelier.

"They'll be listening at the door so don't speak too loudly," she said in a whisper.

Pen smiled and nodded. "Where did Katie keep her clothes, the ones she wore to the places her father didn't want her to go?"

Moira sucked her bottom lip in and reached up to fiddle with the gold cross around her neck as she considered whether or not to tell Pen anything. The cross matched Katie's, also with her name inscribed into it.

"We kept them at the school we go to, St. Mary's. There's an old building there. It used to be a stable or carriage house or something, but now they just use it for storage. In the upper part, no one even goes there. It's musty and falling apart. That's where we keep all our things, the makeup and dresses and shoes we don't want our parents to find."

Penelope couldn't help a grin. Moira sheepishly matched it with one of her own. It quickly faded.

"But I checked there today when she didn't show up to class. Katie never skipped school unless she was sick; the sisters are such *gorgons* about that. She didn't look sick at Mass yesterday, so I knew it wasn't that. I thought maybe she had skipped school to do something special, and I wanted to see what dress she had decided to wear. But all her things were gone, every bit of it!"

"Which was a surprise to you?"

Moira nodded furiously. "I mean, she always talked about leaving home for good. We had a plan in place and everything. But she wanted to wait until she was eighteen. She figured the studios in Hollywood wouldn't hire her until then."

"She wanted to be an actress?" Penelope said with a smile.

"Yes, we both did. Her mother thought all the dance lessons were just a hobby. A safe enough thing to keep her out of trouble."

"What about acting classes?"

"Oh no, her parents would have never allowed that. Dancing is respectable. But acting is for—" she blushed before continuing. "You know."

Penelope had an idea, and bristled a bit. Her mother had been a performer, back when such a thing was probably even less respectable than it was gradually becoming, what with film and all.

"We just enjoy watching the pictures so much, and both of us perform in plays at school. Our teacher says we have natural talent." Her cheeks flushed in a pretty way. Penelope could see both Katie and Moira as film stars. Katie would be brash and bold. Moira would be the beautiful ingénue.

"So you and Katie planned to leave at some point?"

"We were saving up to get on a train and go west."

"So maybe something happened to speed up her timeline? Had some man offered her a role in a film perhaps?" It would be easy enough to prey on the hopes and dreams of some poor girl with stars in her eyes.

Moira looked momentarily upset about that idea, then shook her head to dismiss it. "No, she would have definitely told me something like that. Katie liked to show off a bit. Besides, we had planned on going *together*. I turned eighteen last month and waited for her, so I don't understand her leaving already and without me."

"And you both had to finish school, of course. You should be done in a month or so, no?"

"Well, yes, that too." She gave Pen a sheepish look that told her finishing school was a secondary thought to the dazzling dreams of getting to Hollywood. "But either way, Katie won't be eighteen until September. I agreed to wait until we're both old enough to go to Los Angeles together. That's why I'm sure something must be wrong."

"What about Tino Messina, do you know him?"

"Yes, Mr. Sweeney already asked me about him. He was supposed to come with us when we went to Hollywood. He had no interest in his father's business. He's much more passionate about plays and performing, like Katie and me."

"Were they a couple?"

Moira laughed and shook her head. "He's handsome enough, but I don't think he's interested in Katie. I think he's a bit...that way? Katie and I never minded. He's very sweet and really funny."

"Right." So that confirmed what Tommy had said. It was no Romeo and Juliet situation. "Did anything seem to be amiss the last time you saw her?"

"No, Miss Banks. We talked as usual Sunday after Mass, making plans to—" She shut up, all of a sudden.

"It's okay, Moira. If it isn't relevant I have no intention of telling your parents or Mr. Sweeney anything. I used to sneak out when I was a girl so I'm certainly not judging."

She smiled. "We planned to go to the speakeasy again."

"Again?"

"We went Friday night. A friend of Katie's from dance class told her about it. It's in the basement of a barbershop, George's Barbershop, just off Bowery on 4th Street. Katie has a crush on the boy who works sweeping up the shop."

"So Katie knew this boy before you went on Friday?"

"I don't think so, at least she didn't act like it. I only saw him from the other end of the bar, but he was an absolute sheik. I guess that's why she left me alone to go talk to him," she said with a frown of disappointment.

"Do you know what they talked about?"

She shook her head. "No, I was too far away to hear them."

"How long was she with him?" This was a promising lead.

"They disappeared out to the back with another couple to go...neck," Moira said, blushing furiously. "Katie liked to show off about all the boys she did that with."

"Including this one?"

Moira nodded, then reached up to fiddle with her gold cross. "She made fun of me because I'd only ever let a boy kiss me, maybe put his hand on my thigh. She said once I got to Hollywood, I wouldn't survive. But I don't think that's what a producer would expect me to do just to be in a movie, not if I'm good at acting, would he?"

Pen figured there were plenty of men in Hollywood who expected just that and more, and would be happy to take advantage of two naïve eighteen-year-old girls fresh off the train.

"There's nothing wrong with waiting until you're ready," Pen assured her, then added for good measure, "There's also nothing wrong with doing what you want to when you feel you are ready, even if some people tell you it's wrong. These are modern times, Moira. Women can have just as much fun as the boys. Just be careful about it."

Moira giggled with embarrassment and twisted the ring on her finger. It was silver with two hands holding a heart with a crown above it.

"That's a pretty ring."

"Claddagh ring. We begged our parents to get them for us when we turned sixteen." Moira's eyes dropped to hers. "Katie's is gold with an emerald heart. She likes to move it to her left hand when we go out because she says it makes us seem older, but kept boys from going too far. I always told her that only makes boys think she's taken, but she said it didn't really count if the heart is pointing out."

"What does that mean?"

"Engaged not married, which would still be cheating I think. But maybe not in the eyes of the Church. Pointing inward is a sin, we figured."

"Do you have a name for this boy at the speakeasy?" Penelope asked, getting back to her investigation.

"Christos. I don't know his last name."

"And this girl from her dance class who told her about this place, do you know her name?"

"She never told me who it was."

"And Sunday, after church, you two made plans to go back?"

"Yes, even though her father was being an absolute tyrant lately. She got caught going to the Peacock Club again. Even *I* wouldn't go there with her. I told her it was too risky. It was hard enough sneaking out on Fridays. Her parents always thought she was spending the night here. But why would she talk about going back to the speakeasy if she was making plans to leave?"

"I think maybe some opportunity presented itself." Or

perhaps Katie just wanted to throw even her best friend off the scent of what she was planning. "Can you think of what might have suddenly happened to give her the money she needed? Something she might have hinted at?"

She lowered her eyelids and shook her head. "No, as I said, she would have told me. Katie never did anything without making sure everyone knew about it. Everyone but her parents, that is." Tears began to fall from her eyes. "Do you think something terrible happened to her, Miss Banks?"

"I don't know, but I do plan on finding out, Moira. Who knows, maybe you'll get a postcard from California in a week or so?" she offered with an encouraging smile.

Moira laughed a little and wiped her eyes, looking back up at her. "I hope that's it. I—I would have told Mr. Sweeney, you know, about the stuff hidden away at school, and the speakeasy, but I didn't want to get her into trouble, just in case. We just liked to dress up and have fun sometimes, act like real flappers. That's all."

"How did she get the money for those clothes?"

Moira swallowed hard. "She stole things, from shops and such. Things she either wanted or thought she could sell for money. Sometimes she just stole money from her parents. She'd go into her mother's purse or her father's wallet. He's always leaving it in his office and he carries so much of it." Her eyes went wide. "Oh Miss Banks, you can't tell Mr. Sweeney I said that. You can't!"

"I won't," Pen said. By now he surely must have known. Katie seemed the crafty sort, so she had probably started small, with amounts he wouldn't notice were missing. Whatever she took prior to the night before, it must have been big enough to fund a life in Hollywood, or at least get started on one.

At least now Penelope had a vague idea of what Mr. Sweeney had been keeping from her.

"I just know something terrible has happened," Moira continued, tears coming back.

"Actually, it might be a good sign that her things are gone. It means Katie left willingly and took them with her." And wherever she went, she wasn't interested in looking like a good Catholic girl.

"So you think she's okay?"

"I plan on finding out. Can you think of anything else that might help me find her? Her parents just want to know that she's okay, Moira."

"If I knew where she was, I'd tell you, Miss Banks, honestly!" She looked on the verge of tears again.

Penelope smiled and put an arm around her. "Thank you, Moira, you've been very helpful."

"I just want to make sure she's okay."

"So do I."

Pen waited for her to wipe her face before she dug into her purse and pulled out a business card. "This is in case anything else occurs to you."

Moira nodded and took it, reading it with curiosity. "You're really a private investigator? All on your own?"

"As I said, these are modern times. A woman can do almost anything."

Moira smiled with delight, then quickly stuffed the card into a drawer in her bedside table.

Pen rose to leave. She wasn't surprised to find Moira's mother lingering in the hallway just outside her bedroom when they opened the door. She looked perfectly unapologetic about trying to eavesdrop on what was said. For Moira's sake, Penelope hoped they had kept their voices low enough for her not to hear. She had an idea there would be an entirely different look on her mother's face if she *had* heard.

"Thank you for allowing me to talk with your daughter, Mrs. Mahoney."

She narrowed her eyes in response and gave one quick nod, obviously eager to have Penelope out of her house. Pen accommodated her by doing just that. Mr. Mahoney was standing watch near the front door, as though worried Tommy on the other side might try to break it down.

"Thank you, Mr. Mahoney."

"Well...good luck to you then," he said gruffly, though she could see the tiniest bit of empathy in his eyes.

Back outside on the stoop, Tommy was settled back on the stone railing, smoking. He removed the cigarette from his mouth when Pen exited the house, the door firmly closed behind her.

"So?" he asked giving her a piercing look.

"How do you feel about getting a haircut?"

CHAPTER FIVE

GEORGE'S BARBERSHOP WAS ON THE GROUND FLOOR OF an apartment building four stories high. Like many first-floor commercial establishments, there was a basement level with a separate entrance opening up to the sidewalk, which most businesses used for storage. Since there probably wasn't much in the way of storage for a barbershop, the owner had seen the value in taking advantage of Prohibition and the wave of illegal drinking establishments that sold overpriced drinks.

Or perhaps some enterprising gangster had coerced them into using the otherwise wasted space for such a venture.

Either way, at that time of day, before the sun set and the fun started, the barbershop was still doing business in the perfectly legal establishment on the first floor. Tommy and Penelope arrived before the after-work crowd, so the seats were only half-filled when they walked in.

It wasn't hard to identify the boy Moira was talking about. He was the only young man with a broom, furiously sweeping away the hair that fell to the floor around each seat. When he looked up at the sound of the new arrivals, Penelope could see why Katie was so smitten. Christos was indeed an absolute sheik.

If Penelope had been five years younger she would have swooned right then and there. Christos's eyes were a mesmerizing mix of blue, green, and violet with lids that seemed permanently lowered with seductive intent. They were situated on either side of a long, noble nose. He had a jawline that could probably slice both bread and granite. His lips were full, almost pouty, and Pen could just picture how enjoyable they might have been during a session of necking for young Katie. His hair was cut in the style popular with young men, shaved closely on the sides, long and combed straight back on top. One dark strand fell into his face, most likely by design. When he eyed Pen, the only woman in the establishment, he made a show of flicking it back as he assessed her, eyelids sinking even lower.

Unfortunately, her gaze lingered long enough for Tommy to catch on that he was the target of their little adventure. Pen had told him all that seemed relevant without getting Moira into trouble. Namely that Katie had taken her to a speakeasy underneath this barbershop on Friday. Blessedly, he didn't ask too many questions. Tommy wasn't the talkative type.

But he was the dangerous type.

"You, with me, now." Rather than wait for Christos to even ask why, Tommy strode over and grabbed the boy by the collar of his shirt, and dragged him toward the entrance. The broom fell with a bang.

Everyone reacted at once.

"Tommy!" Penelope protested.

"Aye, what are you doing with my son?" A man yelled in accented English.

The other barbers were almost as vocal and the clients rustled with dismay in their chairs. Tommy ignored them all as he led the boy out like a dog being dragged away by its collar.

"Let him go, *now!*" Penelope demanded once they were outside.

Tommy lost some of his steam and released the boy. But his expression was menacing enough that Christos remained frozen in place.

The door opened and the boy's father stormed out, ready to unleash his own bit of steam.

Tommy stopped him in his tracks with nothing more than words. "I work for Mr. Sweeney. I know what kind of business you're running in that basement there," he pointed to the closed double doors on the sidewalk, "which means you know who he is, even if he ain't running things in this part of town. You interfere with this, and getting caught by the police will be the least of your worries."

The man seemed perfectly torn now. The urge to protect his son conflicted with the knowledge that causing trouble might make things worse for both of them.

"I just need to ask a few questions, that's all," Penelope assured him in the same patient tone she had used with the Mahoneys. "Tommy's not going to hurt him."

The man, presumably George of the business's name, worked his jaw, and glared at Tommy, then his son (probably knowing he was a troublemaker) before escaping inside. She heard the sound of his accented voice trying to reassure the customers and his barbers that everything was fine.

"Did you have to rush in like a bull going up against a matador?" Pen snapped at Tommy.

He leaned in closer and met her with a steady gaze.

"We need to find Katie by Friday, Pen. I'm just makin' sure that happens."

"I can handle it from here," she said.

Tommy seemed ready to argue, but relented, realizing that Penelope had gotten them this far. He steeled his gaze, tilted his head, then backed off, though only a few steps.

The boy had remained perfectly silent through the entire ordeal. His cunning gaze had bounced back and forth between both parties, already sizing up the situation. By the time Penelope focused on him, he was completely closed off, a guarded look on his face. It was the act of someone who was used to getting himself into, and more importantly, out of trouble.

She sighed, realizing she would have to chip away at his resolve with a bit of direct talk. Working with Tommy Callahan, and Mr. Sweeney by proxy wasn't going to be easy.

"Christos?"

"Yeah," he replied, all bravado and defiance.

"And what's your last name?"

He hesitated before answering. "Papadopoulos."

No wonder that hadn't been included in the shop name. Greek by the sound of it.

"Do you know a girl named Katie Grace Sweeney? She was here Friday night. And by here, I don't mean getting a shave and a haircut."

"I'm not too good with names," he said, though she could see the flicker of fear and surprise flash across his eyes when she said the last name, Sweeney. He didn't have the accent his father had, so he'd probably been born in New York and toughened by the city since birth.

"Oh, yeah?" she retorted, mimicking his tone. "That's odd because your father seemed quite familiar with the last name, so I'm guessing you are too. If you still want to plead ignorance, I'm sure *Mr.* Sweeney will be happy to make an introduction, and it won't be a fun one."

That instantly erased the facade.

"On the other hand, you can answer my questions, truthfully and honestly, and neither you nor your father will have to worry about him darkening your doorway."

"I swear, I didn't do nothing with no gal who goes by the last name Sweeney. Or the first name Katie, for that matter. What am I, stupid?"

Penelope didn't bother answering that question.

He exhaled and pushed back his dark hair. "Friday? I suppose, yeah, I was with a coupla gals. I didn't exactly bother with last names, you know?"

Tommy stepped forward and pulled out the photo of Katie. "This girl, she look familiar?"

He glanced at the photo and instantly averted his eyes. "Nah, she don't look familiar."

Penelope sighed. "I used to play poker for a living and you know what I've noticed?"

"What's that?" Christos asked, eyelids lowered to reflect his feigned disinterest.

"When someone is lying, their eyes shift in some way at the exact moment the lie escapes their lips. A blink, a dart to the side, an eye roll, something like that."

Suddenly his eyes were wide open, trained hard on her. "I've never seen the girl, okay?"

"Then there's that."

"What?" A wrinkle of worry.

"When they're doubling down they keep those eyes focused on you, like a snared rabbit trying to ward off a predator, not realizing they've already been caught."

"Well, buggerydo, lady, maybe I should just keep my eyes shut all the time, elsewise I'd always be caught lying."

"I was you, I wouldn't make light of this, boy-o," Tommy said in a dangerously low voice.

"You're not in trouble. Mr. Sweeney doesn't care what you did with her in the back alley."

"Hey, wait a second!" He put his hands up defensively, panicked eyes darting to Tommy. "I didn't do anything with her in no back alley."

"So you *do* know her?"

"I..." he blinked realizing he had set a trap for himself. "Okay, yeah she was there. I talked to her and that's it. But she said her name was Stacy, not no Katie, certainly not Sweeney."

"Stacy? What the hell kinda name is that?" Tommy asked.

"I thought it was strange too, but that's what she told me it was."

Penelope had never met a Stacy before. She wondered what was the significance of choosing such a unique fake name, especially for a girl. Was it because it rhymed with Katie?

"But you went outside with her at one point?" she prodded, getting back to the point.

"Again, just to talk."

"How stupid do you think we are?" Tommy said.

"Not stupid at all," he replied, looking him right in the eye. He turned his direct attention back to Penelope. "She and this other girl I was sitting with, they spent the whole time at the table yammering about girl stuff." He rolled his eyes.

"Who was this other girl?"

"Some girl named Anna," he said, making a point of staring hard at Pen. "I didn't get a last name."

"Had she been in here before?"

"Maybe, I don't keep track."

"Can you think of any reason why Katie might have picked this place out of all the speakeasies in New York?"

At first, Christos looked offended, as though she'd insulted the establishment. Then, he rolled his eyes to the side and smirked. "Nick, the front guy ain't too concerned about age."

"Did the two of them know each other beforehand?" Pen wondered if it was the girl from Katie's dance class.

"Not from what I saw."

"What does she look like?"

"Blonde, blue eyes, pretty enough," he shrugged again and gestured to the photo Tommy still had in his hand. "They could have been sisters. I guess that's why they got along so well from the start. Anna was already with a guy named John when she asked if I wanted to join the table. I think she was trying to make him jealous." He offered a wicked grin.

"And then Katie came over and approached you?"

"Yeah. She asked my name, flirted some. Then she and Anna got to talking. They went on about her dress and that got them going. At least until she suggested we go outside to the back, because there were so many people it was getting kinda cramped. I wasn't about to argue. Only as soon as we get out there, they get to talking again. I shoulda known, Catholic girls only let you go so far anyway. I got as far as a kiss before she shoved off. Me and the other guy eventually gave up and went back inside."

"How do you know she was Catholic?"

He chuckled. "I saw her taking off that cross around her

neck as she walked up to the table. The ring too. I've known enough Catholic girls in this city to know what those mean. I took it as a good sign. I guess I should have known better."

"Was Anna Catholic as well?"

He smirked. "Nah. But all the same, she wasn't going no further than that Stacy was. I think they really did just want to talk."

"What did they talk about?"

"Like I said, girl stuff. Clothes, jewelry, hair, actresses, makeup, shopping—girl things." He rolled his eyes with disdain.

"What was she wearing?"

"Which one?"

"Both of them, I suppose."

"Anna? Some swanky silver number, all sparkly and whatnot, and a silver thing wrapped around her head."

"And what was Katie wearing?"

"Blue, like silk or something. And a black feather in her hair."

Another dress Pen doubted she would have found in Katie's closet.

"What kind of blue? Baby blue? Peacock blue? Cornflower blue? Royal blue?"

He gave her a bewildered look. "I dunno, *blue*. Medium blue, I guess?"

Penelope gave up. "Anything else?"

"Other than the coats they came in wearing?"

"Tell me about them."

He sighed as though next she'd ask him what perfume they had on. "Anna's was a fur, brown. Don't ask me what kind of brown, just brown. Katie had a black coat, wool I think, with a bunch of feathers sticking up around the collar."

"And was there anything special about their makeup?"

"Like how?"

"What was each girl wearing?"

Now, he looked even more bewildered. "Um, lip stuff, I guess? I got it on my lips when I kissed Stacy. It was red."

"And Anna?"

"Same."

"Has Katie been back since then? Did she say anything, anything at all about leaving home? Running away to Hollywood? Talk about her upcoming plans?"

"No, nothing like that at all. And I haven't seen her since then."

"What time did she leave that night? Was it with Anna?"

"She left about one in the morning with that gorgeous friend of hers who stayed back at the bar. A real Sheba, that one; even at a distance I could see that much. I wouldn't have minded her joining us." He grinned and waggled his eyebrows. "Anna and John stuck around for a while, but left soon after. I found another gal to dust off with."

Penelope couldn't think of anything more to squeeze out of him. "Okay, you can go back inside."

He cast a quick, wary look Tommy's way before quickly rushing back into the barbershop.

"So, what do you think? Who's this Anna?"

Penelope said, nibbling on her lower lip. "I'm almost certain she's the girl from Katie's dance class who told her about this place. But it's odd they would pretend not to know each other."

"What do you think that means?"

"I'm not sure yet. Either way, I suppose we won't know until we talk to her. We need to call Mrs. Sweeney and get the name and address of this dance class."

"The Parisian Dance School? It's closed on Mondays."

"How do you know?"

"I had to drive Katie there a few times, make sure she was actually going to class and not someplace else," Tommy replied with a disgruntled twist of the lips.

Penelope imagined playing nanny and chauffeur wasn't exactly what he'd signed up for when he joined Jack Sweeney's gang.

"In that case, I suppose it's time we give Lulu the bad news."

CHAPTER SIX

PENELOPE HAD HOPED THAT VISITING MOIRA, THEN Christos, would shake loose an obvious clue that would help Penelope discover Katie's whereabouts before they had to tell Lulu about Mr. Sweeney's threat. Sadly, she was even more confounded than ever.

There were still several hours to go before the Peacock Club officially opened for business. Monday would be a slow night, but establishments that quenched the illicit thirst of a drink-happy public always did brisk business no matter what day of the week it was. Even better if they provided entertainment at the same time.

Lucille "Lulu" Simmons was usually a Thursday to Saturday act, but Tommy had somehow gotten in touch and told her to meet them there before the club opened.

The mug who was guarding the door, looking ten times more threatening than an ogre, humbly nodded when they entered. One thing about working with Tommy was that he had a way of making everyone exceptionally polite.

Lulu was already sitting at a table in the empty club having a drink. The look on her face when the two of them approached indicated it was strongly needed. She probably knew trouble was brewing. Penelope wondered just how much Tommy had told her when he called.

Pen usually saw Lulu in the evenings at the Peacock Club. It was rare to see her in a day dress, but she wasn't surprised to note that it was as fashionable as her evening clothes were. She had a fox stole wrapped around her to beat the mid-March chill. The dress underneath was indigo silk with a deep purple brocade lace overdress. It ended with a rippled hem that showed off her long brown legs almost to the knee. Now that Pen knew about Lulu and Tommy, she wondered if he was the one buying her such nice clothes. But no, for as long as she'd known her, going on almost five years, Lulu had been dressed to the nines. Surely they hadn't been together that long without her knowing?

Penelope felt rather stuffy by comparison in her dress with a large dot pattern and long puffed sleeves. It had a pleated skirt and ruffled bib, which had seemed rather smart in the office that morning.

"Tommy Callahan and Penelope Banks. The two of you coming in together can't be anything good."

They joined her at the table. "How much has Tommy told you?"

"Only that you both needed to meet with me."

Penelope cast a brief look of irritation at Tommy then turned back to Lulu, who didn't look happy. "You know how you always wanted to be involved in one of my cases?"

"I don't remember putting it quite that way," Lulu said in a cautious tone.

"Well, now you are," Penelope said trying to sound optimistic.

"That does nothin' to ease my mind, Pen."

"I can see that. There *is* something to be said for having a say in the matter." Pen was hoping Tommy would be the one to step in and relay Mr. Sweeney's subtle threat, but he seemed content to maintain his usual silence, only talking when necessary.

"Are either of you going to tell me what this case I'm supposedly working on is?" Lulu's dark, cat-like eyes danced back and forth between the two of them.

Tommy sat back and pulled out another cigarette to smoke, making sure to exhale away from Lulu, perhaps to protect her singing voice. He always did that. A subtle act of consideration Pen should have picked up on earlier.

"I suppose I'll be the one to tell you," Penelope said testily. "It's Jack Sweeney's daughter. She's gone missing and he's hired me to help find her."

At the name, Lulu went visibly tense. "And this concerns me because...?"

"He seemed to have reason to believe you might...help things along."

Lulu narrowed her eyes, which slid back and forth between the two of them once again. "Did he?"

"It's because of me," Penelope said apologetically. "I owe him a favor."

"Really?" Lulu said, one side of her mouth curled up with a half-smile, not entirely believing her. She slid her eyes to Tommy. "And this one is here because...?"

"He's an *advisor*," Penelope said, drizzling sarcasm all over the last word.

Lulu coughed out a harsh laugh. "Considering Tommy is the reason she's probably gone, I fail to see what he'd have to contribute."

"Criticism will get you nowhere, songbird," Tommy said, grinning around his cigarette.

Lulu glared at him. "Just how did my name come up in all of this?"

"She knows about us," Tommy said around his cigarette, his eyes stony.

"You told her?" Lulu exclaimed.

"I guessed," Pen said apologetically. "And...well, Mr. Sweeney knows too."

Lulu's expression went slack, and her face became a few shades paler. She fell back into her seat and took hold of her glass, finishing the contents in one swallow.

Tommy snapped his fingers at someone behind the bar as he studied her. A moment later a man scurried over to refill her glass.

"I'll take a bourbon, the good stuff." Tommy turned to give Penelope a questioning look.

"I'll take gin. I don't care if it's the good stuff." Sometimes the not-so-good stuff was poisonous enough to strike exactly the right note.

The man simply nodded and scurried away.

Waiting until he had disappeared in the back somewhere, Lulu spoke.

"Just how entangled am I in this business?"

Pen hesitated to answer, but Lulu wasn't dumb. Her smarts are what had helped Pen out more than a few times. She exhaled, a crease of worry coming to her brow.

"That bad, huh?"

"He only threatened to keep you from singing here... and anywhere else in New York."

"Only," Lulu repeated softly with an ironic chuckle, as though Pen had suggested she was under threat of being cast into hell.

"But that's not going to happen because Pen here is going to find Katie before our deadline," Tommy said, staring at Lulu but speaking in a tone reserved solely for Penelope.

"That's right," Pen said, also in a voice reserved for him. She softened it when she addressed Lulu. "I already have a few leads."

The man came back with their drinks, making sure to bring the entire bottle of bourbon and an empty glass for Tommy. Penelope took a long, grateful sip of her gin. It was indeed the good stuff, going down quite smoothly.

"What is it you need from me, Pen?" Lulu asked, reserving all her venom for Tommy from behind her drink as she took a sip.

"Can you think of where Katie might be? Or why she would have decided to leave home now, before she even turned eighteen?" Penelope asked, getting them back on track.

Lulu shot Pen a wan smile. "So Kathleen Grace Sweeney finally ran away from home, then."

"How do you know she ran away and wasn't kidnapped?" Pen asked.

"Who would be stupid enough to do that? The fact that she's Mr. Sweeney's daughter aside, I pity the fool that has to keep watch over her. I ain't never met such a headstrong girl in my life, and I say that knowing both myself and you, Miss Banks," she said with a teasing smile. It disappeared quickly. "Besides, that girl's been itching to leave since she learned how to sneak out of the house at night."

"And you know all this because...?" Penelope was now even more alert.

"We've both seen her in here," Lulu said, giving her an exasperated look. "Before Tommy finally snatched her right out, she'd try and sneak her way to me, pestering me to teach her more about what I do, asking me if I had any connections in Hollywood. As though I'd know about that. Someone convinced her that movies would eventually have sound and singing would be a part of the game. She wanted to make sure she had all the talents necessary."

"I suppose any advantage would have helped. She's pretty, but there are probably a thousand girls just as, if not more pretty in Hollywood hoping to be a star."

Lulu just arched a brow as she took another sip.

"Did she ever mention a girl named Anna? Maybe someone from her dance class?"

Lulu laughed. "We didn't exactly have long confidential conversations, Pen. I knew better than to get myself too *entangled* with that girl. You see the mess she's gotten me into without even trying."

"Well, we can sit here drinking and fretting about it or we can work on finding out where she's gone. We only have until noon on Friday."

Lulu coughed out a sharp, angry laugh. "Delightful."

"Let's start by asking what caused her to leave now, all of a sudden," Pen said, just to shift the conversation to something more productive. "It seems Tino Messina has also fled. We should assume they're together."

"Did you say, *Messina*?" Lulu asked, giving Pen an incredulous look.

Pen flashed another apologetic smile. "Oops."

"Oops is right. I swear, if I could go back in time, I'd oops that little girl's behind right into—"

"Now, now, this isn't productive. The good news is, she had a stash of clothes hidden which is now gone, so that suggests she left willingly."

"And just where did you pick up that little nugget, Pen?" Tommy asked, though the cunning look on his face told her he already knew she'd learned it from Moira. She certainly wasn't going to tell him about Katie's stealing habit.

"I learned it from someone you aren't going to bother again, not as long as I'm on this case," she warned. "In fact, we run this case my way. I won't have you or Mr. Sweeney's men terrorizing anyone who can help us. Believe it or not, it can do more harm than good."

"So long as we find her in time, I don't care," Tommy said.

"Neither do I," Lulu said.

Penelope nodded. "Now then, Moira also said Katie *had* planned to leave when she turned eighteen, that they were going to go out to Hollywood together. But her birthday isn't until September."

"So what made her decide to move up her exit date?" Lulu asked

"Either an opportunity she couldn't pass on or some threat. I'd put my money on the former. There aren't too many people who would go around threatening Jack Sweeney's daughter. So what lucrative opportunity or buried treasure did our future starlet come across recently?" Pen asked, mostly thinking out loud.

"Her daddy does own quite a few lucrative businesses around town. Maybe the girl decided to go into the family business?" Lulu said, giving Tommy a sardonic look.

"Open her own gin mill?" Penelope offered, not serious.

"Hell, she probably has more connections than her father when it comes to friends with money. He probably has her spending time with the Astors and Vanderbilts."

"I can tell you firsthand that New York's elite are probably more criminal than Mr. Sweeney," Pen said with a laugh, realizing the gin was getting to her head.

She cast a quick look Tommy's way, hoping this bit of

uncensored talk wouldn't make it back to Mr. Sweeney. He stared at them with his standard placid fare.

"No, our darling Katie wouldn't have the patience for all that nonsense. Besides, it's hard to run a speakeasy when you're trying to make it big in Hollywood," Lulu pointed out. "Still, she isn't foolish enough to head out to California on a wish and a dream. No, what your girl had was a stroke of luck. One thing you can say about her is, she knows how to take advantage of every opportunity."

"It would have to be big enough for Tino and her to get a train to Los Angeles, and live for a while, until they landed roles," Pen said thoughtfully.

"So, we focus on finding out what this golden opportunity was," Lulu said, with a wave of the hand. She arched a brow Tommy's way. "Care to help us gals out, Tommy? You'd know better than anyone what she may have stumbled upon."

Pen was surprised to see a mild wrinkle of consternation in his brow. The cigarette in his hand was burning down to ash as he held it mid-air, studying them both more intently.

"Tommy?" Pen urged.

"I need to make a phone call."

He shot out of his seat and stabbed his cigarette into the ashtray. He gulped down the bourbon left in his glass and practically slammed it back down onto the table, before walking off.

The two women were left in stunned silence.

"What was that about?" Penelope finally asked.

"I have no idea."

"He's been keeping something from me, I can tell. I can't do my job if I don't have all the facts," Pen said, feeling irritated once again.

"I know better than to coax anything out of him when it comes to Mr. Sweeney."

"I suppose I might as well use this time to tell you what I've learned so far today." Pen told her everything about that day's adventures, including the bit about Moira saying she stole things even from her parents.

"That little devil," Lulu said, not without a trace of amusement. "Do you think that's it? She stole something big this time?"

"Big and illegal, more illegal than usual for Mr. Sweeney. Otherwise, why wouldn't he tell me? It's not as though I don't already know about his criminal livelihood."

Lulu began to nibble her bottom lip with worry. "I don't like this, Pen, not one bit."

"Neither do I. But, at the very least, our only job is to find Katie, safe and sound. If we happen to stumble upon her source of money, then so be it."

Lulu sighed and sipped her drink. "I suppose I'm coming into work with you, then."

Penelope brightened up. "It'll be fun, just like old times."

"Not exactly," Lulu said, pursing her lips.

"Nonsense, you were always good at scoping out the cat with the biggest pockets, this may end up being the same thing. You have a good nose for people. You might find private investigating grows on you, Miss Simmons," Pen said with a smile.

"I tell you one thing, when we find Little Miss Sweeney, I'm going to be the first one to give her a good spanking, all this fuss she's causing."

"I'll be right behind you."

They both laughed, tapped their glasses together, and drank.

Tommy came back out, looking even more stone-faced than usual. "This case is temporarily on hold."

"What?" Both of them exclaimed at once.

"You heard me. Neither of you does anything, *anything*, to try and find Katie until you hear from me."

He left, once again leaving Lulu and Pen in stunned silence.

"Perhaps this means you no longer have to worry about Mr. Sweeney using you as a pawn?"

A humorless smile appeared on Lulu's face. "I know Tommy too well. He was worried, which is a rare thing. If anything, I'd say things suddenly went from bad to worse."

CHAPTER SEVEN

"Penelope, you're here early," Jane greeted the next morning when Pen arrived. She had finally become comfortable calling Penelope by her first name. Considering Pen was going to be Jane's maid of honor in a few weeks, that was a good thing.

"Yes, it seems we are currently without a case once again...at least temporarily speaking."

"You found Katie?"

"No, but it seems Mr. Sweeney isn't all that keen on me finding her anymore."

Pen suspected it had to do with the conversation between Lulu and her the day before. Something they'd said had led to Tommy's phone call. Katie's sudden windfall was apparently dangerous territory. It made Pen all the more curious as to what it was.

Was the secrecy to protect him or to protect Katie? Perhaps someone else?

"At any rate, that leaves us free to peruse the newspapers and discuss your wedding. I think it's a grand idea to keep it small and informal, but I do wish you'd let me splurge a bit. What good is my money if I can't spoil my friends?"

"Penelope, you already paid for our honeymoon in Paris *and* my beautiful dress."

"Well, your parents wouldn't!" It had been enough of a burden just to get her awful (at least in Pen's mind) parents to agree to attend. They hadn't particularly liked Jane's first husband and they turned their noses up at the idea of a second marriage. "Besides, there's no reason you and Alfie should start your happily ever after in debt."

"As you said, it's small and informal. It's all settled. Everyone I like and care about will be there. I'm just happy to finally start my life with Alfred."

"Yes," Pen said wistfully.

"Speaking of relationships..." Jane began. She bit her lip and colored a bit. "Are Lulu and Tommy really...?"

"It seems so, and right under my nose!"

"Do you think she'll bring him to the wedding as her guest?" The idea seemed to thrill Jane. "Wouldn't that be something for my parents to behold! They'd never speak to me again."

Pen's mouth hitched up on one side in amusement as Jane actually laughed over the idea of it. She really was a changed woman from the timid little thing who had come into Penelope's office only a year ago.

"At any rate, if there's no wedding talk to be had then let's see what scandals await us in the newspapers. I'd like to see if that mayor I voted for is up to any more delightful shenanigans."

Before Penelope could make it to her desk, she heard the front door to the office open. She looked at Jane and lifted her brow in surprise. Since she was already standing she took it upon herself to greet their visitors. Perhaps it was

Tommy coming to tell them he had been given permission to start investigating again.

Instead, the door was opened by a young man, followed by an older man. Both wore expertly tailored suits and sported serious expressions.

"Miss Penelope Banks?" The younger man greeted. "My name is Barton Tyrell, I'm the personal secretary of Mr.—"

"Charles Easton," Penelope finished for him. She never forgot a face or a name.

Charles Easton was a bona fide shipping tycoon. Seeing him in her office, presumably to hire her, was even more surprising than seeing Jack Sweeney had been the day before. Pen at least had some connection to Mr. Sweeney. Mr. Easton was more likely to consort with Penelope's father, with whom she still had a rather tenuous relationship.

Mr. Easton was the success story that American dreams were built on. He was the son of a tea and coffee merchant who had been very comfortable, but not quite wealthy. Charles used his knowledge of international trade to build a shipping empire which had made him one of the wealthiest men in New York City, if not the country. He'd married late in life, to a much younger debutant that bore him one daughter before she drowned in a sailing accident in Newport.

"Won't you please come in?" she said, putting on a professional smile.

Jane was already out of her seat when they entered. "Can I get you tea or coffee?"

"Coffee please, black," Mr. Easton said, taking the seat at Penelope's desk.

"I'll have the same, with milk if you have it," Mr. Tyrell said, taking the other seat.

"Of course," Jane said.

While she made their coffees, Penelope took her seat behind the desk opposite them.

"I have to say it's a surprise to see you in my office. While I'm certainly good at what I do, I didn't imagine my praise had reached your ears."

He studied her, the expression on his face becoming even more severe.

"So, how is it that I can help you, Mr. Easton?" Pen asked.

"My daughter, Amethyst, has gone missing," he replied in a brusque tone.

Jane had just walked in with their coffees, and she started enough to have both cups jostling on their saucers. She collected herself and handed them to each man, catching Penelope's eye with a look of surprise as she did. Pen subtly arched a brow in return, before giving her attention to both men.

"Missing, you say?"

Mr. Easton nodded to his secretary, who procured a photograph of his daughter. Not that Penelope needed one.

Amethyst Easton was a constant fixture in the society pages, usually involved in something harmlessly scandalous. After a year as a private investigator, Penelope saw the value of *occasionally* perusing the gossip rags. The last antic of Amethyst's had been frolicking in the Bethesda Fountain in Central Park at midnight fully clothed.

It would seem Amethyst's latest misadventure had landed her in slightly more trouble than usual, and someone had taken her. Unless she too had willingly run away from home.

Once again, the photo presented a far tamer image than what Penelope knew of the seventeen-year-old girl. In it, Amethyst was wearing a formal gown and posed with a demure smile toward the camera. She had blonde hair, a shade darker than Katie's. She also had eyes that were a light color, presumably blue. Otherwise, her features were sharper, making her look slightly more sophisticated than Katie, who still had remnants of a babyface.

"I presume you want to hire me to help you find her?"

"I do."

Penelope sat back and considered Mr. Easton before responding. This case was too coincidental to be anything other than connected to Mr. Sweeney's. Two daughters missing? Both fathers, prominent in their own way? And both deciding that Penelope Banks of all people should be the one to find them?

"Have you gone to the police?"

His secretary and he exchanged glances before he responded. "I have alerted the proper authorities."

Not exactly a yes or no. Penelope figured pressing the matter would lead to even more ambiguous answers or him completely shutting down that line of questioning.

"Why is it you've come to me specifically?"

"I'm going to be perfectly frank with you, Miss Banks. Certain information has come to light that leads me to believe that my daughter's disappearance may be entangled with another of your cases."

Penelope's mouth hitched up on one side. "Which case is that?"

"There's no point in being coy, Miss Banks. We both know you are working with Jack Sweeney, whose daughter has also gone missing."

Zounds, how the heck did he know that?

"Why do you suppose the two cases are connected?"

"I've questioned friends of hers who mentioned that Amethyst and this—Katie? Kathleen?—had only recently become friendly with one another. I can't imagine what they could have in common. I learned from certain members of the police department, that she too had gone missing. I naturally concluded it was related."

"Does your daughter take dance lessons at the Parisian Dance School?"

"Yes, I was told that's where they met. What do you know about it? Does it have something to do with my daughter? What have you learned?"

"Not much yet," Penelope said thoughtfully.

At least now she knew which girl from Katie's dance class told her about the speakeasy.

This also meant Katie already knew "Anna" when they met at the speakeasy. So why pretend they didn't know each other? And why the fake names?

"I think you need to tell me everything you know Mr. Easton."

He narrowed his gaze. "What is it *you* know? Tell me now."

Before Penelope could tell him that wasn't exactly how things were done, the door to the outer office opened. The newest arrival breezed in.

"Well, I'm here. I suppose we should—" Lulu, who Penelope had urged to come in the day before despite Tommy's warnings, stopped short when she saw there were two men in the room with Jane and Penelope. "Oh, my apologies."

"This is Mr. Easton and Mr. Tyrell," Penelope said.

"And this is a *private* meeting," Mr. Tyrell said, giving Lulu a dismissive look.

"This is one of my associates, Lucille Simmons," Penelope said in a curt voice. "She's helping me with a case, the very one you seem to be interested in."

Mr. Tyrell looked ready to argue on his boss's behalf, but Mr. Easton waved it away.

"Never mind that, if it's regarding the Sweeney girl, then she can stay. Perhaps the more minds working to find my daughter, the better. Considering some of the activities Amethyst got up to, this Lucille—"

"Miss Simmons," Penelope corrected.

His mouth tightened before continuing. "*Miss Simmons* may be useful in this case."

Miss Simmons remained in the doorway, looking as though she would have preferred being unceremoniously dismissed. With a subtle nod from Penelope, she walked over to take the chair next to Jane's desk. Lulu gave Pen a quizzical look. She returned one that said she would explain later.

"I haven't agreed to take your case, Mr. Easton," Pen reminded him. "And until *you* tell *me* what *you* know, I can't. Furthermore, I would assume you'd expect me to extend you the same courtesy of discretion that I do my other clients."

His mouth tightened with displeasure. Mr. Tyrell looked no less displeased. Whether or not they got up and left would tell Penelope more than enough. He had come to her for a reason, after all.

Mr. Easton relented, offering one sharp nod. "You've no doubt read about some of my daughter's exploits in certain papers like the *New York Tattle*. I've done what I can to try and control her. I'm a devout Christian, so I thought a mandate that she attend church with me every Sunday would help curb her wanton ways. Unfortunately, she was left a decent sum from my beloved wife who died so tragically. I can't keep her under lock and key all day and night. As you probably know, I have a business, an *empire* really, to run. The combination has led to...the degeneracy you see in the tabloids."

"Perhaps the lock and key were the problems," Penelope bristled. She was beginning to note a trend. Most of what she'd seen was Amethyst having a bit of fun, hardly degenerate.

"When you have daughters of your own then perhaps you can begin throwing stones, Miss Banks."

Penelope retracted her claws, accepting that he had a point. It was easy enough for her to criticize a parent, having never raised children of her own.

"Still, as a daughter myself, one who also had a father that believed in locks and keys, it was bound to lead to rebellion. But let's move on, what can you tell me about your daughter, particularly in the week before she went missing?"

"There is a young man, John Foster, he's the son of my Chief of Operations. She's been spending time with him." Mr. Easton nodded to Mr. Tyrell, who produced a large envelope from his briefcase and slid it across the desk to Penelope.

"This is all of his information," Mr. Tyrell said.

John must have been the boy that Christos mentioned "Anna" was with at the speakeasy. Perhaps when Pen talked to him—she had already decided to take the case—he could explain why Katie and Amethyst had gone by fake names and pretended not to know each other beforehand.

Mr. Easton continued. "He's nineteen, and currently a student at Columbia University, so I *assumed* he was sensible enough to keep her in line. He often works with his father, learning the ins and outs of the business. I believe he is interested in one day taking his father's place. His father is nothing short of trustworthy and above reproach. With John, Amethyst was at least beginning to show an interest in the shipping business. When Amethyst went missing, naturally I questioned him. As it turns out, he may not have been as positive an influence as I'd hoped."

"Why do you say that?"

"He confessed to accompanying my daughter when she went to a speakeasy on Friday. He claimed it was her idea, that she introduced him to the place. That's something I once would have been disinclined to believe. Now, I'm not so sure. I asked Amethyst's friends and, one of them, Eliza Hemsford, to whom she's closest, told me about Katie Sweeney. Naturally, when I heard the last name and discovered who her father was, I was appalled. Then, when I learned she too had gone missing, well..."

"I can see why you think they're related," Penelope said with a nod. "When did Amethyst go missing?"

"Friday."

"What makes you think she hasn't simply trotted off to Nantucket for the weekend?"

"Amethyst has been known to disappear, off to some party, or visiting friends in other cities, even without telling me. But she's always either back by Sunday in time for church, or has a good explanation for her absence. It's the one rule I have and, I'm proud to say she's abided by it. It's now Tuesday and she has yet to return or get in touch. According to our housekeeper, she arrived home hours after midnight on Friday." His jaw twitched with irritation. "That's the last anyone, including John, has seen of her."

So Amethyst went missing before Katie, and presumably Tino Messina. More importantly, right after that meeting at the speakeasy.

"Did John tell you anything about what happened at the speakeasy Friday night?"

"He didn't mention anything that might explain her disappearance."

"Did he mention the names Anna or Stacy?"

The instant look of confusion on his face told her he hadn't. "Who are they? Are they related to this?"

Interesting that John wouldn't have revealed those names to Mr. Easton. Perhaps like Moira, he was so intimidated by Katie's father that he left certain important, yet self-incriminating, facts out. Penelope was now quite eager to talk to this John Foster.

"I suspect your daughter may have gone by the name Anna on Friday night. Can you think of any reason why? Does the name have any significance?"

Again, he looked thoroughly perplexed. "None that come to mind."

"And you're *certain* you've never heard the name Stacy?"

"No, is that Irish? I know they sometimes have unusual names."

Having no familiarity with Irish names, Penelope disregarded the question.

"Other than this dance school, you can't think of any connection to Katie? Perhaps mutual friends? Other places they both might have met or spent time together?"

"My world and that of Jack Sweeney's do not mix," he said in a clipped voice. He cleared his throat before continuing. "However, I know that Amethyst liked to dabble in low places. Still, I'd like to think she at least kept her distance from the criminal underworld."

Penelope left that alone, but in her periphery, she could see Lulu's mouth twist into a wry smile, but her eyes were full of venom.

"You said that Amethyst inherited money from her mother. Would it be enough for her to run away and live on? Perhaps use to fund a venture she thought might be lucrative in the short term?"

A rather satisfied smile appeared on his face. "As it turns out, no. It wasn't much to begin with, and all her partying and indulgence has dwindled it down to nothing. Once upon a time, I had a designated amount promised to Amethyst when she turned eighteen. I terminated that the moment she first made the front page of the *Tattle*. Now that her own money has been spent, she's tried various ways to persuade me to change my mind, to no avail. I thought for certain that would be the impetus for an end to her sinful ways, but it seems I underestimated her. Of course, this disappearing act may be some immature attempt to curry my guilt—running away as though she were still a child. Really." He shook his head with disappointment.

"I see," Penelope said. So both Katie and Amethyst recently had their wings clipped in one way or another. It may have made them desperate to find a way out, perhaps desperate *and* reckless.

"Do you have any idea what Amethyst wanted to do with her life? Perhaps become an actress or performer of some sort?"

"If she did, she certainly knew better than to tell me about such an absurd notion," he said, outraged. "A girl of Amethyst's stature has no place on the stage, or worse the film industry. As it was, I had hoped under John's influence she might one day take over, perhaps even expand the business as I did with my own father's company, despite her being a woman."

"We do have our faults," Penelope said with a pat smile.

He pursed his lips. "I'm not opposed to women in business Miss Banks. It's simply a fact that society expects less from the fairer sex. I note that despite your own extremely generous windfall, you've decided to occupy yourself with a worthwhile endeavor. It's to be commended."

"Thank you," Penelope said diplomatically. "Are you sure you can't think of any other connection between Amethyst and Katie, or perhaps you and Mr. Sweeney?"

Both he and Mr. Tyrell glanced at each other, then turned back to Penelope. "None at all."

Pen noted the way his eyes shifted just before his denial. He was lying.

"Mr. Easton, the more I know, the more likely I'll be able to find Amethyst."

"There's nothing more," he said tersely. "Just keep me apprised. I'd also appreciate knowing when or if you find Kathleen Sweeney."

"I'm afraid I can't discuss other cases with you." He opened his mouth to protest and she quickly continued. "*However*, if there is a connection that might help find Amethyst I will be sure to inform you."

He grumbled with irritation.

"If there's nothing more?" she pressed, giving him a piercing look.

"Nothing," he said, staring back at her with an unwavering gaze.

"Well, I suppose my first step is to talk to John Foster," Penelope said, picking up the envelope Mr. Tyrell had given her.

She wondered what lies he would tell her.

CHAPTER EIGHT

When Charles Easton and his personal secretary had left, the three women in Penelope's office all stared at each other thinking the same thing.

"Am I going to be the one to say it?" Lulu finally asked. "That man was lying out his mouth, at least about there being nothing more to this."

"He was. He has some connection to Mr. Sweeney. It may not necessarily be criminal, but it is something they didn't want to tell me. Now, I'm certain Mr. Sweeney was lying or keeping something back too. But why would both men lie when their daughters are missing? Furthermore, why did both girls lie about knowing each other at the speakeasy? Since we can be pretty certain Katie ran away from home, I'm almost certain Amethyst did as well."

Pen addressed Lulu. "Has Tommy told you what was so urgent yesterday?"

"I haven't even heard from him since then."

"Whatever it is, I'm sure it's related to whatever Mr. Easton and Mr. Sweeney are keeping from us. Right now, you and I are going to talk to this John Foster, Lulu."

"You want me to come with you?" Lulu asked uncertainly.

Penelope grinned. "You have no idea the distracting effect you have on people, Miss Simmons. I think the best way to catch our Mr. Foster in any lies is to discombobulate him."

"I have no idea what that means, but flattery will get you everywhere, Pen," she replied with a laugh.

"So Jane, I leave it to you to once again do research. Obviously, see if there are any updates in the tattle presses about Amethyst. Charles Easton owns the Easton Shipping Company. Find out anything you can about shipping, importing, and exporting, or his business in particular. And keep at it with Mr. Sweeney or any recent events in organized crime."

Jane looked hesitant, so Pen asked what was wrong. "Well...you told me that Mr. Callahan said we shouldn't do anything?"

"*Technically*, I'm not working on the Sweeney case," Pen said.

Jane didn't look all that convinced, no doubt remembering his menacing presence in this office from yesterday.

"Tommy's not going to take it out on you, Jane."

"If he does, I'll be the first one to set him straight," Lulu assured her.

Jane smiled with embarrassment at how skittish she was being.

"If he comes by, you tell him we've gone out to work on a *different* case since he forbade us from working on Katie's," Pen said loftily. She turned to Lulu. "Alright Miss Simmons, let's see what lies we can tear from John Foster, because I'm one hundred percent certain he's also going to be hiding something."

Penelope had called Leonard, her chauffeur, to drive them up to Columbia University where John Foster was a freshman. She hadn't been surprised that Mr. Tyrell's packet of information would include his class schedule, including which buildings his classes were held. John's father had probably been all too willing to give his boss anything he needed, especially since his son was spending time with Mr. Easton's daughter.

That late in the morning he should have just been exiting his English class at the Teacher's College, just off the main campus.

Penelope had attended Columbia's sister school, Barnard College, located right across Broadway. At least she had until her mother had died during the Great Influenza, and her path in life had gone a bit wayward.

Being on the campus again was almost enough for her to think about going back and finishing her degree. Her father had only paid her way the first time in the hopes that she'd find a suitable husband. Now, a degree seemed almost pointless. Still, there was something worthwhile in the accomplishment itself.

Knowing that the ever-fashionable Lulu was coming into the office that day, Penelope had dressed a little more chic that morning. It was a surprisingly warm early-spring day, so she'd donned a loosely fitted, gold dress with a gauzy overlay and a tiny beaded design. It just barely reached the knees, which was a recent trend in fashion of which Pen heartily approved.

Of course, Lulu, never to be outdone had worn a maroon sleeveless dress with a vee neckline and a handkerchief skirt over a beaded, straight edged chemise top and a matching beaded belt. The two of them cut quite the striking pair as they waited for John outside of Horace Mann Hall.

"So this is what college is like," Lulu said, looking around at the classical buildings bordering Broadway in that part of town. Columbia wasn't too far from Harlem, but Morningside Park, with its staggering cliff, created quite the buffer separating the two.

They perked up when the student body began pouring out through the front doors. A clog in the flow occurred as every member of that stream stopped to take a lingering look at the two very stylish women waiting out front. It was no doubt an unusual sight after class, especially when one of them was colored.

Pen realized the problem after only a few seconds.

There had been no photo included in the packet of information. Even if there had been, so many of the boys looked almost identical in their jackets and ties.

Thinking quickly, she nabbed the attention of the boy nearest to her. He was short and seemed particularly guile-less. He had a piggish sort of nose and bulging eyes that gave him an unfortunate appearance. Not a likely candidate for someone Amethyst would spend time with. He gawked and his cheeks went violently red when she homed in on him.

"Say, you there, boy-o."

"Uh, y-yes?" The other boys nearby stopped as well, perhaps wondering what made him so special.

"Do you know a John Foster?"

"John? Ah...yes, ma'am, I do."

"Care to point him out?"

His face fell slightly, but he turned to scan the sea of male faces around him. She saw his brow lift once he caught sight of him. Her gaze followed the direction in which his hand lifted to point him out.

"That's him, coming out just now. The one on the far left."

He was a tallish boy, too ordinary to be handsome, but certainly not unattractive. The blond, curly-haired boy next to him was talking and laughing, but John looked distracted, staring at the ground in worried thought.

That was their boy, alright.

She wondered what it was Amethyst saw in him. Perhaps it was the lack of anything exceptional, at least physically, that was the appeal. Most fathers wouldn't look at a boy like John and think he was bad news.

Penelope turned back to the boy who had pointed him out.

"You're the absolute berries," she gushed, turning him into a perfect beet. She almost wanted to lean in and kiss his cheek just to see how red he could go. Instead, she spared him. He was near to fainting just from staring at the far more exceptional Lulu.

She grabbed Lulu's hand and led her toward John. With his head down, he only noted their presence once his friend stopped talking in order to gawk at them. John's eyes flashed up and he blinked twice, staring at Penelope in puzzlement.

Penelope was glad she had thought to accost him by surprise. It wouldn't give him much time to think of a lie for them. She'd had just about enough of those, thank you very much.

"John Foster?" Pen confirmed.

"Why?" he asked suspicion coloring his gaze.

"I'll take that as a yes. We need to talk to you, I think you know what it's about."

"You going to introduce us, John?" the other one asked with a smirk. It only caused John to frown in irritation.

"Actually, this is rather private. Lulu and I need John all to ourselves," Pen cooed, batting her eyelashes. The other fellow lost his smirk, drowning in all the possibilities as his eyes flicked back and forth between the two women. Lulu added a wink just to make things even more confounding.

Pen used the moment of discombobulation to hook her arm through John's and drag him away. Lulu took his other arm and they walked him north up Broadway further away from campus.

He finally found his voice, and disentangled himself from Pen and Lulu. "Hey now, what's this about?"

"I wouldn't protest, John. Mr. Easton isn't very happy with you, and I think you know why. He's hired us to find his daughter."

"I had nothing to do with Amethyst running away."

"Well now, that is very interesting. How do you know she ran away?"

"I-I just figured." He shrugged and looked uncertain.

"Why?" Lulu asked.

"Wait, do you think someone *took* her?" he asked, gaping in horror at the idea.

Pen and Lulu exchanged a glance. "That's what we're trying to find out, John. Why don't you tell us everything that happened Friday night, starting with why Amethyst went by the name Anna?"

"I don't know, it was some joke she wouldn't let me in on." He frowned in resentment.

"The other girl who was with you, Stacy, what can you tell me about her?"

He looked puzzled. "She was just some girl who came over and began talking with us."

"Bobbed blonde hair, wearing a blue dress? She came in with a dark-haired friend?"

"The pretty one with freckles? Yes, but she stayed back at the bar. At least Stacy gave that Christos fellow someone to talk to besides Amethyst." He worked his jaw with residual irritation, probably mentally comparing himself to the much more handsome Christos.

"Amethyst gave no indication that Stacy might have been Katie or Kathleen from her dance class?" Pen didn't want to bring the Sweeney name up just yet.

He shook his head. "No. As I said, she called herself Stacy. And Amethyst said I should call her Anna. I just figured it was one of the eccentric games she played when she was bored."

"And you didn't recognize either of the other two girls?"

He widened his eyes with exasperation, as though he had already answered the question ten different ways. "*No*, I'd never seen either of them before."

"Why did Amethyst bring you along?"

He gave them a defiant look. "Why wouldn't she?"

"I'm guessing she usually took you along on account of you being old enough to get her into places. So why'd she need you Friday night? Supposedly the man who covers the front isn't too hard-nosed about age."

"Maybe she likes me," he scoffed.

"And maybe you were hoping for a little hanky-panky?" Pen suggested.

"No, it wasn't like that! I just—I figured it couldn't hurt to make nice with her. Mr. Easton has connections." His lips twisted into something cynical before he continued. "And he obviously isn't as stingy with her as he is with everyone else, so she was always flush with kale."

75

"It doesn't concern you that she's the boss's daughter? One wrong step and she could ruin you."

His eyes flashed in panic. "I honestly only go with her to these places to make sure she's alright. That dizzy girl would jump into a pit of crocodiles just for the fun of it if there was no one to stop her."

"Any idea what pit she might be in now?"

He bit the inside of his cheek and looked off to the side, shaking his head no. "I don't get it. She wouldn't just... disappear, not without telling her friends. She loved being scandalous that way, making a spectacle of everything."

Yet another thing Katie and Amethyst seemed to have in common.

"Did she mention anything about a new opportunity? Maybe something that might make her money?"

"Why would she need money?"

"Her father seems to be fed up with her adventures jumping into crocodile pits. He's cut her off, and it seems the vein of money she relied on before will soon be running dry. I suppose that saves you the trouble of having to look after her."

He narrowed his eyes at the hint of scorn in Penelope's voice. "Well, maybe that's a good thing. She was bound to get herself in over her head one of these days."

"What did you talk about with her that night before Stacy came over to join you?"

He shrugged and rolled his eyes. "Nothing much, just the usual, until that buttinsky Christos came over." He scowled before moving on. "I know Amethyst was just using him to make me jealous. She liked teasing people, and not just boys. At any rate, I was glad when Stacy finally decided to join us. Amethyst shoved him off on her. But then all they did was ignore both of us to talk about women's nonsense, clothes and makeup and such. That's why I was glad when she suggested we—"

He stopped short, realizing what he was about to reveal.

"We already know you went out to the back alley, John."

"Nothing happened, I swear!" he said, his eyes wide with pleading.

Lulu coughed out a laugh.

"I'm not lying," he insisted. "Amethyst decided she wanted to keep talking with this Stacy. I thought it a bit dirty to play us like that. Why'd they drag us outside for privacy if all they were going to do was talk girl stuff?"

That was a good question. Maybe Katie wanted to know where to buy more fashionable clothes for her new life? But it seemed like she already had a good handle on that, if that stash of hers was any indication. Penelope remembered the dress she'd seen her in at the Peacock Club had been rather modern and flashy. And all one had to do was open a few issues of the society pages to know that Amethyst didn't need any help when it came to fashion.

"You...aren't going to tell Mr. Easton about that, are you? About us going outside to the alley? I don't think he'd believe me when I say nothing happened."

Lulu and Pen looked at each other, sly smiles on their faces.

Pen gave him an overly censuring look. "Only if you keep yourself available for further questioning, and tell me anything you might learn."

"I don't know what else to say. Amethyst was no angel, let me tell you. I wouldn't be surprised if she was on a boat to the French Riviera or halfway to Argentina on a lark, just to mess with her old man. I was already starting to think it wasn't worth it, spending time with her."

"Well, she wasn't doing anything with her father cutting her off recently."

"I suppose not," he said, tilting his head in thought. "Listen, I'm supposed to be at a theater club meeting over lunch, can I go?"

Pen eyed Lulu, who shrugged, having nothing to add.

"Go on, but remember what I said about being available. We might have more questions." She dug into her purse and pulled out a business card to hand to him. "In case something occurs to you."

"Sure." He didn't seem too enthused, but he took the card and jogged off.

Pen turned back to Lulu. "So what do you think?"

"I think some things don't add up. Why drag those poor boys outside thinkin' one thing was going to happen and then just talk with your supposedly new friend?"

"Maybe there was too much noise and they couldn't hear themselves, but they wanted to stay safe in an alleyway?"

"Too much noise? In a speakeasy? There's a sure way to bring the police down on you." Lulu laughed.

Pen joined her. "Right. Maybe Stacy also wanted to make someone jealous. She left Moira at the bar to take the boys outside."

"It seems we have two little devils on our hands. That doesn't bode well. They're the wiliest. And why use fake names?"

"Both girls have rather infamous last names, for different reasons. Neither boy seemed to know Katie Sweeney, which was probably the whole point." Pen sighed. "Whatever is going on here, Katie and Amethyst are definitely in on it together."

"Maybe they both went out to Hollywood together?" Lulu said with a wry look.

"Which gets us right back to what's probably the most important point. How'd they get the money to strike out on their own?"

"So where do we get answers?"

"Start at square one, the dance school where it all began."

CHAPTER NINE

PENELOPE HAD LEONARD DRIVE HER AND LULU TO THE Parisian Dance School located on 47th Street and Broadway, a bit of a drive from the one-hundreds where Columbia was situated. Thus, she and Lulu used the time to consider all the possibilities, no matter how absurd. They even asked Pen's chauffeur to join in.

"Hidden treasure," he said, his voice filled with confidence. "You'd be surprised what's out there just waiting to be found. I heard that the Titanic had over fifteen million dollars worth of valuables lost when it went down, including a Renault CB. Breaks my heart to think of it. I mean, yes all those people dying was a terrible thing too." He looked abashed.

Pen grinned at him. "Of course you'd think about cars."

He shrugged and cocked a half smile. "It's what I know."

She considered that as he continued driving. What did Katie and Amethyst know, and how had they used it to finance their plans?

Amethyst's father was in shipping, which opened an

entire world of possibilities from illegal liquor, to the opium trade, to arms dealing, to stolen artifacts, to yes, even sunken treasure.

It was interesting how so many of those possibilities tied in with interests a gangster might have. Mr. Sweeney mostly dealt in gambling and liquor and kickbacks from businesses. She had learned in her last case that he also had a few fingers in stolen goods and fraudulent replicas. Again, an entire world of possibilities.

"Whatever those two gals are up to certainly isn't legal."

When they arrived at the dance school, she was met with a surprise. Tommy Callahan was leaning against a parked car just outside the front doors, smoking a cigarette and looking none too happy.

"Pineapples! What is he doing here?" Pen protested before Leonard opened the door for them to exit.

"Well, well, well," Tommy said, glaring as he pulled his cigarette away. "If it isn't two ladies who are doing exactly what I told them not to do."

"I didn't realize my *father* was working on this case with me," Penelope retorted.

"You'd better not be getting ideas about spanking us," Lulu sassed with a perfectly unconcerned smirk.

His eyes glimmered as they settled on her. "Don't give me any ideas, songbird."

"At any rate, we're not working on Mr. Sweeney's case," Penelope said.

"That so?" he asked, one eyebrow now arched her way. "And what case would you be working on?"

"How did you even know we'd be here?" Penelope asked instead of answering his question.

"Imagine my surprise when I showed up to your office today to find *yous two* were out and about working on a case

—a case that absolutely, definitely isn't Mr. Sweeney's." He was mimicking Jane, who had obviously been too adamant in her assertion Pen wasn't working on Mr. Sweeney's case.

"Don't tell me you bullied that poor girl into ratting on us," Lulu scolded.

"She's fine," he breathed out with a cloud of smoke, the cigarette still clenched in his teeth. "You got a loyal gal there, Pen, you should be proud."

"One who apparently deserves a raise. So how did you know we'd be here?"

"You ain't the only one who's got detective skills, girly. I figured you'd make your way here at some point, at least if you're any good at your job, which apparently you are. Now let's get to twisting some screws." He flicked the cigarette away and pushed away from the car he'd been leaning against.

"There will be no twisting of screws," Penelope said. "I'm handling this case, remember. After all, I'm not working for Mr. Sweeney—or am I?"

"Only if you're with me," he said, giving her a warning look.

"What is it that had you leaving so early yesterday?"

"That's between me and Mr. Sweeney," He said with a smile that didn't reach his eyes. He then gestured to the front door.

Penelope exhaled in frustration and headed toward the door. "Come on, Lulu."

"I think I've discombobulated enough for today, I'm fine staying out here," Lulu said. She turned to Leonard with a pert smile. "Leonard here can keep me company."

Leonard grinned, consummate tomcat that he was. "This job gets harder and harder every day, Miss Banks."

Penelope laughed.

Tommy glowered.

The two of them entered and found the foyer lined with awards, framed letters, and photographs of Cara Pippin, the woman who ran the school. She was a gaunt, but regal woman who seemed incapable of smiling in any of her pictures. According to several of the accolades, she had once been a ballerina with the Paris Opera Ballet. The name of the school was no doubt used to highlight that fact.

It was a time of day when there were few classes, so they had the foyer to themselves as they greeted the woman at the front desk.

"Good afternoon, I urgently need to speak with Miss Pippin. We're here at the request of Mr. Charles Easton." Penelope decided to use the name that would have the most influence at a place like that. Mr. Sweeney's name had its uses, but she doubted it carried much weight in a proper dance school.

She noted Tommy glance her way at the mention of Mr. Easton's name, though it didn't seem to stir anything more than mild curiosity in him.

"Oh, she mustn't be disturbed right now. She spends this time of day practicing before classes start later on."

"It is rather important."

"I'm sorry miss, I simply can't."

Pen understood. Based on the photos she'd seen, Cara probably wasn't the most lenient boss. She'd have the poor girl for dinner if she interrupted her practice time.

Tommy leaned in closer and met the young lady with a surprisingly charming grin. "Say, how many studio rooms does this school have?"

Two deep dimples formed in her cheeks as she coyly smiled back. "Four, the large one where most students take their classes, and three smaller ones for more advanced or private students."

"Right, and the school has the whole floor to itself? That's impressive."

"Two floors! The bigger studio takes up almost the entire first floor, save for the changing rooms. We have quite a few students."

Which meant Cara's office was upstairs. She'd most likely be practicing in one of the smaller studios up there. Pen almost admired what Tommy was doing.

"Thanks doll, you're a gem," Tommy said with a wink.

Only when Tommy pulled away and casually strolled past the desk, did she realize her mistake.

"Wait a moment!"

"We'll only be a few minutes," Penelope said rushing after him.

"You *can't!*" The girl protested, scurrying to catch up with them.

Tommy ignored her, taking the stairs past the foyer to the second floor. They both heard the sounds of classical music coming from one of the studios. He pulled the door open despite the receptionist's protests behind them, and strolled right in.

The same woman from the photographs was inside, bent in an impressive stretch. She looked like something from Ancient Greece in a chiton, stockings, and ballet slippers. Her hair was viciously pulled back into a bun but she was otherwise plain, no makeup or jewelry.

"What's the meaning of this?" Cara straightened her body and stared at Tommy and Penelope with her nose already turned up, as though they'd brought in a whiff of something unpleasant when they entered.

"I'm so sorry Miss Pippin, they just rushed right past me!"

"Good afternoon Miss Pippin, my name is Penelope Banks, I'm a private investigator, and this is my...partner Tommy Callahan. We wish to speak with you about two of your students, Kathleen Sweeney and Amethyst Easton. They've both gone missing and I'm working on behalf of their fathers to find them."

Cara studied Pen up and down, frowning as she lingered over her legs. It was enough to have Penelope looking down at them wondering what flaw she saw. Yes, they were a bit thin, but shapely enough. Hardly worth sneering at.

She completely ignored Tommy.

"Get out!" she hissed.

"If we do that, I'll have no choice but to go directly to the police and involve them. In fact, I do believe your school lies within the district that a detective, who is a dear friend of mine, services."

That was a lie, as Detective Prescott serviced the Upper East Side of Manhattan, and they were firmly on the West Side. Still, it was enough to put the fear of God into Miss Pippin.

"Fine," she seethed, gesturing with a violent flick of the wrist for her receptionist to leave them.

When it was just the three of them, she glared at Tommy and Penelope. "How dare you come to my school in the middle of the day to—"

"We'll be blessedly brief, Miss Pippin," Pen interrupted in a cheerful tone, which did nothing to appease Cara's outrage. "I've come because, as I stated, it seems both Amethyst Easton and Katie Sweeney have gone missing."

"And what does this have to do with my school?"

"Both girls attended dance class here, and we believe this is where they may have conspired to run away at the same time."

"Kathleen Sweeney and Amethyst Easton?" She coughed out a sharp laugh. "That is highly unlikely."

"Why is that?"

"I never once saw those two associate with one another." She cast an unimpressed look Tommy's way, as though she knew exactly what he was. "Understandable when you consider their vastly different breeding."

If he was offended, he didn't show it. His cool, green eyes remained settled on her with perfect impassiveness.

"So you never saw them talk or spend even a few moments together?"

"Not at all. They were as different as two girls could be."

"How so?"

Cara exhaled with impatience. "Kathleen was nothing more than a fascination. Everyone knew who her father was. If I'd known when her mother first brought her, I never would have signed her on as a student. Girls who are sheltered unfortunately have a habit of being intrigued by those who are more worldly or dangerous. Kathleen, despite her stubbornly papist affectations, *was* such a girl. After the fact, I couldn't very well expel her. Still, for all her disruptive behavior, she did take the class itself seriously, and showed quite a bit of promise as a dancer."

"Disruptive behavior?"

Cara pursed her lips with distaste. "This school focuses on *classical* forms of dance, ballet, ballroom, even *some* of the Latin dances. We do not indulge in various other *primitive* forms." She shot a look Tommy's way. "Or any *peasant* dances."

Again, Tommy remained perfectly placid. He studied Cara with cool amusement, which was perhaps even more dangerous than any outburst he might have laid upon her.

"And Katie? She encouraged this kind of dance? I assume you're talking about dances such as the Charleston?"

"Among others. Much like the music that so often accompanies it, it lacks structure and decorum. A trumpet here, a jazzy piano tune there, and *drums*?" She gave a sharp laugh. "No, Miss Banks, I'm not training girls how to dance in nightclubs or jazz bars like common harlots. I'm training them to be the wives of future diplomats, royalty, perhaps even the First Lady of the Land. Could you imagine Grace Coolidge kicking her legs about and flapping her arms while some brass instrument blares in the background?" She visibly shuddered at the idea, then turned to Tommy with a sneer. "Or doing a jig to some fiddle player?"

"Well, at the very least, your students will learn to have discriminating tastes," Penelope said.

"Exactly," Cara said with a cold smile, the sarcasm lost on her.

"And Amethyst?"

"Admittedly, she may not have taken the class as seriously as Kathleen, but she at least knew how to conduct herself while she was here, the epitome of elegance and obedience. Again, it's in the breeding."

Cara obviously didn't read gossip rags like the *New York Tattle*.

"Did you ever hear either of them go by the name Anna or Stacy?"

Cara just stared back looking perfectly baffled.

"I'll take that as a no," Penelope said. "What about

outside of class, did you ever see them associate with one another before or after lessons?"

"I don't concern myself with what the girls do once they leave the studio room. In fact, I make it a point to quickly retire to my office before they can pester me with too many questions. I focus only on what happens from the moment they enter that door. Before that and after they leave is none of my business and I don't make it such."

"I find it hard to believe that you are that willfully blind."

Cara gave an exaggerated sigh. "No, I have never, *not once*, seen Katie or Amethyst talk, laugh, chat, or so much as look in one another's direction. Even the girls who tend to gravitate toward each of them don't interact with each other. And is it any wonder? One is the daughter of a prominent New York resident the other is an Irish gangster's daughter. One handles herself with grace and dignity, the other makes a mockery of the art of dance. And I would be highly surprised if Amethyst Easton was *Catholic*." She wrinkled her nose as she uttered this apparently offensive word.

"How do you know Katie was Catholic?"

"I have a strict no jewelry rule during class. She patently refused to remove her cross or that ring on her finger. Even when I threatened to cancel the entire class, she stubbornly persisted." She cleared her throat and absently smoothed back her hair, but offered Tommy another glare. "I have since then made an exception for religious ornamentation."

Penelope wondered what threat Katie had used to bully her into backing down. Despite her wanton ways, she was obviously quite the devout Catholic. Still, Christos had told Pen that Katie removed her necklace and ring at the speakeasy. Why so casually take it off there, but put up such stubborn resistance at dance class?

"You have your answers. Are we done here?" Cara said, all her venom mostly reserved for Tommy.

"After you tell me the names and addresses of the girls Katie and Amethyst spent the most time with."

"Absolutely not!"

"Need I remind you how urgent this matter is, and to what lengths Mr. Sweeney is willing to go?" Tommy threatened in a low, cool voice.

"There are also the police, who I'm sure would be happy to interrupt one of your classes to get the names. I suspect the parents of your students wouldn't like that very much," Penelope added.

"Fine! Whatever gets you to leave. But when asked, you did *not* get the information from me."

"I can agree to that."

"Amethyst was popular with most of the girls, but Eliza Hemsford seemed to be the one she was closest to. As for Katie, she was always with Moira Mahoney, another Irish Catholic, but at least she has *some* sense of etiquette."

Moira was a student there? Pen wondered why she hadn't mentioned that. Surely she would have recognized Amethyst at the speakeasy. Obviously, another round of questioning was in order.

As for Eliza, Mr. Easton had mentioned her earlier. Pen had already planned to talk with her.

"Now, if you don't mind?" Miss Pippin hinted.

"Of course, and we apologize for interrupting you," Pen said in such a charming manner it had Cara narrowing her eyes with suspicion. Pen pulled out a business card to hand to her. "In case you think of anything else useful."

Cara stared down at it as though it were a slimy toad.

She sighed, then snatched it from her hand. Pen suspected it would be in pieces in the trash before they even left the building.

As they headed back outside, she gave Tommy a wry smile. "She obviously isn't a fan of Erin Go Bragh. I'm surprised you handled yourself with such equanimity."

"Priorities, Pen, priorities," Tommy said, narrowing one eye toward Lulu and Leonard quite obviously hitting it off through the glass front doors. "That lady knows I work for Mr. Sweeney. I got Mick written all over me and I ain't ashamed of it. Where to, next?"

"I'm going to confirm a few things with Eliza and Moira...alone."

His gaze snapped back to her, obviously not liking that.

"I'm not deliberately keeping you in the dark, Tommy. But you might as well be the Spanish Inquisition when it comes to eighteen-year-old girls. Priorities, remember?"

He nodded, then focused his disgruntled attention on Leonard and Lulu, who were now laughing at something Pen's chauffeur had just said.

"You just remember what's at stake here, Pen."

CHAPTER TEN

Penelope decided to start with Eliza for the next round of questioning. She sent Lulu back to the office with Leonard. She told her to have Jane order a late lunch for the three of them as they pored over all the information they had thus far. Leonard, Lulu, and Jane could possibly be a formidable investigative force.

In the meantime, Tommy drove her to Eliza Hemsford's home. Her father was a partner at a financier firm, and Penelope's father owned an investment firm. Thus, the Hemsfords and Banks were names that were mutually familiar. That's how Penelope had recognized Eliza back at the dance studio.

Clarence Hemsford was more than happy to have Penelope talk to his daughter, no doubt wanting to remain in the good graces of men like Charles Easton and Reginald Banks. He'd called and instructed his wife to give Penelope access, being that she was home from school.

"I don't know where Amethyst is," Eliza said, a tart smile already plastered on her face before Penelope could even ask her first question.

"You don't seem all that concerned about what may have happened to her."

Instantly the smile disappeared. "Well, of course I am. Obviously. It's just...I have no clue where she could be."

"So you don't suspect kidnapping?"

"I, well..." She shrugged and looked confused, then, for some reason hopeful. "I suppose that's a possibility?"

Penelope hoped acting wasn't her dream as well. She was terrible at feigning anything.

"Eliza, how old are you? Seventeen? Eighteen?"

"I just turned eighteen," she said with a pleased smile.

"And Amethyst is still seventeen. That limits what she can do on her own. Her father is understandably concerned about her and just wants to make sure she isn't in any trouble."

"Amethyst is always in trouble, and she always gets out of it." She giggled, then caught herself.

It was time for Penelope to use what little acting skills she had.

"Young lady, this isn't a laughing matter. The police are involved at this point," she lied. "Do you really want to go to prison as a coconspirator because you and your friend decided to waste police resources searching for a girl who has decided to play a prank on her father?"

Eliza's eyes went wide and her mouth opened and closed a few times before an eruption of words fell from it.

"I swear I don't know where she is, Miss Banks. All I know is she kept talking about a plan she had to make extra money, and get back at her father. That she didn't need his money because she was going to make her own, tens of thousands probably. That she was working with someone, someone that would make him positively livid if he ever found out, but she never told me who it was. I swear!"

Was Katie this mysterious person? If anyone would make Charles Easton livid, it would be the daughter of a gangster like Mr. Sweeney. But what were they plotting?

"Alright," Pen said in a soothing voice. At least she was finally getting answers. "Do you think it could be Katie Sweeney? Did you ever see the two of them talking in secret, perhaps before or after dance class?"

"Yes, but that was only the past couple of weeks or so. I didn't really understand it, Amethyst used to make fun of Katie—not to her face of course. Then, all of a sudden they were chatting and giggling in secret after dance class like best friends. I thought maybe..." Eliza frowned and stared down at her hands.

"You thought Amethyst and Katie were now making fun of you?"

She reluctantly nodded.

"Not so enjoyable when you're on the receiving end of it."

She shook her head.

"This plan of hers, when did she first tell you all of this?"

"She's been hinting at it for a week or so now. I thought her disappearing like this was just a part of it, that she'd come back with all kinds of fanfare after making her money, maybe throw a big party or something. That's the kind of thing she would do."

"But you have no idea what she was planning or with whom she was planning it?"

"No, I swear I don't. I was just waiting for the big announcement." She wrinkled her brow, finally showing the first signs of concern. "You don't think she's actually in trouble, do you?"

Penelope considered all the ways a stubborn, overly-confident, reckless seventeen-year-old girl—someone exactly like she once was—could get herself into trouble. Yes, she thought it was very likely that Amethyst had done such a thing.

There was no reason to worry Eliza with that possibility.

"I'm going to find out, but I need to know everything in order to do that," she hinted.

"That's all I know, Miss Banks. Amethyst had a plan to make money, a lot of money."

"And Katie?"

"She only just started making nice with her recently. Wait...do you think *that's* the person she was planning something with? Is Amethyst getting into organized crime?"

How organized could it be with someone like Amethyst? Still, people had a way of surprising you. Penelope was certain she had surprised a few people, including her own father.

"I don't know what's going on, but I plan on finding out."

There was nothing more to be asked, so Penelope thanked Eliza and left. Tommy was, as usual, leaning against his car with a cigarette planted firmly between his lips. Penelope was sure to go home that night smelling like an ashtray at that rate.

"What did you learn?"

"How involved is Katie with her father's business?"

The dry look he gave her was touched with a bit of mirth. "That girl is more swaddled than a newborn baby. She knows what he does, she's not completely stupid, but we all know better than to discuss it when she's around, let alone bring her into it."

"Let me rephrase. How likely is it that she knows enough to get started on her own?"

"Let *me* rephrase, when hell freezes over. She might as well be poison to anyone who works with her for all the pain they'd eventually feel if Mr. Sweeney found out."

Penelope sighed in frustration, but wasn't surprised.

"Is that what that girl in there said?" He pointed his cigarette at the door of the home Penelope had just exited.

"All she knew was that Amethyst was working with someone to make a lot of money. I just assumed it was Katie."

"Whatever it is, it don't involve any of Mr. Sweeney's businesses."

"Perhaps the Messinas?"

"We don't involve kids, that's a rule. Especially not girls. The Italians are particularly strict about that."

"Naturally," Penelope said in a wry tone.

Tommy grinned. "Whatever it is Katie got herself mixed up in, it ain't illegal."

"There are many different kinds of illegal, Tommy. You'd be surprised what people like this," Pen gestured back toward the fine home behind her, "get away with."

He laughed. "I doubt I'd be all that surprised. And who says we don't already work with people like this?" He again gestured toward the home.

"At any rate, now that I know a little bit more, I need to talk to Moira again."

After the exercise of getting past her parents once again, Penelope was with Moira in her bedroom communicating in whispers. It was later in the day than the last time Pen had been there and she could hear the muffled sounds of Moira's siblings being perfectly rambunctious somewhere in the home.

"Four brothers," Moira said, closing her eyes and exhaling a sigh of discontent. "Now you know why I can't wait to leave. Still, at least I get my own bedroom."

As an only child, Pen would have welcomed the distraction of siblings, even if they left her as perfectly vexed as Moira was.

"Moira, I need you to tell me the truth this time," she said in a voice low enough that anyone listening at the door might not hear.

"What do you mean?" Moira said, her far too innocent expression giving her away.

"Why didn't you tell me you recognized the other girl from the speakeasy? It was Amethyst Easton, wasn't it?"

Moira opened her mouth to protest, then snapped it shut and sighed. "I'm sorry about that, I just—I didn't want to get her into trouble."

"Why would you care about what happens to Amethyst? She wasn't your friend, was she?"

"No, not really, but she knows people in Hollywood. One of her friends is a producer who said he could maybe put Katie and me into one of his films."

"When was this?" Pen asked in surprise. According to Eliza, Amethyst and Katie had only been friendly for the past week or so.

Moira looked up at Pen from beneath eyelids lowered with guilt. "Amethyst had a party a little over a week ago that Katie took me to. That's where we met him. Please don't tell my parents!"

Zounds, Cara Pippin was right about these girls being worldly. Speakeasies, parties, Hollywood producers?

"Did he make promises to you?"

"He said he could cast us, but only when we're both eighteen. I promised Katie I would wait for her. I didn't want to go to Hollywood alone, it would have been terrifying!" She swallowed hard, her eyes wide with alarm at the very idea.

She was certainly beautiful enough for the screen, but she needed a bit more gumption if she was going to make it out West. Maybe it had been a good thing to wait on Katie, who apparently had the personality to get her way in life, at least according to Miss Pippin.

"So, just to be clear, you *did* know it was Amethyst at the Speakeasy?"

"Yes, ma'am," she said apologetically.

"But she went by Anna, Friday night? And Katie went by Stacy?"

She wrinkled her brow in confusion. "Anna? Stacy? Who are they?"

Pen recalled that Moira had been too far away to hear what had been said Friday. "Can you think of any reason why they would have used different names?"

Moira shrugged. "Maybe it was a game? Katie liked to tease boys, she always told me it was a good way to get their attention."

Knowing what little she did about both Amethyst and Katie, Penelope could see that. They both craved attention, and perhaps that had spilled over into their conspiracy to escape.

"Or maybe she didn't want anyone knowing she was Mr. Sweeney's daughter. Maybe she didn't want the boys to know who she was? Her father's name scares a lot of them off."

So the change in names might have had something to do with either Christos or John. Pen thought about re-interviewing each of them once again, and felt her exhaustion set in. This case was just taking her around in circles it seemed, orbiting something which she had yet to get a firm grasp of.

"I'm sorry about not telling you I knew it was Amethyst. I should have said something, maybe it would have helped and you would have found Katie by now. Honestly, Miss Banks, I don't even care about going to Hollywood anymore. I just want to make sure she is okay."

"I'm sure Katie is smart enough to be safe. Someone who is cunning enough to sneak into speakeasies and clubs, but also likes to read, that's someone who can take care of themselves."

Moira gave her a confused look. "Who said Katie liked to read? Katie hated books. She preferred plays and films, maybe newspaper articles just for anything scandalous."

"Really?" Pen said thoughtfully. "That is interesting."

"How so?"

"It presents a more clear picture of things. Thank you for your help once again, Moira. And again, if you recall anything, just get in touch using the business card I gave you."

"I will. Sorry again about not mentioning I knew it was Amethyst."

"I understand, fortunately it hasn't hindered my case too much."

Penelope rose to leave. Mrs. Mahoney was once again standing right outside the bedroom door unapologetically. Pen flashed a smile and left.

Tommy was, as per usual, casually standing with his

cigarette. This time all he did was raise his brow in a questioning manner.

"I have a question for you. The Sweeney home, how well do you know it?"

"I've been often enough. Seen almost every room. Why?"

"What rooms are next to the library?"

His curiosity was palpable, but he answered. "It overlooks the back of the house. On one side is the dining room. The other is Mr. Sweeney's office. Then it opens up into a kind of open area leading to the front of the house."

Mr. Sweeney's office. So that's why Katie had been pretending to read in the library Sunday night. She'd stolen what she needed from his office, then pretended to listen to records as she gathered up anything she wanted to take with her and made plans to escape. After her mother had wished her good night, she'd left with it.

If it had been money, Mr. Sweeney would have told her. No, it was something bigger, something expensive, and something he definitely didn't want the world to know about.

"Why do you need to know about the house?"

Pen scrutinized Tommy. "It would help if you told me what it is that Mr. Sweeney doesn't want me to know."

"That wouldn't help either of us."

"Even if it meant finding his daughter?"

"Not worth it. Why did you need to know about the library?"

"Just retracing Katie's steps the night before she disappeared," Pen said as she got into the car with him.

Tommy studied her, not entirely believing her answer. "If you know something, you need to tell me."

"I don't *know* anything. In fact, I have more questions

than answers right now." But there was a third party to this equation. Perhaps she'd find answers there. "I think it's time we spoke to the Messinas. Or is that out of the question?"

He shrugged. "I could set up a meeting." His mouth curled up on one side. "I suspect he'll be amenable."

CHAPTER ELEVEN

Back in the office, Penelope and Tommy found Lulu, Leonard, and Jane enjoying their lunch and entertaining each other with stories from the newspapers in front of them.

"Here's one," Leonard said, reading from the *New York Register*. "'Mae West is Cooking up Something Spicy for Broadway,' written by the lovely Katherine Andrews."

"And here I thought Kitty had gotten out of the tabloid business. Besides, everyone knows how *spicy* Mae West is. How is that news?" Pen said, walking to look over his shoulder.

"It says here this play could land her in jail, at least according to those who've read the script."

"I'll make sure I buy my tickets early then," Pen said with a smirk.

"The current title of the play is *Sex*."

"*What?*" Jane said with a sharp laugh of disbelief, which made Lulu laugh.

"Maybe I should check with Kitty, see if our missing

girls landed themselves in a play they shouldn't have?" Leonard suggested.

"If it's a play that's going to land everyone in jail, it's hardly a profitable endeavor. Furthermore, we are *not* bringing Kitty into this case. We have enough chefs in the kitchen as it is." Pen said, turning to scowl at Tommy, who seemed perfectly disinterested in this upcoming scandalous play.

Penelope pivoted her attention to give Leonard a warning look. She wasn't sure how involved he and Katherine "Kitty" Andrews were, and it was none of her business, but she knew they had definitely been seeing one another. Kitty seemed to go for the naughty boys, especially those with devilishly blue eyes and tall, strong builds. Furthermore, she had a nose for trouble. Kitty would absolutely devour a case that involved both Jack Sweeney and Charles Easton, and even more so, their wayward daughters.

"So I'm assuming there was nothing related to this case that any of you found, then?"

"Sorry, Penelope," Jane said before her expression brightened again. "Though we do have a name for the customs agent who was found murdered yesterday morning, Connor Davidson."

Pen turned to give Tommy an expectant look.

He returned a dry smile. "Not one of ours, Lady Pen. We stay far away from the feds, especially when it comes to bumping them off."

"I'll just have to assume you're telling the truth."

Tommy shrugged. "He's far more likely to be the dirty work of the fine, upstanding citizen from your other case. Weren't you the one telling me those types are just as criminal as I am?"

Pen thought about it for a moment. "He was found roughed up and then shot. Who would do both?"

"Someone looking to get information from him, then wanting him to stay permanently silent." Tommy said it as easily as if he were reciting a recipe for cake. It sent a chill down Pen's spine, but she couldn't deny it made sense.

"I suppose you have your uses after all," she said. He smiled with sardonic amusement. "Speaking of which, do you think you could set up that meeting with the Messina family?"

He briefly closed his eyes, as though to say yes, then walked out of the office without a word. Pen stared after him, her mouth falling open. She was used to him being tight-lipped—an occupational necessity, she supposed—but this complete lack of communication was getting irksome.

"I suppose I'll have to wait for him to deign to call me back," she said at the door that closed behind him.

"Oh, he will. I'll make sure of it," Lulu said.

"Have a sandwich, Penelope," Jane urged. "You always forget to eat when you're on a case. That's why I ordered more than necessary. I suppose it's too late to offer Mr. Callahan one now."

Pen shot her a grateful smile and walked over to grab one. She turned to Lulu as she plopped down into a chair. "I don't know how you stand it. The man is incapable of proper communication."

"Sometimes I wonder myself. It all seems like more trouble than it's worth. My family would absolutely *not* approve. And his? Well, his father basically sold him to Mr. Sweeney when he was thirteen, he was the oldest of ten, all Irish twins. So Tommy doesn't much care what they have to say about things."

Penelope was almost as ignorant about Tommy's background as she was about Lulu's. She had once prodded her for more information, just to get to know her better. Lulu had made it quite clear there was a firm line between that world and the Peacock Club, which included Penelope. Pen had only recently learned Lulu lived in a home that was practically a mansion up in Sugar Hill, and that was due to her helping on another case.

But this information about Tommy cast him in a new light. It was no wonder he was so silent and assessing. His own family had given him up, perhaps for practical reasons, but it still had to hurt. He'd probably be appalled at the idea Penelope sympathized with him, but she did.

"Um, how did you and Tommy, um, decide to be...a couple?" Jane asked timidly.

Lulu smiled and tilted her head. "A couple? Now there's a word." She breathed out a laugh. "It was gradual. I was taking a break outside after a set. He came out to have a smoke, and we just started talking. Then, it happened again...and again...and again. That was three years ago."

"Three years?" Pen said in shock, sitting up straighter.

Lulu laughed. "I suppose that means we've hidden it well. Not that it will do any good." She looked off again with a frown. "Maybe this case is a sign I should move on, not just from Tommy but the Peacock Club. It only proves how vulnerable I am. Maybe follow my mama's advice and marry a nice pharmacist, have a lot of babies."

Pen suspected there was a "nice pharmacist" who was indeed vying for Lulu's attention. A man who probably only knew her as Lucille Simmons.

"But you love singing," Pen protested. "The two don't have to go hand in hand."

Lulu turned to offer her a wan smile. "It isn't that

simple. There are...other considerations. But never mind that. What did you find out today?"

Penelope stared at her for a moment longer, then exhaled and told them everything.

"So that's the gist of it. Moira swears she doesn't know what the final plan is or what started it all, neither does Eliza. I'm certain Katie stole something from her father, but I have no idea what it was. We're not much closer to finding any of them than we were when this all started, except for being certain they were working together on something."

"Let's get the chalkboard!" Jane said, popping up before Pen could stop her. Perhaps it would do some good to have it all laid out in front of her.

On one side Jane wrote Katie's name, then underneath began writing Stacy. "Do you think it ends with an I-E or a Y? Perhaps an E-Y?"

"Put all three," Leonard suggested, finding the process interesting.

Jane wrote out all versions: Stacie, Stacy, and Stacey. On the other side, she wrote "Amethyst" and underneath she put "Anna," then "Ana" for good measure.

"What else?"

"List all their crimes and misdemeanors," Pen said, only partially in jest. "Katie was a habitual thief, constantly snuck out, disobeyed her teachers, and had a secret hiding place right underneath the noses of the nuns at her school. Amethyst liked to make a public spectacle and ran right through her inheritance. She was also the one to introduce Katie to the speakeasy."

"Though she did go to church faithfully with her father every Sunday," Jane noted.

"Only as a way to curry favor with Dear Papa," Pen said.

"You might as well include what their fathers do. No matter how sheltered a girl is, she picks up a thing or two," Lulu said, a cryptic smile on her face.

"Amethyst's father is in shipping, and well, Katie's is in almost anything illegal."

"Not mutually exclusive, I'd say," Leonard pointed out.

"Agreed."

"True."

Pen and Lulu both concurred at the same time and laughed.

When Jane was done writing, they all stared up at the board trying to make the connection. Finally, Penelope sighed with frustration.

"Until we know what both Mr. Easton and Mr. Sweeney are hiding, I simply can't figure this out. Perhaps an old-fashioned search party is in order? These two girls come from money. So I doubt they are holed up in some abandoned tenement building."

They all continued to stare at the chalkboard until the blaring of the phone broke the silence, causing them all to jump. Pen rushed to answer first.

"Your wish has been granted, Lady Pen," Tommy's voice said before she could even ask anything. "Carlo Messina has agreed to meet with you and me in exactly two hours. I'll drive you."

He hung up without a goodbye. After knowing more about him, she was inclined to be less irritated at his abrupt nature. Still, she once again, wondered how Lulu put up with it. She thought back to how Tommy had spoken to Mrs. Sweeney, and even the charm he'd turned on for the receptionist at the dance school earlier. Perhaps he had an endearing side.

"It seems I have a meeting with Carlo Messina. Let's hope this sheds some light on things."

Pen didn't need an interpreter to read the expressions of everyone else in the room. Even Jane knew of the Messina family. Their handiwork was a constant in the crime section of every paper in town. No one crossed them and came out of it unscathed.

CHAPTER TWELVE

PENELOPE HAD THOUGHT ABOUT TAKING HER GUN WITH a jade handle to meet with the Messina family. Then, she realized it would do no good. There was no way Carlo Messina, head of the family, would allow a meeting without searching her purse, especially if she was escorted by Tommy Callahan.

It was evening by the time Penelope and Tommy arrived at Mulberry Street, which was Little Italy's version of Broadway. The meeting was held under the terms of the Messinas, which meant an Italian restaurant in the heart of their home territory. It wasn't the first time Penelope had visited that street for a case, but she had certainly not met with the head of a crime family the last time.

"Are the Sweeneys and Messinas at war or not?" Penelope asked Tommy on the drive there.

"It's complicated."

"So uncomplicate it," Penelope said in a testy voice.

Tommy sighed. "There are some...misunderstandings about issues concerning the shipments of a certain product."

"You don't have to be so cryptic, I know you're talking about alcohol."

Tommy just stared ahead, continuing to drive without answering.

"Quite the lucrative business. I can see how that might cause someone to resort to drastic means like kidnapping."

"As I already said, we don't mess with kin, certainly not children. If Mr. Sweeney was even stupid enough to do something like that, he would have gone after Messina's oldest, Mario. He's the one already involved in his Da's business."

"Does Mr. Messina feel the same when it comes to Mr. Sweeney? Katie is his oldest."

"But a girl."

"Ah, her one failing."

Tommy shot her a wry smile. His smile cooled as they turned onto Mulberry Street. The last time Pen had been there, Leonard couldn't even get the car through due to the congestion of the street markets. Somehow a path had been cleared for Tommy to arrive, like God parting the Red Sea. Perhaps in that part of New York, Carlo Messina was akin to God.

"Should I let you do the talking?"

"This is your meeting, Pen. I'm just here to observe."

"What?" Penelope looked at him in alarm. "You're not even going to make introductions or something in that manner?"

"He ain't the King of England."

Pen took that into consideration, then remembered why she was there. Three young people were missing. That eased some of her nerves. Besides, she had met with one head of a gang, Mr. Sweeney, several times. Still, this felt far more formal.

Outside of the restaurant, two men in suits were standing guard.

"We're here to see Mr. Messina. I'm Penelope—"

"He's expecting you, Miss Banks," one of them said with a face of pure granite. "We need to check for weapons."

Penelope's eyes dropped down to the vested dress with a pleated skirt she had changed into, wondering where she could have possibly been hiding a weapon.

"Those are the rules, miss," he said in a tone that wasn't remotely apologetic.

"Fine," she said, throwing up her hands. He at least had the decency not to enjoy himself as his hands lightly patted her up and down. He made her open her purse, then grunted in satisfaction. Yes, it was probably a good thing she hadn't brought the gun. It might have given the wrong impression.

Tommy's inspection was understandably more thorough. They quickly found the gun under his jacket that he hadn't even bothered to try and hide.

He grinned. "Force of habit, boys. You understand."

The man scowled. "I understand I could use this right now to—"

"Gentlemen, please. We're just here about two missing young people. Tommy is very sorry for his oversight, aren't you Tommy?"

"My apologies, fellas."

There was a stare down that sent a ripple of danger through the air.

Penelope coughed to get their attention. "Do you think we can meet Mr. Messina now?"

The mug stood firm for one second just to make a point, then backed up and opened the door for them.

"How could you forget that?" Penelope hissed with annoyance.

"I didn't forget. They would have been suspicious if I hadn't come armed."

"Zounds," she muttered.

"You should probably start carrying around the toy I got you for your birthday, the way this case is going." Just as Pen had figured, the gun Lulu had given to her had come from Tommy.

"I'd rather use my brains." She didn't want to tell him the gun had already come in handy in a prior case.

"You better hope those brains stay in your head. A gun could help with that."

"Pineapples," Penelope cursed, feeling suddenly weak-kneed.

It was a quaint restaurant, big enough for only about ten tables, all covered in white tablecloths. On each, a candle sat in an old wine bottle, already half melted. Carlo Messina was seated at one with a candle that was lit, giving his dark, handsome face an eerie glow, even though dim, electric lights were also on. Two more men in suits stood on either side just behind him. The restaurant was otherwise empty.

Not for the first time, Penelope had the distinct feeling of deliberately entering the lion's den.

Carlo was a bit older than Jack, but presented himself in a completely different manner. Save for the darker skin tone, he could have easily been a senator or even Pen's own father in his expertly tailored three-piece suit. He even offered them a smile worthy of the mayor of New York as they approached. There wasn't a hint of animosity or sinister intent.

"Miss Penelope Banks and Tommy Callahan," he said,

gesturing to the two chairs opposite them. "Please, sit. Can I get you something to drink? Coffee? Water? Something a bit more...potent? I have a nice Primitivo, imported specially."

"No thanks," Tommy said curtly.

"Primitivo? That sounds divine," Pen said, truly interested despite the circumstances. It had been so long since she'd had red wine. Champagne and cocktails, or straight liquor was the usual fare at any club, speakeasy, or party. It was rare to find actual wine, at least any worth drinking. Six years after selling it became illegal, any wine connoisseur holding on to their pre-Prohibition stock was hesitant to open a bottle for anything other than a very special occasion. Mr. Messina apparently had no such reservations... unless this meeting turned out to be special in its own way.

That was something Pen didn't want to think about.

Mr. Messina laughed congenially, then snapped his fingers. The man on his right immediately exited to get the wine and glasses for them. He returned with a bottle that certainly didn't look like it had been collecting dust in a cellar for six years. Penelope read the label on the bottle: D'amico Vineyards.

"I would offer food, like a gracious host, but the kitchen is closed for the moment."

"We're fine," Tommy said in a level voice.

Messina's man uncorked the bottle, then poured three glasses despite Tommy's objections. Mr. Messina and Penelope raised theirs. Tommy demurred for only a moment, before picking up his glass and lifting it. Pen suspected there was some hidden power game in all of this that she would never be privy to.

"*Salute*," Mr. Messina said, looking Penelope in the eye and then, much more piercingly, Tommy.

"Salute," Pen repeated.

Tommy remained quiet.

Penelope took a sip from her glass, savoring it.

"Good, yes?"

"Delicious," Penelope hummed in earnest appreciation. She took another lingering sip, then reluctantly set the glass down to focus on Mr. Messina. "But we aren't here to enjoy the wine. Mr. Messina."

"Ah yes, my son, Tino."

"And Mr. Sweeney's daughter."

"I see Jack has to hire a woman to do his business for him." There was a taunting glimmer in his eye reserved specifically for Tommy. The two men on either side of him chuckled for effect.

"A woman who is very good at what she does," Penelope said in a sharp tone.

"Yes," Mr. Messina said, taking another sip and swallowing as he eyed her. "I'm familiar with your work, Miss Banks. It is the only reason you are sitting here right now. We look after our own down here, and welcome those who have done the same for us in the past."

Penelope knew which case he was talking about. Though that one had been a decidedly less daunting face-to-face meeting.

"I only seek justice is all. If someone is innocent and wrongfully accused, I'm happy to help."

Mr. Messina lowered his head to cede the point. "All the same, your efforts have been noted. *You* will always have safe passage in this part of town." His eyes flicked to Tommy and a glint appeared that made it quite clear she was the only one of them afforded such a benefit.

"I appreciate that, Mr. Messina. I hope that extends to getting information that might help me find Kathleen Sweeney?"

He shrugged. "I had nothing to do with the disappearance of Jack's daughter."

"And your son? Are you not worried about him?"

A subtle smile touched his lips. "If Tino wants to be his own man, who am I to stop him?"

"Even if it takes him to Hollywood?"

He coughed out a laugh. "Only if he promises to introduce his *papà* to Greta Garbo."

That got another hearty laugh from his men.

"I hardly think this is a laughing matter, Mr. Messina. A girl has gone missing. Your son has as well, but you don't seem at all worried, at least not about his welfare."

He considered her over his glass. "You told me you were good at what you do, Miss Banks. What do you suppose happened?"

Pen took a breath before speaking. "I think they ran away together. But not in the way you might have hoped."

"And what is it that I've hoped?" He asked, all prior hints of bonhomie disappearing under a dark look.

"That they might have conveniently eloped?"

He arched a single eyebrow. "Conveniently?"

"Well, a marriage between the Messinas and Sweeneys works out better for you, the groom being your son and all."

He smiled again.

"But no, I understand they are just friends."

His smile disappeared.

"Friends who had plans to go to Hollywood as soon as they were both eighteen. Friends who I think stumbled upon something that was quite valuable. Enough to forgo waiting until they were all eighteen to leave home."

Mr. Messina's eyes shifted to Tommy with scrutiny, and interestingly enough, curiosity. He had no idea what Penelope was talking about.

"And what would that quite valuable thing be?" Carlo asked.

"That's what I'm trying to find out."

Mr. Messina's eyes remained on Tommy. Penelope turned to find his face perfectly impassive, no hint at all as to what he was thinking or even feeling.

"If you're worried about me telling the police, Mr. Messina, I can assure you that my only interest is in finding Katie and—"

The way his eyes snapped back to Penelope silenced her.

"You think I have it? *That's* why you're here?"

"Have what exactly?"

He narrowed his eyes. "Are you trying to trap me?"

"I'd like to think I'm not that stupid." Penelope suddenly felt lost.

He breathed out a quiet laugh as he studied her. His eyes slid to Tommy, and despite meeting the same impassive expression, he didn't seem to like what he saw.

"This meeting is over," he said tersely. He shook one finger in the direction of the ever placid Tommy. "Next time Sweeney needs information, tell him to be man enough to come to me himself. Or at least be respectful enough not to send a dame in to do his dirty work."

"*Excuse* me?" Penelope said, offended.

Mr. Messina glared at her. "I don't appreciate being used this way, Miss Banks. I would have thought you unworthy of this, based on what I've heard. It seems I was wrong."

Before she could even respond he gestured to his men.

They came around to stand next to Tommy and Pen. He took that as a sign they were dismissed and stood up. Penelope remained seated.

"I haven't finished my wine. I also haven't gotten any answers."

Carlo stared at her with incredulity, then he laughed. "I admire your bravery, Miss Banks. Perhaps I wasn't mistaken about you. What answers did you come expecting to find? Other than the fact that I don't have this supposedly valuable thing you're looking for?"

Tommy took his seat again, and the meeting resumed.

"Has Tino ever run away before?"

"He has nothing to run away from."

"Of course not," Pen said dryly. She doubted that, and suspected Mr. Messina did as well. "If he *were* to run away, can you think of a place he might hide?"

It was a long shot. All three children had to know their fathers would be searching the most obvious places, as in buildings they owned. Then again, Mr. Messina wasn't exactly on the hunt for his son.

"I don't know. However, I do know that should someone in this city be...*unwise* enough to involve themselves in this by hiding these runaway children, they would find themselves in a very unfortunate position. Not from me, of course. I trust my Tino. Mr. Sweeney's princess...well, she does have a reputation." He sent a small smirk Tommy's way. He was wise enough not to react.

"Mr. Sweeney and you have been in disagreement with certain shipments or something of that sort, I understand. Can you tell me about that?"

"Jack knows what that is about."

"Ah yes, but I don't." Penelope casually sipped her wine.

He considered her for a moment, then a conceding smile appeared. "Fine. Mr. Sweeney knows that anything south of 4th Street is my territory, especially east of Broadway, this includes the piers. I don't appreciate our agreement being violated."

"What makes you think it's been violated?"

"I know what comes into lower Manhattan, even if Jack thinks it's well-disguised. I know how he supplies his establishments. But for the past several months, crates with no paperwork are suddenly disappearing from warehouses before my men can even get a peek? None of the five families know anything about it, which means it must be his business. Does he think I'm stupid?"

Even though his eyes bored into Penelope as he spoke, she knew that message was for Tommy. Still, that business about piers and boats was interesting.

"Do you know Charles Easton?"

There was a glimmer of recognition in his eyes, which didn't mean much in and of itself. Anyone involved in importing—even of the illegal variety—would know the man.

"Personally?" He grinned. "I haven't had the pleasure of being invited to dinner."

"And business-wise?"

"Again, I haven't had the pleasure."

"So I can assume you aren't smuggling this fine wine in on his ships?" She took another sip.

Mr. Messina laughed. "We don't need the help of American aristocrats to do our business, Miss Banks. The kind who look down their noses at us, all while sipping their fine brandy and whiskey in their private clubs, which we supply." He narrowed his eyes with suspicion. "Why do you ask?"

"His daughter has gone missing as well, Amethyst Easton. She's around the same age as your son and Mr. Sweeney's daughter."

Next to her, Tommy didn't so much as twitch, but she could sense his irritation at having given Carlo Messina that bit of information. Penelope didn't care, so long as it gave her answers.

"Well," Mr. Messina pondered that news, with a thoughtful look. He sipped his wine, allowing the information to simmer in his head. He swallowed and focused on Penelope again. "And you suspect the two girls are working with my Tino?"

"I do." Again, she could sense Tommy's irritation.

Mr. Messina grinned and lifted his glass in salute, a mask of levity coming back. "It seems I have underestimated my youngest son."

There were several ways that could have been interpreted.

"He might be in trouble."

"Then he should come to me for help," Mr. Messina said indifferently, casually sipping his wine.

It was useless. The only thing Penelope had learned was that Carlo Messina had no idea what his son was doing with Katie or Amethyst, or where they might be. He also didn't seem too concerned. She wasn't sure if it was the hubris of a man used to instilling fear in anyone who might cross him, or the hope of a father who thus far had misunderstood his son.

Penelope finished her wine. "One final question. Do the names Stacy or Anna mean anything to you?"

He stared back with no reaction. "No."

"I thought not. Well, this has been quite helpful," she said in a sardonic voice.

Mr. Messina smiled, but there was a sinister tinge to it. "Yes, it has."

"I appreciate you meeting with me, Mr. Messina."

"As I stated, you are always welcome in this part of town, Miss Banks. If you do find my son, please tell him to write. I'm very curious about this adventure of his."

"I just hope I find him before anything unfortunate happens to him or the two girls," she hinted.

"Should that be the case, I will handle it myself." All humor had disappeared.

On that note, Penelope decided it was time to leave. She reached into her purse and pulled out a business card. "In case you discover something that might help me find them."

Mr. Messina seemed amused by it, but took the card all the same. If he wanted to get in contact with her, she was fully aware he had his own means.

Penelope rose, but couldn't help staring at Tommy's untouched glass of wine with disbelief and frustration. What a waste.

As languid as a cat, Tommy also rose from his chair and strolled out the front door ahead of her. He held out his hand to the one who had taken his gun. After a momentary glare, he handed it back, but not before emptying it of all the bullets.

Tommy just offered a dry smile before leading Penelope back to the car. He was gracious enough to open the door for her before getting in on the driver's side.

"Well, that wasn't helpful at all. He's just as clueless about Tino as Mr. Sweeney is about Katie."

Tommy shrugged nonchalantly.

Pen breathed out a sardonic laugh. "Do I at least get to know if my theory in there was correct? Does Katie have something valuable? Something she may have stolen from her father?"

Again he shrugged.

"I'll take that as a yes." She turned to fully stare at him

as something occurred to her. "Zounds! You were using me! You wanted to find out if Messina did in fact have this valuable thing, and I was the only way you could get a meeting!"

He met her with eyelids lowered in dry amusement. "It seems you *are* very good at what you do, Miss Banks."

Penelope fell back in her seat with exasperation. "Does Mr. Sweeney even care about finding his daughter?"

"She'll be fine. Anyone who knows who she is knows better than to mess with her."

"And those that don't know?"

"Will be dealt with."

Penelope stared out the window, wondering how she had gotten wrapped up in this mess.

"Finding Katie is and always will be my priority, just so you know. Amethyst as well."

"That is what you were hired for."

"At least now I know what I was really hired for."

"What's that?"

"Finding this *very valuable thing*."

"I wouldn't focus on that if I were you."

"Oh, and why not?"

"As I've already told you, that's gonna get you into a lot of trouble—Lulu as well."

Tommy drove Penelope home, dropping her right in front of her 5th Avenue apartment building. He was even enough of a gentleman to make sure she walked through the front door. She said hello to the evening doorman and took the resident elevator up to her floor.

"Miss Banks, you received a hand-delivered message late in the afternoon today," her butler, Chives greeted as she entered.

"Really?" Perhaps someone she had spoken to had decided to get in touch with urgent news. But why send it to her home rather than her office? That was the number and address on the business card that she'd been handing out.

She took the envelope and opened it:

I have what you're looking for. Jeanette Park, behind the door left of the band shell. Midnight. Come alone.

Penelope reread it in puzzlement, her head filled with questions. She surmised it had to do with her current cases. She also assumed she wouldn't find the three young people hidden away in a storage area for the band shell, a memorial dedicated to the merchant seamen from the Great War, located in Jeanette Park.

But what *would* she find?

CHAPTER THIRTEEN

Penelope had been a bundle of nerves all through dinner with Cousin Cordelia. She hadn't told her older cousin about either case, as it would have only opened the door to questions Pen shouldn't have answered. Even Cousin Cordelia knew about Mr. Sweeney and the Messina Family. She would have positively fainted if she'd known Penelope had personally met with the heads of both criminal organizations in the span of forty-eight hours.

No, the case already had too many players involved. Penelope was keeping the message she received to herself until she knew exactly what lay in wait in Jeanette Park.

But she wasn't going alone, especially at midnight. She had alerted Leonard that she needed his services. Rather than seem put out, he'd sounded excited at the prospect. He'd seen and overheard enough about the case to know he had reason to be intrigued.

Pen also made sure to bring her jade-handled gun with her. For once, she was glad of her association with Tommy Callahan.

Leonard was tactful enough to drive in silence, which

gave her time to think. As he drove down South Street that bordered the East River, Pen realized that Jeanette Park was located right across from the piers. In fact, as Leonard slowed down to approach, she noted that Pier 6, where Connor Davidson's body had been found, was directly visible from the tiny park.

"Just pull around so you're behind the stage," Pen instructed.

Jeanette Park was a small, triangular wedge carved into the southern tip of Manhattan. It was really just an open area, surrounded by benches. At the western end sat the Great War merchant seamen memorial, which had been converted into a lifted stage shielded by a half dome. There were lights in the park and on the street, but that only made the figures lying prone or slouched on the benches and skulking in the shadows seem that much more ominous.

Even knowing the 1st Precinct for the NYPD and a firehouse were both within walking distance didn't help ease Penelope's trepidation. Neither would have men who could be there in time, should the worst happen.

"I should really come with you, Miss Banks."

"I'll be fine," she assured Leonard. "I've got my gun and I'll be quick."

Despite her fears, she wasn't about to lose the most promising lead she had thus far because she'd failed to follow the simple instructions to come alone.

"Just keep the car running and stay alert. Beep the horn if something looks suspect."

"Will do, Miss Banks." He looked as though he wanted to argue, but he didn't.

Penelope opened the door, and waited, her gun drawn. She left her purse, taking the flashlight she'd thought to bring with her instead. She was fully prepared to put the zotz on this mission if it looked like an ambush. She didn't see anyone looking suspicious nearby, so she cautiously got out. Once she closed the door behind her, she quickly skittered to the gate surrounding the park and entered.

Pen ignored the transients in the park and rushed to the door to the left of the stage. She tugged at it, probably harder than she should have, fully expecting it to be locked. Instead, she nearly fell back as it easily opened. She noted that the lock seemed to have been picked.

It was dark inside, and she was glad for the flashlight. She certainly didn't want to waste time searching for a switch or light pull. Instead, she turned it on and swept the small area ahead of her. Not seeing or hearing anyone, she walked in, pointing the gun and flashlight ahead of her into the darkness.

"Hello," she whispered, then waited. "Katie? Tino? Amethyst?"

There was no response, save for some concerning skritches warning her that her only company was of the four- or six-legged variety.

Was she the victim of some practical joke?

Pen walked in a few steps further, ready to call out again. Then her foot hit something small on the ground before her. It was solid and immobile, but it still had her heart in her throat, thinking it was a rodent.

"Pineapples!" Pen hissed, kicking at it in frustration.

Penelope heard the sound of a piece of paper whispering against the ground. She lowered the flashlight and saw the paper right next to the object she had bumped into. It read: For Penelope Banks. The object next to it was covered in cloth. She picked up both items and rushed back out.

So this was what she had been summoned to get. The

object the paper had been lying on top of was inside an empty sugar sack. Whatever was inside was round, like a coffee can. Penelope didn't waste time opening it there, as the park denizens were getting curious about the most recent visitor.

Pen rushed back to the car and got in, slamming the door behind her. Leonard wasted no time driving off.

"Everything go alright?"

"Well, I didn't find any of our missing individuals, but someone did leave something for me," she said. She put her gun and flashlight back into her purse, then unpacked what had been left for her.

The sugar sack opened to reveal a coffee can. The smiling face of the woman advertising Ideal Blend Coffee did nothing to settle her beating heart as she opened the top. Inside, something had been swaddled in much finer cloth than the sugar sack. Penelope reached in and gently pulled it out, noting that the cloth was a silk scarf, quite nice. What she uncovered was even more impressive.

"Zounds!"

CHAPTER FOURTEEN

PENELOPE STOOD IN THE LIBRARY OF HER APARTMENT staring down at the object on the side table underneath a lamp.

It was a gold egg.

For how small it was, it was surprisingly intricate, which made Penelope believe it was real gold. Everything from the ribbed outer shell to the three-legged stand to the floral garland draped around it was most likely made of real precious metal. There was a diamond (a gem) set in a diamond (a shape) on the front. Holding up the garland were three blue stones—sapphires?

Penelope noticed a seam circling the middle, which meant that it opened up. She hesitantly picked up the egg, which was about the size of a real chicken's egg. Carefully, she opened it and blinked when a small clock popped up. The tiny hands also had tiny diamonds in them. She closed it just as gingerly and set it back into the base.

With her hands on her hips, she stared down at the egg and breathed out a long slow breath.

"So...this is that very valuable thing."

Pen had no idea what to do with it, not just the egg itself, but the news of her having it. She certainly wasn't going to tell Tommy. Nor Carlo Messina or Jack Sweeney, for that matter. She saw no reason to tell Charles Easton either. Lulu and Jane were probably trustworthy, but this would be an unnecessary burden of information. She'd even managed to keep Leonard from finding out on the drive home, and he'd been tactful enough not to inquire.

There was of course Richard. But he'd quickly turn into Detective Prescott when he saw it and then force her to tell him about the circumstances leading up to it. No, that would—

"Penelope, whatever are you still doing up?"

Penelope jumped, her heart clawing up her throat at the sound of Cousin Cordelia entering the library.

"I'm sorry, dear. I didn't mean to frighten you. I just got up to— Oh, what a darling little egg!"

Pen watched in horror as her cousin rushed over to pick it up from the stand to admire it.

"Such intricate detail. It reminds me of those eggs made for the poor tsar and his wife in Russia, you know the ones."

"Fabergé?" Penelope croaked out.

It was exactly what she had suspected. It wasn't just any egg, it was no doubt an authentic Fabergé. Supposedly after the Romanov family had been murdered, the Bolsheviks had ransacked the palaces, nationalized the House of Fabergé, and taken control of all the eggs in the Kremlin Armory. Even at the time, Penelope hadn't been alone in assuming at least a few pieces had gone "missing" during all the chaos of the revolution.

And this one was small enough to easily be smuggled away underneath a coat or even in a pocket.

"Yes, Fabergé," Cousin Cordelia said in agreement, still

admiring the egg in her hands. "They were so lovely, I suppose it was inevitable other jewelers would have started replicating them."

"They must be in vogue once again," Penelope said, gingerly taking the egg from her cousin and placing it back in the stand.

"I wouldn't have thought you'd be one to buy one for yourself. You always seemed so averse to jewels and expensive trinkets. Fine dresses and shoes are all well and good, but something like this, well, it could be timeless."

"Indeed. Or priceless," Pen muttered, staring down at the egg.

"Oh my, I haven't walked in on a present for me have I?"

"No," Pen said, nibbling her bottom lip distractedly.

"Oh."

Pen snatched her attention away from the egg to acknowledge Cousin Cordelia, who looked as though she'd been stricken. "Oh, Cousin, I didn't mean it that way. You know I'm happy to buy you any little figurine you'd like, no matter the price. It's just that this one is, well, it's part of a case I'm working on. I think..." She turned her attention back to the egg and inhaled before continuing. "I think this might be an authentic Fabergé egg."

"Oh!" Cousin Cordelia stared down at the egg, now in alarm. She brought her hands up, as though they were covered in blood. "How could you let me touch it! To think, the poor tsarina may have held this very egg in her own hands!"

"It's the hands that have since held it that I'm worried about," Penelope said, turning her attention back to it.

"However did you come into possession of it? Wait! I'm

not sure I should know the details. I'd hate to be arrested as a coconspirator in all of this."

"Don't worry, Cousin, you won't be."

"You should hand it over to the authorities this very instant."

Pen nibbled her bottom lip in response.

"*Penelope?*"

"It isn't that simple. There are two—possibly three missing young people. I have a feeling they're in trouble, especially now."

"What sort of trouble—no, I don't want to know!" She put a hand up to stop Pen before she began. She lowered it and gave Pen a sheepish look. "Unless you think it will help to tell me?"

Cousin Cordelia was never one to miss a good bit of thrilling news or gossip.

"It's probably best that you don't know." It would be all over the wealthy matronly set of New York before the end of the day. "And you can*not* tell anyone about this egg, Cousin."

"Pen, what sort of gossip do you take me for," she scoffed.

She ignored that to save her cousin's pride.

"At the very least you should tell Detective Prescott. This is no simple matter for a private investigator, Penelope. This could very well be an international incident. The Bolsheviks might be at our door at any moment!" That seemed to give her an attack. "Oh, where is my medicine?"

"I'll pour us both some."

Pen walked out to grab the bottle of gin from her small bar. She brought it back in with two glasses.

"Illegal alcohol is hardly medicinal," Cousin Cordelia said, pursing her lips.

"And yet it has the same nerve-settling effect. You can take two teaspoons of your medicinal brandy, come morning. Right now, we both need this."

Pen was in no mood to remind Cousin Cordelia that her "prescription" medicinal brandy was almost three years expired and the "medicine" was just as illegal as what Pen was currently pouring for her.

"Cin cin," Pen said, lifting her glass before taking a long swallow.

Her cousin plumped her bottom lip out, but took a sip all the same. When she brought her glass away, she squinted one eye at Penelope. "What exactly do you plan on doing with it, Penelope? We can't very well keep it here."

Pen twisted her lips in thought. "Yes, you're right of course. I'll...I'll call Richard in the morning, that's what I'll do. I need time to think. Besides I can't call him now, it's only—"

"Oh no·you don't! I know for a fact that you've called him at an earlier hour than this, young lady. I'm not saying you're in over your head, dear, but this," she stabbed a finger at the egg, "is a sign that you shouldn't be handling things on your own."

Even without knowing the parties involved, Cousin Cordelia had a point. Everyone involved in this case seemed to be holding secrets and operating with urgency, so it had to be authentic. Penelope hated to think she wasn't capable of anything on her own, but if the egg was a real Fabergé, certainly the authorities needed to be notified.

"You're beginning to sound like my father."

"Don't be silly, I'm hardly that terrible."

Pen coughed out a laugh. Cousin Cordelia smiled and took another long sip.

"You should drink more often. It makes you smarter than me," Penelope said.

"You should drink less, it makes you think I'm smarter than you."

Pen laughed again, and Cousin Cordelia joined her. When they finished, the sobering reality hit.

"I suppose you're right. I'll call him now."

Pen finished off her glass of gin and took a breath. Cousin Cordelia was right in that it wouldn't have been the first time Pen called Richard at odd hours of the night. This wouldn't even be the most problematic reason she'd had to call him. Still, she at least trusted him to do the right thing, even if that conflicted with her case.

She went into the hallway to pick up the phone, connecting to him via the number she had well-memorized by now.

"Hello, Richard," she said, trying to sound cheerful.

"Penelope," he said in a deep, groggy voice that sent a shiver of delight through her. "This is becoming a rather irksome habit of yours, calling me at indecent hours."

"I think you'll agree this one might just be worth it."

"That's what you said the last few times."

"I don't believe I've ever used those exact words."

"Yes, I suppose you would know better than I would." He sighed heavily and Pen could picture him sitting up in bed. Another shiver, this time more delightful went through her. "I assume this is related to a case of yours?"

"One I can't talk about over the phone."

"Of course not."

"Again, it'll be worth it. At least...if something is what I suspect it is."

"Well, your suspicions have a habit of being true, or at

least worthy of a visit at...good grief, one-thirty in the morning?"

"If you manage to get tired again after this, then you can sleep here. Though, I have a feeling you won't."

"Alright, you've tempted me enough. I'll be there soon."

CHAPTER FIFTEEN

"IT'S AN EGG." RICHARD STARED DOWN AT THE GOLDEN figure with an expression that didn't seem very impressed.

Penelope observed his handsome face, dark eyes framed by thick lashes, and strong features. She was on the side of him that offered a view of the burn scar rising out of his collar and creeping up to just below his right jaw. He had received it during the Great War after his plane crashed.

The noise of his arrival had roused her orange, long-haired cat, Little Monster. He navigated his way between the legs of Pen and Richard until she picked him up to drape over her shoulder. It was the only way to settle him, and she stroked his long fur as he softly purred in her ear.

"It's not just *any* egg! It's a Fabergé," Cousin Cordelia exclaimed. She had taken it upon herself to have another finger (or two) of gin before his arrival.

"We don't know that," Penelope said, though her doubts seeped through in her voice.

Richard stared at her, his brow slowly furrowing with disbelief. "You don't think this is an authentic Fabergé, do you? I mean, yes it's a very convincing replica...*surely?*"

"Considering the circumstances, I think it might be authentic."

His brow smoothed out, growing suspicion coloring his narrowed eyes. "What circumstances are those?"

"Before I explain, I want to impress upon you the fact that this is a legitimate case. I have yet to break the law...knowingly."

"That doesn't reassure me."

"I'd also like to point out that should our own daughter ever go missing, you would want as many resources dedicated to finding her as possible."

"I'm not even sure where to begin with that..." He stared down at Penelope's abdomen, his eyes widened with alarm.

"Zounds, no, not that!" Pen exclaimed with a nervous laugh, cutting a quick glance to Cousin Cordelia in hopes she hadn't noticed where his eyes went. "Obviously, we'll both be waiting for marriage to even consider having children."

"Naturally," he said, with a degree of relief.

"Well, at least you two are being careful. In my day, it wasn't so easy to prevent such things."

Both Penelope and Richard turned to Cousin Cordelia in surprise.

"What makes you think...?"

Cousin Cordelia waved a dismissive hand at Penelope. "You two are hardly inconspicuous. You're twenty-five, Penelope. And Detective Prescott is quite handsome. The scar only adds something dashing about him." She gave him an ossified smile. "I'd have been surprised if you *hadn't* been doing something. Heaven knows I couldn't wait with Harold!"

Penelope coughed out a laugh. Richard just coughed uncomfortably.

"Perhaps you should tell me about this case, Penelope," Richard said, his voice gruffer than it needed to be.

"Yes, of course," she said, thinking about where to begin. "On Monday, Jack Sweeney came to my office."

"*What?*"

"Because his daughter has gone missing," Penelope quickly added.

"Which sounds like a matter for the police," he said in a censuring voice.

"She's seventeen, Richard, and there are no signs of foul play. They'd hardly put all their efforts into it. Besides, I suspect he already has a few members of the force working on it." She arched a brow accusingly. He matched it with one of acknowledgment. "It seems Carlo Messina's youngest son, Tino, has also gone missing."

"This keeps getting better," he said in exasperation.

"And the seventeen-year-old daughter of Charles Easton has also gone missing."

He became more alert. "And you think they're related?"

"Mr. Easton seems to think so. After a bit of investigating, so do I."

"Before we get into that, what does all of this have to do with the egg?"

"I think either Katie Sweeney or perhaps Amethyst Easton stole it in order to fund their independence. Considering both of them are used to a certain standard of living, they must have expected quite a bit from the sale. If it was just a replica, even in authentic gold and gemstones, that would hardly do it. Thus, I have to assume it must be worth far more than the sum of its parts, as in an *authentic* Fabergé. That would be priceless."

"Apparently not, if what you say is true," he said, staring down at the egg with new eyes. He turned his attention back to Pen. "And how did you come into possession of it?"

Penelope walked Little Monster out into the hallway and set him down. She closed the door on his mild meow of protest. She walked over to pull the note out of her purse. "I received this by hand delivery today."

He read it, and she could see the same confusion on his face that she felt about the whole thing.

"So one of these girls stole it, only to give it up...to *you?*"

"Yes, which means something must have gone wrong."

"Or maybe they just got scared and decided to forego their plan of running away?"

"So where are they? And which of them stole it?"

"Tell me everything you've learned thus far."

"Alright, but just remember, despite who I have been working with, I haven't broken the law."

His jaw visibly tightened, but he nodded.

Penelope noted that Cousin Cordelia had fallen fast asleep on the sofa in the library. That was for the best, as she didn't need to hear any of what Pen had to say. Penelope turned back to Richard and told him everything. He didn't say anything when Tommy's name came up, but she could see the hard glint of disapproval in his eyes. Those eyes brightened in horror when she got to the part about meeting Carlo Messina in person.

"I see," he said in a measured tone after she was finished. "We have a crime boss's daughter, the son of the head of one of the five Italian criminal families, and the daughter of a man who owns a shipping business. It's not hard to figure out why they came together. Plenty of illegal and stolen property comes in on almost every ship that makes it to port, even those that are completely legitimate.

"So, some enterprising Bolshevik, realizing communism wasn't to his tastes, decides to make a nice penny by squirreling away one of the famous Fabergé Eggs at some point during the revolution. And it eventually ends up in the hands of either Katie Sweeney or Amethyst Easton. Either daughter might have the connections to know a way to sell it on the black market, especially if they were working together with Tino Messina."

"Obviously, the only concern I have is finding them and making sure they are safe. Unless they all go running home first thing in the morning, I think we have to assume they might be in danger."

"What about these two boys with them Friday night, John Foster or Christos Papadopoulos? I think it's interesting that both of them were included in this little meeting at the speakeasy."

"I'll try talking to them again, now that I know what the big secret was. They might cave if they know the egg has been returned."

Richard scratched his jaw, just to the side of his scar. "A group of young people, none older than nineteen, trying to pull this off? It's no wonder it went off the tracks."

"I wouldn't underestimate young people. We were both that age once. You went to war. I went...well, that's a story for a different night."

Richard gave her a scrutinizing look.

Penelope quickly moved on to something that had just occurred to her. "The man who was murdered and left at Pier 6, Connor Davidson. Does the department have any more information or leads on his death?"

"Do you suspect it's related?"

"A customs agent, killed and found near the piers? And in the same timeline as our missing girls and the discovery of this egg? An egg which I found not too far from where his body was?"

"I can look into it. If it is related, that only makes things more dire for your missing kids."

"Unless they participated in it?" Pen suggested.

He shook his head. "I read the circumstances of his death. That was done by someone used to being violent." He gave her a pointed look.

"Tommy swears it wasn't the handy work of Sweeney's men."

"Well, if he says so."

Pen ignored the sarcasm in his voice. "At any rate, unless we do in fact learn it's related, let's leave that case to the police. I'd rather focus on finding these three."

Richard sighed and ran a hand over his thick hair. "You're right. Since we have possession of the egg, we *should* focus on them. Let's review everything."

"Right," Pen began, thinking about the chalkboard back in the office that listed everything known so far about each girl. "Perhaps these fake names are part of—Pineapples!"

She had exclaimed loudly enough to startle Cousin Cordelia out of her slumber with a snort.

"Oh, Penelope, how could you let me fall asleep in front of Detective Prescott? It's perfectly indecent."

"Sorry, Cousin," Pen said still distracted by the insight that had come to her. "I was just about to tell Richard that I may have figured out these fake names, especially now that we have the egg. Stacy and Anna. I had wondered why *those* names, as Stacy in particular seemed unusual. But if you switch them they become Anna and Stacy."

Richard and Cousin Cordelia stared at her without comprehension.

"Anna-Stacy?" Again, they seemed lost, and Pen

laughed, throwing up her hands with exasperation. "Anastasia!"

"Like the surviving Romanov?" Cousin Cordelia said, eyes wide.

"I'm pretty sure they determined she was in fact killed with her family. Wasn't that confirmed?"

"I don't believe it," Cousin Cordelia said, her chin lifted in stubborn denial. "I know there were several frauds trying to get rich off of her legacy. All the more reason she's had to go further into hiding. She's out there somewhere, I know it. Perhaps she's come for the egg?" Her eyes were wide with excitement at the prospect.

Pen stared down at the Fabergé. "That's a wrinkle to this case that we don't need. Someone knows about this egg —either Mr. Easton or Mr. Sweeney, I'd say, perhaps both— and is bound to come looking for it. Throwing a surviving Romanov into this will only make it more of an international mess."

"Which is exactly why we need to take this higher than the NYPD," Richard said. "Frankly, knowing how many men on the force Mr. Sweeney, and frankly, Mr. Easton may have on their personal payroll, I don't trust it in our custody."

"Agreed."

"As for the feds, there are a few men I know personally from my time in the war who I would trust with this. They're in the State Department, which is probably fitting. They handle most international affairs, at least when we aren't at war. This is bigger than the FBI if it involves international smuggling."

"Now wait just one moment. This is directly tied to both of my cases, I'm certain of it. It's one of the few helpful clues I have. If we hand it over to the federal government, we'll never see it again. Further, we don't even know if it's an actual Fabergé."

"Something which the State Department will be able to determine."

"And if one or all of these missing three ends up dead because someone came looking for it?"

"Don't you suspect it was one of the three who left the egg for you in the first place?"

"Well, yes, but...until I know why, I'd rather not just hand it over so casually. After all, the only people who know I have it are you and Cousin Cordelia."

"And whoever sent you that note."

"Yes, and I suppose Leonard knows I have something special, though I didn't show or tell him what it was."

"Which is exactly four people too many."

"Leonard is trustworthy."

"I'm sure. But there are many ways to get information even from trustworthy people."

Pen shuddered at the prospect. "So what do you suggest?"

"It's the middle of the night, so there isn't much I can do, or really *want* to do at this hour. My friend in the State Department, he's in Washington D.C. He'll have to catch a train here, which will take some time. I'll call him first thing in the morning. In the meantime, I'll stay here with the egg."

"*Here?*" Cousin Cordelia exclaimed.

"It's safe enough here for now. Your building has a doorman at least and is situated on a visible and active street. Even if someone did know about it, they'd have a few obstacles to get to me...and my gun."

"Oh dear," Cousin Cordelia cried.

"It'll be fine, Cousin. We'll keep it hidden, on top of Richard staying here." Pen turned to him. "And what are you going to tell your friend when he asks how it came into my possession? Are you going to reveal all the circumstances surrounding this?"

He gave her a sardonic look. "As far as I know, you received an anonymous message and acted on it. At least until these young people are found, safe and sound, I'll leave it at that. Truthfully, he'll probably be most concerned about getting the egg back to the proper people, for diplomatic reasons."

Pen knew what that meant. "The Bolsheviks? I wouldn't be surprised if they melted it down for scrap."

"Or you could deliver it to Anastasia," said Cousin Cordelia. "It rightfully belongs to her."

"And if she's alive and in hiding, who better to return it to her than the federal government?" Richard said, managing to keep a straight face.

"Fine," Pen said in resignation, looking at the egg longingly.

"Good. Now then, I'll stay here in the library tonight and keep watch for the safety of both of you. In the morning, I'll make the call and the feds can take over from there."

"Thank you, Richard."

"Of course." He grinned. "I do have to hand it to you. You were right, this was worth it."

Pen laughed and walked over and picked up the egg, realizing it might be the last time she'd ever see it in person. Now that she was almost certain what it was, there was a degree of gravitas attached to the situation. She was staring at a piece of history. Like her cousin, she wondered if the tsar and tsarina had held the same egg in their hands.

Where would it end up?

Perhaps Anastasia was indeed still alive and this would be the very thing to bring her out of hiding?

CHAPTER SIXTEEN

Despite the excitement of the night, Penelope eventually succumbed to sleep. The next morning, after getting dressed, she rushed to the library. She found Richard sitting in one of the chairs, reading a book and enjoying a cup of coffee.

He lifted it toward her and grinned. "Chives took pity on me, and didn't ask any questions. Good man."

They had put the egg in a secure location behind some of the books on one shelf. It wasn't much, but at least it kept the egg from remaining out in the open for anyone to view. They were still without a maid, something Penelope had oddly bad luck with, so that saved some of the trouble.

"I think you should go in to your office today as though nothing has happened. Obviously, don't mention the egg to anyone, not even Jane or Lulu, though I know how much you trust them."

He was right. There was no need to involve more people than necessary. Besides, by the end of the day, the egg would be out of their possession and the federal government's problem. Still, she walked over to push the books aside and look at it one last time.

"An actual Fabergé," she said with a smile, picking it up from its stand one final time. "I can see why so many people would be after it."

"Perhaps that's why Amethyst or Katie gave it up, maybe they felt they were in over their heads."

Pen thought about the girl in the red dress from the Peacock Club, throwing a fit as she was dragged out by Tommy. Then, she thought of the girl splashed across the pages of the tabloids.

Both were immature and rebellious, though perhaps good at scheming and planning. She didn't know much about Tino, but she doubted he was enough to turn this caper of theirs into a failsafe plan for independence.

After breakfast, Penelope had Leonard drive her to the office, as Richard had told her to do.

"Did last night's adventures lead to any development in the case?" Leonard asked as he drove.

She was glad she hadn't shown him the egg. It would have embroiled him in all of this, and she had a feeling that wouldn't be good for him.

"It only created another puzzle. Fortunately, Detective Prescott is handling it. I doubt it's even really related to my current cases," she added just for good measure.

The traffic light had just turned, allowing them to proceed when Penelope heard the sounds of a police siren. She didn't think much of it—police sirens were part and parcel of living in New York City—until the car sped up right next to hers, then deliberately cut them off. Leonard was forced to come to a screeching halt, which nearly had Pen tumbling into the front seat.

"What the hell?" Leonard exclaimed in anger.

Two uniformed policemen exited their car and stormed over to Pen's door. One abruptly opened it and leaned in to address her.

"Miss Penelope Banks?"

"Yes. What is the meaning of this?"

"I need you to come with me, Miss Banks. Now." He was just short of being polite, considering who he was talking to. However, the look on his face left no room for argument.

Pen's mind instantly went to the egg. Had they found out about it? Had they already raided her apartment to take possession of it? Was Richard in trouble? Cousin Cordelia would no doubt already be into her medicinal brandy.

"What is this about, officer?"

"Please come with me, miss. I'd hate to have to take you into custody by force."

Her mouth fell open in shock. "Am I under arrest?"

"No Miss Banks, but you do need to come with us."

Pen wanted to stand her ground, but she knew that would only make things worse. They might commandeer the whole car and decide to take Leonard as well.

He twisted around in his seat to face her. "Miss Banks, do you need me to—"

"You stay out of this, pal," the cop said, not nearly as congenial with her driver as he'd been with Pen.

"It's fine Leonard. But please go back to my apartment, if you would. Richard should still be there. Make sure he knows I've been taken by two uniformed policemen." Pen made sure to make it sound as offending as it was, perhaps worse. She'd used Richard's first name rather than "Detective Prescott" so as not to get him into trouble if he wasn't already. Still, she trusted that Leonard knew what to do.

Penelope exited the vehicle, chin held high with

outrage. The officers at least had the decency not to take hold of her arm as they escorted her, though they did stand close enough to prevent her from fleeing. Still, it was insulting when the back door of the police car was opened and they silently indicated she should get in.

She frowned and got in. They wordlessly closed the door on her, then got into the front seats and drove off.

"Where are you taking me?"

They stared ahead without answering.

The further south they went, the more Penelope's stomach dropped. It became quite evident that they were headed in the same direction Leonard had driven her just before midnight.

Had someone from the 1st precinct seen her pick up the egg? Why had they waited until now to arrest her? How had they even known what she was doing? Perhaps it was for breaking into the door of the memorial? No, they wouldn't have gone to all this trouble for a woman of Pen's stature just for opening an unlocked door.

Despite the officer's assurance that she wasn't under arrest, she knew she was in some sort of trouble.

"I demand that you tell me what this is about, right now!"

Still no answer. Not even so much as a glance her way. They remained stone-faced, staring straight ahead.

"I have a right to call my attorney. I also have a right to know why I've been taken! Do you know who I am?" She hated using that threat, but she'd seen how effective it was when used by others.

They had no fear of her threats, which only made her more concerned.

Pen sat back and nibbled her bottom lip in thought as she stared out the window. When they drove so far they had passed both the police station and Jeanette Park, her brow wrinkled with confusion. There wasn't much left of Manhattan beyond that.

Where were they taking her?

They turned west and Penelope sat up to pay more attention. They were heading to Battery Park. Or perhaps the aquarium in Castle Clinton situated at the southern tip of Manhattan? Both were within walking distance of where she'd been last night.

She could see another police car parked ahead. The car she was in came to a stop next to it. Again without any word, both policemen exited. One opened the door for her. As much as she itched to remain in place unless they told her more, she welcomed the release from her temporary prison. Her curiosity also had her scooting to get out of the car.

The reprieve was temporary. The two men crowded her on either side, wordlessly guiding her into Battery Park. Penelope expected the park to be filled with people, even in the middle of the week. Instead, a handful of officers were holding everyone at bay, angrily informing them that the park was closed and they needed to move along.

Penelope was led further in toward one of the grassy rises surrounded by pathways. She came to a halt when she saw, from a distance, the two men who weren't police officers standing there. One was the bulky, well-dressed figure of a man who had spent his youth in boxing halls. His broad back was to her, but she recognized the stance of authority he always carried with him. The three officers giving him wary looks and keeping their distance only punctuated it. Next to him was another unmistakable, tall, lean figure, standing in profile. As always, he was dressed in a white suit.

"What are they doing here?"

"Come along, miss," the officer said, finally taking hold of her arm to urge her forward.

Tommy was the first to see her, turning to give her an unreadable look. He muttered something and Mr. Sweeney's head shot up. He spun around and Penelope once again halted, this time at the expression of pure rage on his face.

When the officer urged her closer, she could see why. Before them was a body.

Pen gasped.

It was another recognizable figure, face down on the grass. A short blonde bob was adorned with a black headband that sported a feather. The sleeveless dress she wore was blue—not medium blue after all, but more of a peacock blue, shimmering in the morning light. Her black shoes on silk stockinged feet were splayed, as though she had merely tripped and fallen in a clumsy manner.

As Penelope was led onto the patch of grass, she could see a ring on her finger. The two gold hands held an emerald heart, all situated on a band around the finger on her left hand so she would seem older.

It was Kathleen Grace Sweeney.

CHAPTER SEVENTEEN

"You tell me what the hell is the meaning of this!" Mr. Sweeney roared as Penelope approached him next to the body on the grassy knoll.

The two officers who had escorted her, or rather kidnapped and delivered her, took several steps back, leaving her at the mercy of his rage.

"I'm so sorry, Mr. Sweeney. You have my deepest condolences," Penelope said, her eyes sliding past him to the girl lying on the ground behind him.

The confounded expression he returned was odd. Did he not think she was capable of sympathizing over the loss of his daughter, despite who he was?

"This isn't my Katie," he snapped.

Was he in denial? Pen was the one confounded now. She took another look at the girl on the ground. She'd only seen Katie a few times in person and then only from a slight distance. Still, she could see subtle differences between that Katie and the one lying on the grass.

This young woman was a bit taller with fuller hips and

a more narrow waist. The hair was also more brassy than strawberry blonde.

Was it Amethyst?

Again, Pen had only seen Mr. Easton's daughter in tabloid photos or at a distance. She was too young to be part of Pen's social circle, so she'd never met her directly. Still, what she'd seen in photos was a girl who was thin to the point of looking rather like a praying mantis, with long lanky limbs, a flat chest, and a narrow torso, all of which were so en vogue recently.

So who was the woman lying on the grass?

Now that she was closer, Pen could see she wasn't face-down. Her head was turned sideways. Out of curiosity, she ignored Mr. Sweeney and Tommy and circled around to look at her face.

It was utterly unfamiliar. Still, Pen felt a pang in her heart at the shock and fear registered on the face of the girl. No, not a girl. This was the face of someone closer to Pen's age than Katie's or Amethyst's. She was in her early-to-mid twenties, missing the youthful softness in her features. Her eyes were brown, and the eyebrows indicated she wasn't a natural blonde.

However, she was quite dead. She'd been shot, twice it looked like from the wounds in her back.

Pen could see there was a thin gold chain around her neck. Whatever was attached to it was underneath her. She slid her eyes up to Mr. Sweeney.

"I assume you've already tampered with her body?"

"What the hell do you mean by that?" His face became even redder.

"I mean, there's no way you found her like this and left her without learning as much as you could before having me dragged here by your hired goons." Pen stood up and looked him in the eye.

"Of course I checked to make sure myself. If you had a daughter, you'd do the same. I had the boys put her back in the position she was found."

Pen sighed. "Let me guess, there's a cross around her neck that reads Kathleen?"

"How do you know that?"

"Because this young woman was trying to impersonate her."

"Well, I can see that much," he roared. "I want to know why, dammit! And where the hell is my daughter?"

Pen ignored him, trying to understand what all of this meant. She thought back to Christos's and John's descriptions of the conversation Amethyst and Katie had held at the speakeasy. They'd discussed makeup, jewelry, dresses... and acting. Christos had also mentioned Katie taking off her jewelry and ring, both of which were on the body.

Had Katie hired an actress to impersonate her? Why?

Penelope tried to work it out in her head. Had the killer shot this woman, then placed the egg in a completely different location nearby for her to find?

No. Pen had received the message in the afternoon the day before. There was no way the body of a woman would have gone unnoticed for that long, especially in such a popular area of the city. She had to have been murdered late last night or quite early that morning. Whether it was before or after Pen had picked up the egg, she wasn't sure.

She studied the woman's body. The heels of her shoes were muddy. Pen's eyes wandered the grass around them, and she saw the marks where the heels had sunk into it. They were spaced far enough apart that Pen could see she hadn't simply strolled up onto the knoll. She'd been running.

Pen's eyes followed the path from which she had come. It led directly to Castle Clinton, with the aquarium inside. It certainly wouldn't have been open that late at night. Perhaps someone who worked there and had a key had let her in so they could conduct their business.

It would have explained why the woman didn't have a coat on. It was still mid-March. The days were pleasant but the nights were still quite chilly, frigid even. It was that period of the month when winter struggled to make one final stand before disappearing underneath the veil of spring. Even if she had been meeting someone inside, she would have worn a coat to and from the meeting.

"We need to find her coat."

"How do you know she had a coat?" Mr. Sweeney demanded.

"It was cold last night. She wouldn't have been out here in just this. She was either meeting someone inside the aquarium or in one of those buildings across the street. The aquarium is closer. We should find out who has a key to open it that late at night."

Mr. Sweeney jerked his chin at one of the officers, who instantly rushed toward the aquarium.

"Do you want to explain this?" Mr. Sweeney demanded waving his hand at the dead woman.

Pen looked around, trying to fit it all together with her own adventures last night. She turned in the direction of Jeanette Park. It wasn't even a ten-minute walk from where they were, but several streets and buildings blocked the way so it wasn't visible from there. Pen wouldn't have even heard the gunshots.

She could see the crowds forming at the edge of the

park, mostly wondering what was going on. Their necks craned to see what she, Mr. Sweeney, Tommy, and the officers were circled around. Fortunately, the young woman's body was behind a slight rise so—

Pen stopped when her eyes landed on one woman in particular. She was perhaps in her fifties or sixties, it was difficult to tell from there. Still, her face was weathered and she sported a large, drooping hat over her graying hair, which was gathered in a bun in the back, leaving a few strands free. She wore knit gloves, the left of which had a hole on the back. Her shoes were sturdy, well-worn, brown boots—more practical than fashionable. The woman next to her, glanced her way as she was jostled by the crowd, then instinctively flinched away, her nose wrinkling with distaste.

If not for the very fashionable coat she had on, the woman would have looked like a vagrant. Even the woman who had made sure they weren't touching suspiciously eyed the coat of fine black wool and a collar with feathers sticking up.

"Never mind the aquarium!" Penelope shouted, rushing across the grass toward the woman.

It took her a moment to realize Pen was coming straight for her. Her eyes widened with alarm and she quickly shouldered her way out of the crowd.

"Wait!" Penelope said, running after her.

The officers behind her sensed her urgency and began running as well. There was only one member of the crowd attempting to escape, and they caught up with her before Pen could.

"Let me go, I've done nothing wrong!" The woman wailed, trying to wriggle free of their grasp.

"What do you know about what happened here?" the officer gripping her right arm growled.

"Nothing," she said in a piteous voice. The crowd around them stared, their eyes filled with hungry curiosity, already devising the story they'd have to tell back at work or home.

"For heaven's sake, there's no need to manhandle her," Penelope scolded as she caught up to them.

They ignored her, dragging the woman into the park back toward Mr. Sweeney. Penelope sighed with frustration, following them.

It didn't take Mr. Sweeney long to figure out why Pen had singled the poor woman out. He eyed the coat, incongruous with the rest of her clothes, all of which were old and worn.

"Where'd you get that coat?"

"It's mine," the woman insisted with a pout.

"The hell it is." He leaned in menacingly. "You tell me what happened last night, or I'll have these officers throw you in a cell so dark and—"

"Zounds! There's no need to threaten her. She isn't the one who killed anyone," Penelope said, inserting herself between the woman and Mr. Sweeney. He gave her an incredulous look as though shocked anyone would have the audacity to defy him. When Pen didn't back down, he glared and worked his jaw, but backed off.

Pen turned around to give the woman an apologetic smile. "Ma'am, were you somewhere around here either last night or early this morning?"

She pressed her lips together, not saying a word. The officer on her right jerked her arm enough to make her cry out in pain.

"I insist you two let go of her this instant!" Pen gave him

a hard look, waiting until he glanced past her shoulder for permission from Mr. Sweeney. He must have given it because both men let go. The woman knew better than to try and run, but she did wrap the coat around her more firmly as though it was a shield against the animosity directed her way.

"Now then," Pen said with an exhale as she smiled apologetically once again. "We know you had nothing to do with the woman lying here. But you did find that coat last night, no?"

The woman hesitated as though wondering whether or not to answer. She also glanced over Penelope's shoulder and swallowed nervously at what she saw.

"It's not hers. She wasn't anywhere near where I found it, and she was already dead besides that."

Everyone seemed to perk up at once. Penelope gave the two officers on either side of her a warning look, silencing them before they could ask questions or otherwise get aggressive.

"Why don't you walk me through how you came to find the coat and the woman?"

"The coat is mine!"

"Of course, and no one is going to take it from you, are they?" Pen deliberately looked around for confirmation. It would have been cruel, considering how chilly it was that day.

"Keep the godforsaken coat, and just answer the damn question," Mr. Sweeney growled.

Pen turned back to her with an encouraging look. The woman sniffed, wrapped the coat more firmly around her, then spoke. "I spend time here in the park, because it's peaceful, see? People like to have their picnics here during the day and sometimes they throw out perfectly good food."

She looked around with a haughty expression as though daring them to ridicule her about that.

"I was wandering along, looking out at the water when I sees this coat draped over the railing, right behind the aquarium. I waited for a bit at first, figuring someone must have left it there and was coming right back. The cigarette on the ground next to it had already mostly burned out, so I figured they was gone for good. So, I took it. It's a fine enough coat, so I tossed out my old one and put this on instead.

"Well, that was that. I thought, lucky me, at least until I came back around and found her," she jerked her chin toward the body, "just lying there. That's when I got scared and left."

"What time was that?"

"I seem to have left my gold pocket watch in my mansion, don't you know?" She scoffed.

"Don't get smart, lady," the officer next to her warned.

"I don't know what time it was. All's I can say is that it was a long time after it got dark and a long time before it got light."

"Midnight?"

"Maybe."

Pen moved on. "Did you see anyone else around? Perhaps someone who looked very similar to this woman but several years younger? Short blond hair, nice clothes?"

"Girls like that know not to be around here that time of night. Not unless they want trouble. Those men from the piers ain't so nice."

"You said you like to spend time down here. Did you hear the gunshots last night? Maybe the woman screaming or calling for help?"

The woman paused too long. "No."

"Ma'am, this is a serious case, you understand that don't you? It's not just a murder but two missing girls who may be in grave danger."

"I didn't see who shot her!"

"But you heard it?"

She twisted her lips, then quickly nodded. "I was resting on one of the benches, see? Closer to the water, over there." She pointed toward Castle Clinton. "Only thing I seen was two people running away. I knew it was gunshots that I'd heard so I skedaddled, hiding behind the aquarium. That's when I saw the coat over the railing."

"*Two* people?" Pen asked in surprise.

"What did they look like?" Mr. Sweeney demanded, stepping forward.

"I didn't see them," the woman protested, cowering from him. "It was dark and they was in coats and hats."

"You must have seen something. Were they women, men? Tall, short? Fat, skinny?"

"Regular. Not fat, not skinny. One was taller than the other. I couldn't tell if they were men or women. Except," she nodded quickly, "one was telling the other that they had to leave. That was a man's voice."

"Did he sound young or old?" Pen pressed.

"He sort of grunted it out so it's hard to say. The other one didn't speak, but they were searching around here as though looking for something. I couldn't tell what, as I had decided it was none of my business."

"You couldn't tell, huh?" Mr. Sweeney said skeptically. He turned his attention to the police officers. "Search her, every damn inch of her."

They began tugging at the coat, pulling against the woman as she tightly held onto it and protested.

161

"Stop, just stop!" Penelope demanded. "She doesn't have what you're looking for."

"And just how do you know what I'm looking for?" Mr. Sweeney squinted one eye at her.

"Because I have it."

CHAPTER EIGHTEEN

Everyone stood frozen in place, staring at Penelope after she told Mr. Sweeney she had what he was looking for. He turned to confront her, looking angrier than she'd ever seen him.

"And just what is it you think I'm looking for?"

"Do you really want me to say in front of the police?"

Something in his gaze faltered. She of all people knew he wasn't afraid of the police, at least not the ones surrounding them at the moment. There was a reason Mr. Sweeney had been granted special privilege to view the body of the anonymous woman before the scene had been officially turned over to the proper authorities. Every officer present was on his payroll.

It was something else he was worried about.

He nodded to Tommy, who took hold of her and dragged her far enough away to be out of earshot. Pen struggled but knew it was in vain. Mr. Sweeney followed at a casual pace.

"You start explaining yourself, missy, and do it quickly," he demanded once they were out of earshot.

"It's gold and round, perhaps egg-shaped?" She didn't want to fully show her hand if she didn't have to.

A spark of familiarity touched his eyes. He took hold of her other arm and squeezed. "Where is my egg?"

"I wasn't aware it belonged to you," she scoffed.

"Don't get smart with me, Miss Banks. You know full well what I'm capable of."

"Perhaps if you'd been honest in the first place, the egg wouldn't currently be with the authorities." She wasn't going to let him know to which authorities she was referring.

A sly smile told her he assumed she meant the New York police. If that had been the case, he'd have it back in his possession by the end of the day, as Richard had suggested. He would be disappointed, but hopefully she'd be safely distanced when he was. "And just how did you come to be in possession of it?"

"I received a message yesterday, hand-delivered, informing me that someone had what I was looking for. It told me to go to Jeanette Park, not too far from here, at midnight."

"I know where that is," he said, turning his head in that general direction even though the much smaller park couldn't be seen from there.

"I figured it was too much of a coincidence not to be related to either case. I had no idea I'd find an egg."

"It was just sitting there?" He snapped his attention back to her, eyes wild with disbelief.

"Not exactly. It was inside one of the storage areas to the side of the stage. The egg was packaged in a coffee can, inside a sugar sack.

That did nothing to ease the shock on his face.

"There was no sign of Katie or Tino, or Amethyst for

that matter. Is there any reason why Katie may have chosen that spot?"

He shook his head, looking distracted, lost in thought. He focused on Penelope again, eyes penetrating her. "Where is this note? Let me see it."

"That's with the authorities as well." She quickly continued before he could explode with anger. "However, I remember the handwriting in detail. If you show me an example of Katie's I can tell you if it was the same."

He still looked as though he was ready to erupt, but he held back, realizing Pen was still working on finding his daughter.

"Speaking of Katie, I assume she stole it from you and was trying to sell it to fund her independence?"

"For your own good, it's best you forget about that egg and focus on finding Katie."

There was a threat there, but not the one Pen expected. He wasn't warning her that he might do something if she meddled. He was telling her there was something much bigger going on.

"What do you know?" Penelope asked.

He gave her a humorless smile. "Just focus on finding Katie."

"Don't you see what keeping things from me has already done? If I'd known about the egg in the first place, maybe that woman would still be alive! Maybe you'd have Katie back by now." Granted, she couldn't see how knowing about the egg would have done either of those things, but perhaps it would make him reveal something.

His expression told her he was already done talking.

"Does it have something to do with Connor Davidson?"

Mr. Sweeney gave a dry, soft chuckle. "I'm not responsible for every murder in this city, Miss Banks.

There's no way anyone is laying the murder of some fed at my door."

"How did you know he was a federal agent?"

His gaze sharpened and he pierced her with it long and hard before answering. "You think I'm too stupid to read the papers?"

She couldn't tell if that pause before answering was out of anger or to give him a chance to come up with an acceptable answer.

"Why did you give me Friday as a deadline? Is something happening then?"

"Just find Katie, Miss Banks. That's what I hired you for." He turned to Tommy. "*You* don't let her out of your sight. I want to know everything she does and everything she learns. Everything! I don't want any more surprises. And you both better damn well find Katie, and soon."

CHAPTER NINETEEN

TOMMY WAS UNDERSTANDABLY TENSE AS HE DROVE Penelope away from the scene of the murder. He stared silently ahead, his eyes like green chips of ice as he gripped the steering wheel so tightly his knuckles went white.

"I suppose you aren't going to give me any more information either?" Pen risked asking.

"Even if I knew more, if Mr. Sweeney don't want you to know, neither do I," he said, staring ahead.

"But you knew about the egg. That's why you left so abruptly from the Peacock Club on Monday."

He didn't respond, as the answer was obvious.

Penelope sighed. "Is there anything you *can* tell me?"

He continued to stare ahead for a moment before turning to her. "Is there anything else *you* want to tell *me*?"

"You officially know everything I know."

A dry smile touched his lips. "Only because I'm smart enough to know that you didn't deliver that egg to the local boys in blue, did you?"

A look of surprise colored her face before she could mask it. "Why didn't you tell Mr. Sweeney?"

"You think I want any more heat from him? It's bad enough I didn't learn about this note you got before he did. I'll let him figure out the egg is with the feds." He turned to scrutinize her. "It is with the feds, no?"

"No, I put it on display in my library," she retorted. She figured the truth disguised as sarcasm would work well enough.

He breathed out a cynical laugh. "I suppose when you've got five million in the bank, it's easy enough to hand something that valuable over. As though the federal government is any more trustworthy than the locals."

"Either way, I've washed my hands of it. My only focus has ever been to find Katie and Amethyst. Even though his father doesn't seem to care, I'd like to find Tino as well."

"Which means I'll be stuck like glue to you, Miss Banks."

"So what now?"

"You tell me, lady detective. Other than getting you that sample of Katie's handwriting, we got nothing as far as I can see. Other than a dead body, of course."

"Right," Pen breathed out, feeling the bewilderment set in. "I suppose before anything, I want to go into the office and at least update Jane so she doesn't worry about why I haven't come in. Considering your men abducted me in the middle of 5th Avenue, I should probably tell Leonard as well."

"First we get the handwriting comparison from Mr. Sweeney's home."

"That's all the way in Morningside! Both my office and apartment are closer and on the way if you drive up along the East Side."

He was silent but seemed to be considering it.

"At least my office first. I can call home from there. That way you can turn west before we even get to Central Park. It will be quick. Lulu may be there as well," she added as an enticement.

He gave her a look of disdain, as though disappointed she would try that tactic. But it worked.

"Fine. You have ten minutes."

He turned to head up Madison. It still took a while due to traffic. Pen decided to use the time productively so he wouldn't change his mind.

"Odd that it was two people involved in that murder. Could it have been Tino and Katie?"

He shrugged.

"Hopefully once the police identify the dead woman, that will give us a lead. She was dressed exactly like Katie was Friday at the speakeasy. That may have even been her coat the woman we spoke with was wearing, rather than a replica."

Tommy maintained his trademark silence, giving her nothing.

When they got to her office, he parked illegally in front and came in with her. She didn't bother asking if he was worried about getting cited.

Penelope rushed into her office, calling out for her associate. "Jane, I'm here. I'm sorry I'm late. There was just a bit of a—"

She stopped when she saw that there was no Lulu sitting with Jane in her office, but there was someone else. Barton Tyrell turned to give her an inquiring look as he sat opposite Pen's vacant desk.

"Mr. Tyrell, how can I help you?"

He stood and offered a placid smile. "Mr. Easton is

wondering about the progress of your case, specifically whether or not you had any updates?" He met Tommy's eye in a way that indicated he knew exactly who he was.

"It's only been a day, but, yes, we have made some progress. I would be happy to update you, but I did have some questions of my own, since you're here. However, I need to make a quick phone call first."

She didn't wait for him to answer, and ignored the disgruntled look he shot her as she picked up the phone to call her apartment. Chives was the one to answer.

"Chives, can I assume Leonard made it back and relayed what happened to me this morning?"

"He did."

"Please tell everyone that I'm fine. It was a simple misunderstanding. I'll explain later." She deliberately left Richard's name out of it, but she was curious. "Has there been any other visitor?"

"Detective Prescott is still here. Mrs. Davies has been keeping him company. Otherwise, no."

Poor Richard, stuck with her cousin all morning while no doubt fretting over what may have happened to Penelope. Still, his agent hadn't arrived yet, which meant he had no option to leave.

"Thank you Chives. Tell Cousin Cordelia I'll explain everything when I get home later today."

She hung up and gave Mr. Tyrell an apologetic smile. "I'm afraid I can't stay as I was on my way to—"

"Nonsense, that can wait," Tommy said, casually taking the seat next to Barton. "Go on and ask your questions, Penelope."

She looked back and forth between the two men, watching them size each other up. Both could have been considered the right-hand men of two very powerful bosses in New York. Mr. Tyrell seemed just as loyal as Tommy was. Considering the finely tailored suit, also a match to Tommy's though done in dark charcoal instead of white, he was rewarded quite handsomely.

Behind them Jane stared wide-eyed, no doubt wondering what was going on.

"You said you had updates?" Mr. Tyrell hinted.

"Yes," Pen began, deciding to reveal as much as she could. Let Mr. Sweeney berate her later. Perhaps it would lead to some insight. "It seems Mr. Easton was correct about the two cases being related. Amethyst and Katie did know each other and met Friday night, presumably to hatch a plan of escape."

She paused before continuing. "Do you know anything about Fabergé?"

Tommy was perfectly still, one leg crossed over the other, but his expression spoke volumes, telling Pen to tread very carefully in what she revealed.

"The jewelry house? I know of the Imperial Easter Egg collection created for the tsar, of course. Sadly, much like many priceless historical artifacts in the East, they've fallen into the hands of barbarians."

"Bolsheviks, to be specific."

"Is there a difference?"

Pen ignored that bit of bias for the sake of priorities. "Have you ever suggested that Mr. Easton use his company to help salvage some of those priceless artifacts?"

He stared at Penelope through narrowed eyes, assessing her. "If you're suggesting something underhanded, I can assure you that isn't the case. Mr. Easton is a devout Christian, and so am I. Yes, he has used his business to *legally*

salvage many a religious or even historically significant artifact, and turn them over to museums, where they belong.
The Museum of Natural History has an entire collection in
his name. To imply something underhanded is slanderous
and, frankly, absurd. Why would he risk everything by
selling artifacts on the black market? He hardly needs the
money."

He had a point.

"Does Easton Shipping do business with Russia, or I
suppose the Union of Soviet Socialist Republics, as it's now
called?"

He offered a patient smile. "Easton Shipping does business with all parts of the world. We certainly don't let
differing politics interfere, at least beyond how it affects that
business." He frowned. "What does this have to do with
Fabergé?"

"It seems Amethyst may have been involved in the
black market purchase or selling of one of the eggs, at least I
believe it's an authentic piece."

He blinked in surprise, then gave a short, incredulous
laugh. "Amethyst? I find that very hard to believe."

"Young women are often underestimated," Pen said
with a tight smile.

He briefly lowered his eyelids in acknowledgment.
"That wasn't meant to disparage your gender, Miss Banks. I,
for one, think Miss Easton is incredibly bright and has quite
a bit of untapped potential. Unfortunately, it seems to have
been frittered away on all the wrong ventures."

"I suppose you would have raised her differently?"

"That isn't for me to comment on." He was being diplomatic, but Pen could see the way his mouth twisted ever so
slightly with disapproval.

"I received a note from someone alerting me to the egg's location. I'd like to compare it to Amethyst's handwriting. Do you think I could get a sample?"

"Of course." She could see the curiosity touch his eyes. "Do you...still have the egg?"

She tilted her head and gave him a sardonic smile. "Is that out of personal curiosity?"

He recomposed himself, taking on a lofty air. "Never mind."

Pen continued with her questioning. "Does Mr. Easton own any properties where she might be hiding?"

He gave her a slightly withering look. "We have searched every holding of Mr. Easton's, as well as every known escape of Amethyst's. She hasn't been found in any of those locations. As I stated, she's quite smart when she puts effort into it."

"It's just that, she's been known to have impromptu parties in unusual places. Abandoned buildings. Empty warehouses. Even the middle of Central Park when the weather is nice."

"I must confess, we hadn't thought to check Central Park for her," he said dryly.

Penelope's mouth twisted into a cynical smirk. "Did she know enough about her father's business to have the knowledge, connections, or resources to sell a stolen Fabergé egg?"

He considered that for a long moment, casting a brief glance Tommy's way. He seemed to put it together in his head, and exhaled with understanding. "So Katie somehow stole a Fabergé egg, then connected with Amethyst, of all people, to sell it?"

"You tell me."

"I'm asking you. Because no, Amethyst alone wouldn't

have had the connections or resources. Her circle, up until recently, has been comprised of flappers, reprobates, rakes, and gadabouts. All very well connected as far as family, *not* in business."

"Including John Foster?"

"He's the exception, of course. Then again, perhaps not?"

"I wonder how many other exceptions she had. She strikes me as rather enterprising when she really wants something."

"Is there anything tangible you have for me to take back to Mr. Easton?" He was getting impatient.

Penelope stared at him for a moment, allowing the gravitas of the information she was about to give to fill the moment. "There was a body of a young woman found this morning."

His reaction was instant. He sat up straighter in alarm, leaning in slightly, eyes wide, nostrils flared, every part of him wanting to know more.

He was genuinely surprised.

Behind him, Jane sported an even more extreme look of shock and horror.

"It wasn't Amethyst. Or Katie Sweeney for that matter."

Mr. Tyrell's eyes narrowed, resentful at having been toyed with. "Who was it then?"

"We still don't know, but she did resemble both girls. She was made up to impersonate Katie though."

"Then I can't really help you, can I?" He sat back in his seat, smoothing down the lapels of his jacket. "I'm going to assume you don't have anything useful yet. I shall report as much to Mr. Easton. So if that's all, I will be—"

"Connor Davidson. Is that name familiar?"

His brow wrinkled in confusion, and he blinked in

recognition. "The man who was murdered Sunday evening? I know he was a customs agent." He seemed to realize what she was insinuating by bringing up his name. "Yes, I'm sure someone in the machinery of Easton Shipping Company has personally interacted with him during the regular course of business. That hardly makes us a primary suspect in his murder, as unfortunate as it was. Besides, Easton operates out of Red Hook in Brooklyn, not the Manhattan piers."

"So you know the details of his murder?"

"I do read the newspapers," he said with a surly sneer. "What does that have to do with Amethyst?"

"What were Mr. Easton and you holding back when you were here yesterday?"

"I beg your pardon?" He was caught off guard by her sudden shift in topics. He wasn't good at hiding his surprise.

"Something is going on, presumably with his business, that you didn't want me to know. What is it?"

He stared at her, lips pursed. "I have no idea what—"

"Do you want to find her or not?"

"If I did know anything, I'm hardly likely to tell you without his express approval, especially in a room filled with...others." He cast a look to Tommy as though to clarify exactly what he meant by "others."

"Have you discovered smuggling within your ranks?"

One blink. That was all it took for Pen to know she had hit the bullseye. He tried to recover by straightening his tie, which only confirmed what she had suspected was true. Really, what else could it have been?

Next to Barton, Tommy snickered. "Not so lily white after all."

Mr. Tyrell glared at him. "If there was any hint of such a thing, Mr. Easton would work very quickly to stamp it out.

New procedures would be put in place imposing more scrutiny from origin to destination. There would be multiple checks put in place to put an end to any such illegal activity." He gave both of them a hard look. "Not that there are any such goings on."

"Of course not, but if there was, it would be likely someone at the top might have orchestrated it. Perhaps someone close enough to Mr. Easton to be trusted."

"I beg your pardon?" He sat up straighter, filled with umbrage.

Pen laughed. "I wasn't suggesting you, Mr. Tyrell." It was a lie, mostly to set him at ease again.

He relaxed, readjusting his tie.

"But Amethyst *was* close with John, who is, after all the son of the Chief of Operations."

He considered that, then shook his head. "Ethan Foster has been fully vetted. He's been with the company since before John was even born. He'd be the first to turn his son over if he so much as suspected something."

"Young people can be quite cunning. Especially with the right motivation."

"Perhaps leave *that* concern to us, Miss Banks," he said tightly. "Again, I would be very surprised if Amethyst Easton is the mastermind behind whatever unfortunate business you were suggesting a moment ago."

She wasn't going to try and persuade him not to underestimate Amethyst yet again. However, *she* wasn't going to make the same mistake. It seemed another talk with Eliza or John, perhaps both, was in order.

"I'll have the handwriting sample delivered to you, post haste. We will look into discovering the identity of this dead woman on our end," he said in a way that suggested he didn't think Pen was worth the effort they had put into hiring her. "However, I'm sure Mr. Easton would appreciate an update all the same directly from you, just in case you learn of it first." He cast a pointed look Tommy's way. "I assume there's nothing else to report?"

"No, thank you so much for stopping by," she said pleasantly.

When he was gone, the smile fell from her face. Penelope didn't appreciate having Mr. Easton send his man in to check up on her, especially after only twenty-four hours of working on his case.

"There was a third girl? And she's dead?" Jane fretted. "And you have a Fabergé egg?"

"It was hardly a girl, but she was dressed the same as Katie had been on Friday. In fact, I'm sure she was hired to stand in for her, but I can't fathom why."

If Katie had been the one with the egg, why would someone hire a woman to pose as her, presumably to get the money? She wouldn't have had the egg, so what was the plan? Show up and just rob whoever was there to buy it? It was foolhardy.

Now that the information was out, Pen told Jane about the note and going to get the egg.

"I, of course, immediately contacted the authorities and delivered it to them," Pen said, giving Tommy a pointed look.

"Speaking of the note," Tommy said, standing as a hint.

"Yes, Tommy and I are going to check the handwriting from the note against Katie's. If it matches, hopefully that means she's alive."

"What should I do?" Jane asked.

The case was getting dangerous and Pen certainly wasn't about to put her friend in any more danger. Jane was to be married in less than two weeks, after all.

"See what you can do to find out either the identity of this woman who was killed, or more about where Katie, Tino, or Amethyst might be. Take Leonard if you need to, that will make things easier than using a taxi." Pen turned to Tommy with a wry but sour look. "After all, I have my own knight in shining armor to escort me around town."

CHAPTER TWENTY

Tommy drove Penelope north again, back to the Sweeney mansion.

There were fewer of Mr. Sweeney's men lurking about, but Mrs. Sweeney was no less morose and worried than she had been on Monday. Her eyes were hopeful when Penelope appeared once again with Tommy, at least until he explained why they were there.

"Was there a ransom note? Is that why?" Her voice was shrill with alarm.

"No ma'am," Penelope said gently. "But Katie may have been in touch, which would be a good thing. It means she's at least alive."

That didn't console her much, and she sighed before silently leading them into a study. She walked over to a delicate desk that looked out onto a side garden where green was just beginning to sprout from the ground. In a few weeks, it would be lush with flowers making a lovely view as Mrs. Sweeney wrote her correspondence.

Hopefully, Katie would be back by then.

Mrs. Sweeney opened the right bottom drawer and

pulled out a long box. "I keep several mementos from the children in here, school assignments they are proud of, and such. This is an essay Katie had to write for school. She scored the highest marks for it."

That probably wasn't the best comparison, as pupils tended to write more formally for important class assignments than they did for hastily jotted notes. Still, at least Pen might be able to eliminate her.

She took hold of the paper and looked down at the loopy script that hinted at a feminine hand. Penelope could tell it wasn't anything like the note she'd been sent. Katie had a habit of not connecting her "e" if it fell in the middle of the sentence, and her lowercase "l" was exaggeratedly round. The writer of the note felt no such qualms about connecting their "e" and their "l" was long, thin, and more slanted.

"No, it wasn't written by her."

Mrs. Sweeney inhaled sharply, taking that as bad news.

"That doesn't mean anything," Pen tried to reassure her. "We still have two other people's handwriting to look at. She could very well be with either or both of them, hiding away somewhere."

Mrs. Sweeney turned to look out at the not yet verdant garden. "I don't understand it. That she'd want freedom this bad, she'd cause me so much heartache, wondering where she is?"

"Girls that age tend not to think of all the consequences of their actions." Pen thought Katie might be far more scared of the punishment she'd get should she return than anything. Her father may very well put her in a convent when she did come back.

"Just find her and bring her back, Miss Banks."

"I'll do my best, Mrs. Sweeney."

Tommy had made the phone call to get a sample of handwriting from the Messinas. Penelope wasn't sure how things worked amongst the various criminal families, but they seemed awfully cooperative, considering. Then again, if they didn't have some semblance of an understanding, New York would have been far more dangerous than it already was.

As one poor woman had found out sometime last night.

Pen shuddered, thinking how close she might have been to murder. What if this duo, whoever they were, had come for her instead? Could she have reacted in time with her own gun? Against two of them? Could she have shot someone?

"Let's make a stop, since we're in this part of Manhattan. Take me to Columbia University."

"Who's there?" Tommy asked as he drove her.

"John Foster, a friend of Amethyst. There are only so many men involved in all of this, and he's one of them. I might as well ask if he has an alibi for last night."

Tommy sped up.

Pen mentally brought up John's class schedule. That day, he had a class called World Politics and Imperialism in the Nineteenth and Early Twentieth Centuries. It was in a building closer to Low Memorial Library, the easily identifiable domed building which was the de facto center point of the university.

As Penelope ascended the stairs in front of it, she turned and looked out on the field beneath them. Memories came flooding back of watching boys in tights tussle on that field during football games. Her father had thought sending her to Barnard would keep her out of trouble. Little did he know how much trouble she would get into with the boys on that campus. The university had built a stadium at Baker Field further north. Pen supposed it was progress, but she couldn't help feeling a bit of nostalgia at the games she'd enjoyed right there.

"I would have thought these college boys were a bit young for you, Pen," Tommy said, misreading her expression with a smirk.

It pulled her out of her memories. She pursed her lips at him and continued to the building where John had his classes. They were just in time to catch a flood of students exiting for lunch. Now that Pen knew what face to look for, it was easier to study the crowd in search of it.

Unfortunately, only one familiar face appeared. It was John's friend with the curly blonde hair, who also recognized her. He grinned and sauntered over.

"Back for John again? I'm starting to get jealous."

"I thought he had a class here at this time."

"I thought so too, but he wasn't in today."

"He wasn't?" Pen became more alert. Next to her, she could also feel Tommy react in that barely perceptible way of his, a slight hitch in his breathing.

It made sense that someone who had just shot a woman might be feeling a bit too overwhelmed to attend a lecture on world politics. Was John at home, wracked with guilt over having committed murder? Perhaps with his partner in crime?

"Probably recovering from his party."

That caught both Pen and Tommy off guard.

"A party?"

"Yes, not that he invited me," he said, hiccuping an incredulous laugh at the audacity.

"How do you know he was hosting a party?"

He laughed again. "I doubt he was the host. John rarely throws a shindig."

"Then how do you know he *went* to a party last night?"

"I assume it was last night. Why else would he be out today?"

Pen closed her eyes and shook her head. Obviously, she was missing something.

"I'm sorry, I didn't get your name last time we met."

His smile broadened. "Oliver Dennis, pleasure to meet you, miss."

Pen quickly shook the hand he offered. He cast a quick look Tommy's way and decided to withhold offering it to him as well.

"Oliver, why is it you think John was at a party last night rather than home sick or just playing hooky?"

He pursed his lips, stuck his fists into his pockets, and rocked on his heels. His eyes darted back and forth between Pen and Tommy, growing suspicion coloring them.

Zounds, was the boy worried about a bit of illegal giggle juice? What had become of Columbia men?

"We're not police officers, Oliver," Pen said in exasperation.

"Well..." He paused to consider it, then he leaned in conspiratorially. "He always comes to me when he needs a bit of the muggle, ya follow?"

No, Pen most certainly did not follow. She thought she was pretty hep to modern slang, but leave it to college boys to devise new ones.

"Muggle?"

He gave her a patronizing look, but there was a strong hint of smug satisfaction at her ignorance.

"That's what they call it down in New Orleans. I'm not surprised you don't know what it is."

"I know what it is," Tommy said in an unimpressed voice that wiped that self-satisfied smile from his mouth.

"Would either of you care to translate for a New Yorker?"

"It's...a special kind of tobacco," Oliver said, looking abashed and once again reluctant to reveal everything.

"Marijuana?" Pen said, a bit too loudly.

"There's no need to tell the world, now is there?" Oliver protested, eyes wide with disbelief.

"*That's* what you're worried about telling us?" Pen had to laugh.

"Well, they're making it illegal everywhere, aren't they? In your time maybe one could even smoke it in class. Things have changed. They're banning everything enjoyable these days."

"In my time?" Pen said, giving him a haughty look. "I'm only twenty-five."

"Exactly."

Pen was set to give him an earful, but Tommy preempted her, looking slightly amused.

"So this John, he asked you for some *muggle*," Tommy drenched the word in sarcasm.

"Yes."

"Did he tell you the party was last night?" Pen asked, getting back on topic.

He shrugged. "I just assumed since he wasn't in class today."

"When did he ask you for some?"

"Yesterday."

"Yesterday? When?"

"Afternoon."

"So, after I spoke to him."

"Yes, ma'am."

"And he told you it was for a party?"

"Why else would he ask for some?"

"For himself?"

Oliver laughed. "John hates the stuff. You should have seen him the first time he tried it. Amateur. No, it was that dish of his, Amethyst, he was always trying to impress. He only ever asks when she's having a party."

Once again, Tommy and Penelope both became more alert.

"Just to clarify, John asked you for some 'muggle' yesterday, but he didn't necessarily say it was for a party. Still, in the past, you've only ever procured it when he was set to attend one of Amethyst's parties?"

"Sounds about right. But he knows the rules. I sell to him at a discount if I get an invite. He's usually fine with that. This time, he said he'd pay above asking price. So I'm thinking maybe it isn't for one of her parties after all."

"You don't say," Pen said. "Did you get it for him?"

"For above asking price? You bet your bottom dollar I did," he said with a grin.

"So you're the go-to man for this stuff?"

"I'm the go-to man for any of your needs, miss." He grinned and waggled his eyebrows.

"But you have no idea where or when this party is?" Pen said, ignoring that.

"No, just that he needed it as soon as possible." He frowned. "Does this mean there was no party last night?"

"Thank you for your time, Oliver," Pen said, extracting them from the conversation as she led Tommy away.

"I'm guessing you don't think John was at any party last night?" Tommy said in a droll voice.

"Do you?"

He shook his head. "So where does the marijuana come

in, then? He smokes a bit, then goes out to kill some dame meant to look like Katie?"

"I don't know, but I do know where we can find out more about this party," Pen said, feeling the first trickle of hope about the case fill her veins.

CHAPTER TWENTY-ONE

"I don't know where Amethyst is."

Penelope had Tommy drive her back to the Hemsford residence. She'd once again gone in alone to speak with Eliza in private, who was conveniently home "sick" from school. Penelope had an idea it was something else that was weighing on Eliza, something related to her best friend.

The senior Hemsfords were less enthusiastic about her visit that time around. No doubt they now knew the circumstances regarding their daughter's best friend and wanted no part of it. Still, it wouldn't have done for them to deny Penelope, for a number of reasons.

Pen took what was offered with good grace, and went up to meet Eliza in her room. Before she could even ask her first question, the girl had blurted out her protest.

"But you do know of a party being held this week?"

Pen studied her reaction. Eliza would never do well in a game of poker. Her eyes went wide, cheeks drained of color, and even her mouth fell open ready to utter a false protest.

"Don't bother denying it. I already know about it. And

after all, you were the one to tell me Amethyst couldn't go a week without having some bit of adventure."

"That doesn't mean..." She went quiet before continuing. "I can't tell you anything, Miss Banks."

Pen sighed. Perhaps it was time to put a bit of fear into the girl. "Do you know what I saw this morning? A dead girl, someone who personally knew Amethyst and is directly involved in why she's disappeared." Yes, a lie, but for a good cause. "Your friend is in over her head, Eliza. If you know where she is, you need to tell me, before she's next."

Her face had become increasingly ashen, and now she looked as though she was struck mute.

Pen softened the blow before delivering what she knew would scare her more than anything. "I promise not to tell Amethyst it was you who told me. But I do need to find her."

"I don't know where she is, Miss Banks."

Pen exhaled with exasperation. "Eliza—"

"No, I mean, I really don't! But..."

Pen waited, realizing that she was on the brink of revealing an important bit of information that was obviously weighing heavily on her.

"I did hear that there is to be a party tonight. The location is going to be published in today's classifieds of the *New York Register*, evening edition. She figured that was a paper no one would suspect her of using, but also one her father doesn't read. I'm supposed to look for the code word Easter Egg."

How apt. And of course it would be the *New York Register* out of all the newspapers in New York. As though the case weren't troublesome enough.

"That's it?"

Eliza nodded, looking morose at having betrayed her friend. "The listing will tell me where the party is located."

Well, this was news indeed. Someone like Amethyst couldn't remain out of the spotlight for long. It was rather odd timing though. A woman was murdered, and the next night a party?

"How did you hear about this party in the first place? And when?"

"By messenger this morning."

"Do you still have the invite?"

Eliza hesitated, then realized she had already revealed too much not to go a step further. She sighed heavily, then rose to retrieve it from her bedside table drawer. The note was in a small white envelope of fine quality paper. Nothing like the thin sheet on which Pen had received her message. The one Eliza handed her seemed more like a calling card.

Pen pulled out the thick white card and read:

Put on your pearl necklace and dancing shoes
Come prepared for good music and bad booze
A Wednesday party is starting at ten
The code word below will help you get in...

For location, see evening edition of New York Register
Classifieds: Easter Egg

"How clever," Pen deadpanned.

"She must be so lonely," Eliza lamented.

"It seems she's taken steps to alleviate that. I assume you're going?"

COLETTE CLARK

"Of course! It's going to be *the* party of the week. And she sent *me* an invitation! It's very exclusive, don't you know?" Her joy at having been included usurped any misgivings she may have had about withholding this information. Or the previously mentioned dead woman.

"You do know her father is still looking for her? You didn't think you should tell him?"

She looked at Penelope as though she was batty. Not for the first time, Pen felt older than her years. How had it come to that? A point in her life where she sympathized more with her tyrant of a father than some silly teenager—a newfangled word she'd recently learned from a member of that group.

"You won't tell him will you?"

Under normal circumstances, Pen would have ignored the ridiculous question. Of course she should tell Mr. Easton. But there were two other souls to consider. Besides, if Amethyst was comfortable enough to throw a party, she was apparently doing just fine for the moment. Until Penelope could make sure all three missing people were fine, she would be judicious.

Who knew, perhaps Tino and Katie would be jazzing it up at this party as well?

"No, but only if you promise not to tell anyone you told me about it."

"Are you crazy? Of course I won't."

"Right then, I suppose that's everything."

Downstairs, the Hemsfords were waiting with matching stoic expressions.

"I trust this is the end of it?" Mrs. Hemsford asked, though it came out as more of a demand.

"Darling, please," Mr. Hemsford censured, though not very vehemently.

190

"I hope to find Amethyst very shortly so I doubt I'll need to disturb your home any further."

Mrs. Hemsford gave a firm nod, and Mr. Hemsford smiled with relief, happily leading her to the door. His smile disappeared at the sight of Tommy on the stoop, smoking a cigarette. All one had to do was look at him to know he was bad business. The door was swiftly closed the second she stepped outside.

"Well?"

Penelope considered him. She planned on attending the party that night, and it would be impossible to try and hide that from him.

"It seems we do indeed have a party to go to." She sighed, ignoring the questioning rise of his brow. "But first, we need to find out where it is. Which means a trip to the offices of someone I had hoped to avoid."

CHAPTER TWENTY-TWO

THE *NEW YORK REGISTER* WAS LOCATED IN MIDTOWN, where most of the action in the city happened.

Katherine "Kitty" Andrews was one of the few female reporters who worked there, mostly as a result of having worked on a case with Penelope the prior year. It was certainly a step up from the *New York Tattle*, her prior gig. Though, it seemed, even at the *Register*, Kitty had been delegated to society news and entertainment.

Penelope was hoping to avoid running into her, as she'd most certainly want to join in on her current case, much as she had prior cases. It wasn't that Kitty wasn't helpful, but she was always looking for an angle she could use to her advantage. Frankly, Pen didn't need the additional burden. It was bad enough being Tommy's prisoner.

Blessedly the Classifieds department was on a different floor than the news desks. Pen approached the only desk in that department, where people could drop their announcements and pay the fee. There was a sign indicating as much, which left little for the woman sitting there to do. That was perhaps why she was absorbed with a magazine instead.

Pen cleared her throat to get her attention. After jumping in surprise, the woman quickly closed her magazine and gave her a guilty smile. "Can I help you?"

"Would it be possible to have a look at the evening edition before it goes to press?"

The young woman blinked in puzzlement. "I'm sorry?"

"The paper that's going out this evening. I'd like to have a look at it, if I could? Specifically the classifieds section. Or perhaps I could just look through the ads that are to be posted? I'm looking for something in particular."

"I don't think I can do that?" She didn't seem sure.

Penelope planted a reassuring smile on her face. "Certainly you can. I'm simply asking to see what's already going to be published. It's a rather urgent matter." She replaced the smile with a solemn expression. "A girl has gone missing."

Now the woman looked scared. "I—I should ask Mr. Perlgut."

Before Penelope could stop her, the woman jumped from her seat and fled.

"Pineapples," Pen hissed. The last thing she wanted was some stuffy superior getting involved and making things official. Her eyes wandered past the desk, wondering if she could simply tiptoe behind it to search around and—

"I understand you'd like to see the classifieds before they are put out to press?"

Pen spun around to see the woman walking back in with her boss. She seemed relieved to place the burden squarely on his shoulders, shoulders which were already set in a way that made Pen think the answer would most certainly be "no."

Well, if they were going to be official about it, so would she. She reached into her purse for her business card. "My name is Penelope Banks, and I'm a private investigator looking for two missing young women. I believe one of them may have placed an ad in your paper and I need to look at it."

After a brief look of alarm, a cool, suspicious look came to his face. "Shouldn't that be a police matter?"

"The fathers would rather they weren't involved."

He stared with even more suspicion. "This is highly irregular. I'm afraid I will have to involve Mr. —"

"Really, I don't see why this needs to be more complicated than necessary. After all, if the paper is going out this evening anyway, why not simply allow me to have a look? It's rather urgent."

"All the more reason for the legal department to become involved. If you could tell me exactly what it is you're looking for, Miss Banks?"

That would be disastrous. They'd surely pull the ad and there would be no party, and thus no Amethyst.

"I'm afraid I can't tell you that."

"Because you don't know or you don't want to tell me?"

"I simply can't say. But—"

"Then, I'm afraid I can't help you," he said, a frown of irritation coming to his face. "As it is, you've already kicked a hornet's nest. We may have to pull the entire section for this evening."

"You can't do that!" Pen exclaimed, startling both him and his underling. She continued more calmly. "I'm sorry, but if you do that, these girls will be in even more danger. Then you'll really have a legal conundrum on your hands, not to mention two very angry fathers. Fathers who you really wouldn't want to upset, I should say."

Now he looked as though he wanted nothing more than to lay the problem at a superior's feet. The woman next to him however looked thrilled. She probably hadn't expected something more exciting in her day than the latest fashions from Paris.

"At this point, I have to insist that you tell me what this is about, Miss Banks."

"As I stated, I can't. For the girls' safety, I can only insist that you publish the section as scheduled. I can promise that no legal repercussions will come to the paper. I can't promise the same if you don't. Now, if you'll excuse me."

She rushed out, ignoring his protests as she left. That had gone perfectly disastrous. Not only had she *not* obtained what she came for, but now there was the danger that she might not get it at all.

In the lobby of the building, Pen finally came to a stop. She'd left Tommy there, telling him she'd have more success without his menacing presence.

"Well?"

"No luck."

He narrowed his eyes with suspicion.

"Why would I lie, Tommy?" Pen said with exasperation. "As it is, I just hope they actually publish the darn ad. Pineapples!"

A subtle smile came to his face at her version of a curse. "Need me to go up and ask?"

"Zounds, no! You'll have them canceling the entire evening edition. No, we'll just have to wait until five, I suppose. But it's well after lunch, I'm going back to the office to have something delivered for lunch," Pen slid her eyes to Tommy. "I suppose I should order something for you as well."

"Why thank you, Lady Pen," he said with a grin.

Tommy drove her back. When she entered the office,

she was surprised to see Richard there. And he wasn't alone.

The man with him didn't look quite as identifiable as the average FBI agent, all of whom seemed to dress in a way that might as well have been a uniform. This man's suit was a little nicer, a little lighter in color, and fit a little better.

He was around Richard's age, presenting bravado and confidence that was barely constrained.

"What are you doing here?" Pen asked, looking at Richard, then in a meaningful way to his friend, presumably up from Washington D.C.

He looked past Penelope to Tommy. "I didn't realize you'd have company, beyond Jane, that is."

"Detective Prescott, I presume," Tommy said in that cool voice of his, now laced with humor. "I suppose it's time we officially met."

Suddenly, Pen no longer cared about lunch as she'd lost her appetite. But Tommy was right, it was about time those two had an official introduction.

"Is there a reason why I'm meeting you now?" Richard slid his gaze to Penelope with a questioning look.

"My client was unhappy about my midnight adventure. Thus, I've been given a chaperone. I'm sure by now you already know Tommy Callahan."

Richard's gaze only sharpened with animosity. "Chaperone?"

"Just to make sure she's safe, detective." Pen could hear the taunt in Tommy's voice.

"I see you have someone with you?" Pen hinted, just to curb whatever battle they were waging.

"Yes, this is Kent Simpson," Richard shifted his gaze to Tommy. "With the State Department."

"A pleasure to meet you, Miss Banks. I was hoping to

speak with you in private about...recent events." He too cast a look Tommy's way.

"Of course," Pen said, also turning to Tommy. "I'm sure Mr. Callahan wouldn't object to a private conversation with a member of the federal government."

Tommy knew better than to argue. "Not at all."

CHAPTER TWENTY-THREE

PENELOPE, RICHARD, AND AGENT SIMPSON WERE IN Richard's car, the only place they could speak without worrying Tommy might be listening at the door. She thought it rather odd that they had both chosen to sit up front, awkwardly twisted to face her in the back seat.

Then she noted it seemed decidedly like an interrogation. Perhaps that was the point.

"I should state that Mr. Sweeney knows I have the egg, or at least had it."

The looks on their faces indicated they were both ready to erupt in protest. Pen continued before it came to a head.

"I had to suss out if he was the one who originally had it."

Richard's brow was still sharply creased in anger. Agent Simpson's quickly softened with curiosity.

"And did he?"

"I'm almost certain of it." She felt no qualms about revealing this information. She had no proof with which to testify in court. Hopefully, a hunch was enough for either the NYPD, FBI, or even the State Department to do what they needed to do and leave her out of it.

"This is interesting." He turned to Richard. "Jack Sweeney could be our man."

"Our man?" Pen inquired.

Agent Simpson's attention remained on Richard, now with an inquiring look.

"You can tell her. She's trustworthy." Richard turned back to Penelope. "So long as the information doesn't get back to Tommy." There was a trace of disdain when he said his name.

Pen glared at him. "I'm not his personal rat. As I stated, I already told Mr. Sweeney the egg is with the authorities. Now, after the murder this morning, he just wants to find his daughter."

"Does he?" His voice was the height of skepticism.

Agent Simpson inserted himself back into the conversation. "I'll tell you as much as I can, Miss Banks. Just so you understand that this is bigger than a couple of kids running away from home."

Penelope decided she would be the judge of that, but remained perfectly placid. Pen had spent too many years playing cards against men like Agent Simpson, who were usually too self-assured for their own good.

"The federal government has only recently been alerted to an increase in illegal imports."

"Only recently?" Pen said with sarcastic wit and a mild smirk.

Agent Simpson wasn't amused. "Something much more serious than a few crates of whiskey and rye, Miss Banks. Ironically enough, the authorities only discovered it while on the chase for such an illegal import. I don't know if you read about the boat that was caught carrying almost a quarter of a million dollars worth of alcohol about a week ago?"

"I did."

"That was our boys," he said proudly, as though he had personally nabbed the culprits. "But frankly, this case involves items that are far more valuable, antiques, historical valuables, that sort of thing. Items like your egg."

"It's no longer *my* egg. In fact, I thought you would be on your way back to Washington with it by now," Pen said, her brow suddenly creasing in puzzlement.

Richard and Agent Simpson glanced at one another.

"As it turns out, this egg might be the key to at least two major federal and international cases."

"Oh?" Pen wondered if they had been targeting Mr. Sweeney all along.

"Oh," Agent Simpson repeated in a mildly patronizing way. He scrutinized her. "Again, everything said in this car is confidential. Prescott here vouches for you, and I'm holding both of you to it. Not a word, especially to your buddy, Tommy Callahan in there."

"He isn't my *buddy*, and you have my word," Pen said testily. She was beginning to wonder how Richard deemed this man so trustworthy. Still, she supposed being a bit of a patronizing rooster didn't necessarily make one unethical.

Kent went through the process of holding her gaze, then Richard's, then hers again, before he spoke. "We believe the customs agent who was roughed up and murdered Sunday night may have been involved in this criminal enterprise, at least tangentially. As a federal employee, the FBI is handling the case. It seems Mr. Davidson had a rather unfortunate gambling habit."

"That's hardly unusual."

"No, but when you hold one of the keys to the United

States, at least as far as imports go, it gives you quite a bit of leverage. No one likes paying duties, tariffs, even the fees involved in getting a product from the boat and headed to the stores. If you can get a man like Davidson to look the other way, or provide the documentation free of charge, that's worth a lot to many people."

"I see." Pen was still wondering if Mr. Sweeney was involved. After all, her connection to him also began with gambling.

Then she wondered why she cared. There was no love lost between Jack Sweeney and Penelope Banks. There was Lulu to consider, though. Would she be targeted by association? Pen couldn't deny also feeling a *tiny* inkling of consideration for Tommy.

"Do you think Jack Sweeney is the one who killed him?" Tommy had seemed pretty convincing in denying it earlier. Still, considering his "career," such a denial was probably old hat by now.

"That's what we're hoping to find out."

"I still don't like it," Richard grumbled.

"Like what?" Pen asked, realizing there was more going on than a simple exchange of information.

Agent Simpson laughed and clapped Richard on the shoulder. "I keep telling my old war buddy here that taking down the Sweeney gang is a win for both of us. The fact that you confirmed Jack originally had the egg means it's all the more likely he's behind this international smuggling operation. And, of course, the murder of one of our own," he added, a somber look suddenly coming to his face.

Pen had the idea that poor Connor Davidson's murder was an afterthought for Agent Simpson. No, that was an injudicious thought. It made sense that the federal government would be more concerned about an ongoing, widespread criminal enterprise that reached the far corners of the world, over the murder of a single compromised agent. Who knew how many countless others had been killed in the time it had been in operation?

"I don't understand what the problem is." Pen studied Richard, wondering what his objection had been about.

Again the two men looked at each other.

"You already have direct access to Mr. Sweeney. I—and I've run this by my superiors so I'm not just throwing darts in the wind—think it provides the perfect opportunity to flush him out."

Penelope erupted with laughter. "Jack Sweeney isn't some simpleton who just landed on our shores with more naivety than sense. He's been doing this probably longer than you've been an agent. There's a reason why he's still powerful and has yet to be taken down, even by the federal government."

"Except now his little girl has gone missing, presumably having taken his egg. That is the gist of it no?" Agent Simpson didn't seem to like having his bubble burst.

Pen became serious again. "And even she seemed to realize that she couldn't take on her father. Why do you suppose it ended up in my hands?"

"Just how did she know to turn it over to you of all people?"

That one gave Penelope pause. It was a question that had been on her mind as well. Pen and Katie had never met before. Yes, she may have seen Penelope at the Peacock Club with Lulu, who she did know, but how would she have known Penelope was working with her father to find her? And how had she gotten Penelope's address?

"It doesn't matter, I've already turned the egg over to you," Pen said giving him a pointed look.

One side of his mouth hitched up in cryptic amusement. "But what if you hadn't?"

"I beg your pardon?"

"Yes, you told Mr. Sweeney that you turned over the egg. But what if he was under the impression that was a lie?"

"Why would he think that?" Pen asked in a curt voice, already knowing the answer.

"Before I explain, let me assure you, you'll be perfectly safe and—"

Pen coughed out a laugh. "Are you planning to use me as bait? And you agreed to it, Richard?"

"No, I most certainly did not," he said through gritted teeth. "But I also wasn't going to speak for you, Penelope. I trusted you to have the good sense to say no all on your own."

Penelope took a moment to appreciate that bit of consideration on his part. She turned to Agent Simpson with a cool look.

"I should probably tell you that my connection to Mr. Sweeney may soon be coming to an end, at least as far as working with him to find his daughter. We've almost located Amethyst Easton, the young woman she was conspiring with. I'm hoping to find all three missing people tonight."

Pen felt a ripple of that satisfaction Agent Simpson seemed to carry about him. Neither of the two men had been expecting that, based on their expressions.

"Tell me everything," Agent Simpson demanded.

Penelope told them about visiting Columbia and John skipping class, about Oliver suggesting a party, then about her meeting with Eliza.

"The *New York Register* wasn't forthcoming at all, so I'll have to wait for the evening edition to come out."

"That's an easy enough obstacle for someone with a badge to get past," Agent Simpson said in a slightly censuring tone. He took a moment to consider the new information. "Why would Amethyst be throwing a party? Is it because her part in all of this is done?"

"That part is none of my business. My only goal was to go, make sure she is fine, encourage her to at least call her father, then report back to Mr. Easton. Hopefully, I'd be able to do the same with Mr. Sweeney and...Mr. Messina."

She realized too late that she had just confessed to knowing yet another criminal. Fortunately, Agent Simpson's only response was a small quirk of the brow. He seemed to be pondering how the new information fit with his plans.

"This might work better. If we can get the girls to speak, then—"

"You mean get Katie to turn on her father? Absolutely not!"

"I have to agree with Penelope, Kent."

"We have a real chance to do some good here, Richard. Need I remind you both that this girl and her friends have committed a very serious crime? A crime that may have international implications. Things are tenuous enough between us and the Soviets. The new folks in charge won't look kindly upon learning we have one of their national treasures. We can create some goodwill by diplomatically returning it and punishing those who stole it in the first place. Furthermore, we could take down an entire criminal gang, and you're balking?"

"What makes you think Katie knows anything, or that she'll speak?"

"Furthermore," Penelope added. "There is a reason she turned the egg back over to me. Because she's already terrified. Now you want her to give evidence against the father she ran away from in the first place?"

"Once we have the two girls in custody—getting Tino Messina as well would simply be a bonus, and a good one at that—I'm pretty sure we could be far more persuasive than their fathers are."

"Now wait just one moment, Kent—"

"Use me instead," Penelope said before Richard could protest further. "The girls are far more likely to talk to me. Once I know more, I could even get Tommy or Mr. Sweeney to talk to me and reveal more...if indeed they are the ones operating this whole thing."

"If?"

"There *is* a possibility it isn't him. Surely you've considered that. I don't even know for sure that he had the egg first. Perhaps he had planned on buying it rather than selling it. It could be the Messina family. It could be Charles Easton, for that matter."

"You don't believe that."

"I try not to pass judgment until I have the facts," she said pointedly.

"Well, Miss Banks, as much as I appreciate your nose for detection, we've looked at every shipping company that operates at all in New York. Charles Easton is the cleanest. The man doesn't so much as smoke cigarettes, and his company is perfectly sound. No money troubles making it necessary for him to have a side business.

"As for why Amethyst is involved in this mess? My guess is either a girl looking for a bit of daring fun with a gangster's daughter, or she has no idea that she's being used somehow. Still, she's also someone who can be used for information if needed."

"All the more reason to use me to get it out of them,"

Penelope insisted. "You have a few young people who have made a stupid mistake. Heaven knows I remember what it was like at that age, and I'm sure you do as well. I see no reason why this one dunderheaded idea of theirs should turn into something they'll regret the rest of their lives."

"This isn't an operation to swaddle them, Miss Banks. A serious crime has been committed."

Zounds, the man was infuriating. "I know what needs to be done. This isn't my first case, just so you know. If laws have been broken, justice should be served."

"Good, just so we're on the same page."

"We are. Still, before I do this, I want to be assured of two things."

"Which are?"

"One, you go after only Jack Sweeney and those directly involved in Connor Davidson's murder and this illegal importing business. You aren't going to widen this net to try and catch any fish who just happened to be in the wrong pond at the wrong time."

"Did you have someone in mind?" He asked, arching a brow in cynicism.

"Lucille Simmons. She's not to be so much as taken in for questioning."

"I don't even know who that is."

"Good."

"And the second?"

"We're going after whoever is truly in charge of all of this, including Connor's murder. If it turns out to be someone other than Jack Sweeney then that's who you arrest."

He breathed out a laugh, as though he was all but certain he had his man. Still, he shrugged and nodded. "Done."

Pen turned her attention to Richard, whose feelings on this plan could have been read all the way from Russia—correction, USSR.

"Don't worry about me. I can take care of myself."

"I certainly hope so, Penelope."

CHAPTER TWENTY-FOUR

AGENT SIMPSON REVEALED HIS REVISED PLAN, BASED on the new information Pen had given him about Amethyst's party. Pen agreed, reiterating that he should abide by her own demands. He agreed, and Richard escorted Penelope out of the car and back into her office building.

Penelope knew Richard considered the men he had served with during the Great War to be his closest confidants and acquaintances. They were mostly scattered across the East Coast or lived in Europe. The few Penelope had briefly met had been far more amenable than Agent Kent Simpson.

"If that's an example of a friend you trust, Richard, then—"

"He's not a friend," he said tightly. "His superior is the one I expected to come. Kent is just some..." He exhaled as though trying to rephrase what he was about to say. "Kent is just ambitious is all. I have to give him credit for that. He's willing to act and go the extra mile when a lot of men are happy to sit at a desk and consider their job done."

She had a feeling he was thinking back to the war. She didn't prod as that was understandably a difficult topic for Richard. He'd lost his childhood best friend during the Great War.

"Speaking of friends," Richard continued, snapping out of his thoughts."You're working far more closely with Tommy Callahan than you first indicated."

"Only because his boss had *your* police kidnap me this morning!"

His expression hardened. "I still want names, Penelope. Who were they? And don't tell me you don't remember."

"Of course I remember, but I'm not diverting attention from this case so you can pursue it and cause even more of a mess. Priorities, Richard."

He wasn't happy, still staring at her, his dark eyes trying to penetrate her resistance. She met him eye to eye and he relented.

"I suppose I'll have to live with that. For now. But with regard to Kent Simpson, if Gregory trusts him, so do I."

"With his plan to browbeat people who are barely older than children?"

"Fortunately, he was wise enough to allow you to do it for him."

That managed to get a smile out of her.

"As for Tommy, it will work better if he doesn't suspect Kent or I are pulling the strings."

"He's not stupid."

"Of that, I have no doubt. But he does want that egg. So long as he knows it's still in New York, he'll do what he has to in order to get it. Which is why I'm staying with you. He can't very well object to that."

"He can, but he knows he can't do anything about it."

"Which is a good thing."

They entered the office and Tommy and Richard had another staring match.

"What happened to your other friend?"

"He's working on getting the location of this party from the paper. It's funny the things one can do when they have a badge," Richard said with a taunting but humorless smile.

Tommy laughed. "Very funny, detective. I suppose in the meantime, we'll all just sit and wait."

"We will. And when the information comes, *I'll* be going with Miss Banks to question Amethyst. Alone."

"I expected as much," he replied with a cool smile. Neither Richard nor Penelope were fooled by it. It was going to be a lot harder than a simple say-so to keep Tommy away.

"I suppose Mr. Government Man has the egg?"

"You suppose correctly." Tommy seemed to be considering that in a way that Penelope didn't particularly like.

They were interrupted by the sound of the door to the front office opening.

"Pineapples, what now?"

When Pen saw who breezed in, her irritation became more profound.

"Really, Pen, if you wanted to know about a party, you should have just come to me. I am a reporter, after all."

"What the devil are you doing here, Kitty?"

"It's Katherine now, at least while I'm acting as a professional reporter. You caused nothing short of a storm in our offices, Pen. Your little disruption earlier eventually made its way to me. My editor remembered I had worked with you on quite a few occasions before. So he asked me to look into it. They had me scan this evening's classifieds to see if anything stood out. The Easter Egg business was just one of a few things that looked odd."

"You didn't tell your superiors which ad it was, did you?" Pen asked with alarm.

Katherine gave her a look of scorn. "Of course not! I made sure to keep it to myself. Do you think I want them handing a possible story off to some *man* to write up on? No siree! I thought I'd come right over to get the full story straight from the source.

"So they are still running all the ads?" Penelope pressed.

"I told them they had to, considering the circumstances."

Before Penelope could breathe a sigh of relief and get the information from Katherine, the phone rang, causing everyone in the room to start.

"Oh for heaven's sake," Pen said, rushing over to grab it. When she learned who it was on the other end, she muttered a silent curse.

"Penelope," Her father's voice greeted in a voice that was sterner than usual, and that was saying a lot. Still, he rarely made a social call, especially in the middle of a work-day, so she was on alert.

"I certainly hope you haven't called for help with an investigative case, Papa. I have my hands quite full at the moment."

"I'm not amused, Penelope. I've received several calls today from business associates saying you've been harassing their daughters?"

Pen very much doubted Moira's parents were among her father's associates, so it must have been Mr. Hemsford exaggerating the wave of terror Pen had been casting through the young members of New York society.

"As much as I've missed a scolding from you, Papa, your timing is rather unfortunate. Any havoc I've wreaked among the families of your associates has been for a very good cause. I'm working on a case."

"Of course you are, and that's just the trouble. I confess I found myself impressed with your abilities in that one instance during the holidays. But of course that didn't involve anyone I personally know. Now, apparently you've become embroiled with Charles Easton, of all people. Why he would go to you instead of the police is beyond me. A good and decent man, who is far more traditional about these sorts of things, perhaps even more so than me. Worse, I've been told you're also working for some gangster by the name of..."

Penelope filtered out the rest, smiling at the room. They all stared back with varying degrees of amusement.

She realized he had stopped talking and she blinked, focusing her attention on the phone call again. "I'm sorry, I missed that last part?"

He heaved an aggrieved sigh. "I trust you'll explain to Charles that you can no longer work for him?"

"Should I tell him my father insisted upon it?"

"Heaven's no! I want no part of this nonsense."

"Well, what excuse should I give him, Papa? Perhaps some womanly ailment that keeps me from doing my job?"

"You know I have no interest in hearing about that, Penelope," he said in an appalled voice.

"I doubt he would either."

"I trust you'll come up with some *decent* excuse. You're a bright young lady. Please don't embarrass me any further."

"Of course, father, I know exactly what to do."

"Good, I'm glad the matter is settled."

When she hung up the phone, even Richard was biting back a smile. Everyone else either laughed, chuckled, or giggled.

"Now then. Let's proceed with this case," Penelope said in a brisk voice. For some reason, the phone call from her father had invigorated her. "Where is this party to be held, Katherine?"

"Perhaps not in mixed company," Richard said before she could speak.

Tommy chuckled and shook his head as though amused by how futile Richard's attempt to keep the information from him was.

"I could have you arrested for obstruction, Mr. Callahan."

"And my lawyer will have me out on bail before the party starts tonight."

"Hopefully, while you're cooling off in a cell, we'll get all the information we need such that there won't be a party."

"Now, now, Detective Prescott, I thought we were friends?" Tommy said with a sly smile. "No need for the antagonism. We all want the same thing."

"I very much doubt that."

"For heaven's sake," Penelope said with a sigh. "I for one think it would be easier to keep Tommy close at hand. That prevents him from otherwise meddling too much." She turned to give him a stern look. "And he promises not to obstruct, interfere, or otherwise misbehave, don't you, Tommy?"

He chuckled again. "I'll be on my best behavior, Miss Banks."

Penelope turned to Katherine who had been watching the little squabble with avid interest and amusement. Pen could already see the words in the article writing itself in her head.

"What is the address on the ad?"

"It's a loft in Greenwich Village." Katherine gave the exact address. "Third floor, knock on door 3B."

"I suppose that saves us having to go through Agent Simpson."

"I'm going with you!"

"Oh no you aren't," Penelope retorted.

"You can't stop me," Katherine said, giving Pen a knowing smirk. "I already know where whatever this is, is happening."

"But I can stop you," Tommy said, giving her a look that often caused grown men to wither.

But Katherine was a different breed.

"Don't think you can scare me, mister. I've seen you at the Peacock Club, so I have a pretty good idea of who you are. Let me tell you, you have nothing on my fellow reporters when it comes to going after a story. You'll have to go ahead and shoot me if you want me gone."

Tommy seemed amused by the way she stood up to him. Even Pen couldn't deny a modicum of admiration.

"This is an urgent police matter, Miss Andrews," Richard said with authority in his voice.

"You're another one who doesn't scare me, Detective Prescott," she scoffed. "After all, I can help! As I said, I already know the location. I'm happy to set up camp until whatever is supposed to happen happens. Maybe I'll have Leonard drive me," she gave Pen a wink.

Penelope gave Richard an exasperated look. He seemed to realize, Katherine would do exactly as she'd threatened, then barrel her way into it if only to get a story. It was better to at least have some reins on her.

He exhaled and nodded.

"Fine, but I have two rules, *Katherine*," Penelope said. "One, you say nothing! This is about three missing young people we're trying to find. Two, you report nothing! At least not until this is all over, and then I'll tell you every-thing I can."

"Agreed," Katherine said, looking ecstatic.

"I assume you don't want me to go along," Jane said, with a smile of amusement.

"Very funny, Jane," she said but couldn't help a small laugh. "Perhaps when Agent Simpson calls or returns, you can tell him we've already headed to the address."

"Of course."

Pen looked at the others. "Oh let's go, I'm ready for all of this to be over."

CHAPTER TWENTY-FIVE

PENELOPE DROVE TO AMETHYST'S LOCATION WITH Richard. Katherine being Katherine (Kitty, during non-working periods), and always up for danger or adventure drove with Tommy. Penelope's only satisfaction was that Tommy would be the last person on earth who would give her so much as a "hello" let alone any information related to the case.

The building where Amethyst's party was to be held wasn't quite as abandoned as Penelope thought it would be. To be sure, it wasn't any place the daughter of a wealthy shipping magnate might decide to live on any permanent basis. Still, it had enough comforts to be a perfect hideout for less than a week, which was about how long Amethyst could apparently last before needing some entertainment.

The front door to the building was unlocked and Richard led the way inside, just to be safe. When they reached the third floor, Pen wasn't surprised to see Tommy and Katherine already there. Pen had seen firsthand how devilishly fast he could drive when he wanted to.

"You should have waited for us," Richard whispered in an angry hiss. "I thought I made things clear."

"As crystal," Tommy deadpanned. "You should be happy I waited for you."

"Should *I* wait for you two to draw pistols and eliminate one another or are we going to proceed?"

The two stared at each other, one hard as granite, the other perfectly insolent. Katherine positively devoured it all. They finally seemed to come to some understanding that only men could comprehend, and stepped apart. Pen went between them to the door marked 3B. There were only two doors on the floor, which meant the loft would be quite spacious, considering the size of the building.

Pen knocked quickly and firmly, so no one inside could claim they hadn't heard her. She pressed her ear against the metal, straining to hear anything. It seemed sturdy enough, but that wouldn't have meant anything if no one was on the other side. Just when she assumed that was the case, she heard the muffled sounds of an argument.

"I hear you in there, Amethyst! It's better to open the door to me than to the police," Penelope shouted as loudly as possible. Tommy cast a sardonic smile Richard's way. Katherine giggled.

Her words must have done the trick. Suddenly the door was opened and the pouting face of Amethyst Easton stared out at her.

"Who are you and how the hell did you find me?"

"I'm Penelope Banks, a private investigator your father hired to—"

"*What?*" Amethyst looked ready to combust. She turned her head to someone else in the space with her. "Johnny, you rat!"

"I didn't tell anyone!" The voice sounded familiar, and

explained John's absence from his classes that morning. He suddenly appeared, looking at Penelope with confusion and consternation.

"Hello, John," Pen said tersely.

"So you *do* know her!" Amethyst punched him in the arm.

"Amethyst," Penelope snapped. "I don't think you understand the gravity of the situation you're currently in. May I come in?"

Amethyst diverted her attention to Penelope, then slid her eyes past her to the three people behind her. "Did my father send those two goons and whoever she is as well?"

"No, they're with me. You might as well let us in so I can explain the situation, which has gone decidedly off the rails from your original plans, I should say."

Amethyst considered her a moment longer, then whined in frustration, stomped her foot, and threw open the door in a fit of despair. As though a ruined party was the worst thing in the world.

A good spanking seemed in order, but Penelope reminded herself that Amethyst probably had no idea that someone had already been murdered over all of this.

Richard, Katherine, Tommy, and Penelope all walked into the large loft. There were worn Victorian sofas and chairs strategically placed on oriental rugs. It created an oddly appealing decor. On a table stood a gramophone and a pile of records. Another table had enough liquor to drown in. A magnificent bed with ornately carved wood was against a wall, looking somewhat out of place amid the streamers Amethyst had already begun stringing across the air. The smell of Oliver's "party favor" also hung in the air.

"So, what is the *gravity* of the situation?" Amethyst said

with so much sass, Penelope reconsidered her idea of a spanking.

"First of all, where are Katie and Tino?"

Amethyst swiveled her head to glare at John.

"I didn't tell her anything! She already knew about them when she talked to me."

"And *you* conveniently withheld vital information, I might add," Penelope scolded.

Amethyst laughed. "As though I'd trust Johnny with any of our plans. No, I was able to keep everything about my running away a secret until today. Isn't it just the cat's pajamas?"

"Not when you consider a woman is dead," Penelope finally said.

"What?" Amethyst asked, her forehead creased with confusion. "Who?"

"You tell me. She was dressed exactly the way Katie was when you two met at that speakeasy underneath the barbershop, complete with her necklace and ring."

Amethyst finally became somber, falling onto one of the worn sofas. "Anastasia's dead?"

Pen could almost feel Tommy and Richard straighten with surprise at her putting a name to the dead woman.

"Is that her name? Anastasia?"

"Well, her stage name. She once made a living pretending to be—she's *dead*?"

"Murdered, last night in fact."

It was probably too much information at once, but Pen felt it was warranted. Amethyst went perfectly white, but she was certainly over her frivolous attitude.

"I need a drink," Amethyst said, rising and stumbling toward the table packed with booze. She grabbed a random bottle and a glass and poured too much.

John also looked quite pale. "Wh—what happened?"

"I thought you two might be able to tell me. What was she doing in Battery Park last night?"

"We certainly had nothing to do with her murder!" Amethyst exclaimed. "I've been here the entire time."

"Alone?" Richard asked.

"Well...yes. I've been in seclusion!" So, no alibi.

"And you, John?" Pen asked.

"Me? As she said, I have nothing to do with any of this. I only even found out where Amethyst was just this morning when she called me."

"It's true," Amethyst said, casting a sour look his way. "Goody boy Johnny here would have just gone running to Daddy. He's been so dull lately." She stuck her tongue out at him. It was an immature response, and Pen could sense an underlying animosity that was still fresh.

"So that business about not knowing what Amethyst and Katie were talking about Friday was just hokum?" Pen gave John a searching look.

"No, silly," Amethyst answered for him with exaggerated impatience. "Katie, or should I say Stacy—don't you think that idea of changing names was the berries? I wanted Anna, because my name already starts with an A. Katie originally thought of Stasia, but that was too obvious, besides, I thought it should rhyme with Katie. So...Anna and Stacy, like Anastasia!"

"We need you to tell us everything, Amethyst," Penelope said, trying to get her back on topic. If she kept straying, Richard might have to finally reveal himself as a detective. Pen was surprised Amethyst hadn't figured it out already. Perhaps it was the scar and standing next to Tommy, who might as well have worn a badge proclaiming himself part of Jack Sweeney's men. "But first, where are Katie and Tino?"

Amethyst shrugged and took a sip. "That's the point. Everyone is left in the dark deliberately. It was to be very cloak and dagger, like a spy mission."

Zounds! They'd been treating the whole thing like a group of kids playing make-believe.

"Except someone is dead," Pen reminded her.

"Yes..." Amethyst said, taking a long sip. "But who would kill Anastasia?" She perked up, a look of alarm on her face. "They didn't take..." She caught herself. "I mean, was there any indication it was a robbery?"

"What would they have stolen?"

"What robbers normally steal," she said her brow furrowed with uncertainty.

Pen turned to Richard for confirmation before finally saying, "We know about the Fabergé Egg, Amethyst."

She choked on the swallow she'd just taken. When she recovered, she plastered an innocent expression on her face. "Fabergé Egg?"

Pen sighed and closed her eyes. "Let's start from the beginning. How did you and Katie even devise this plan?"

"She was the one to come to me. It was a few weeks ago, after dance class. Before then, I really didn't associate with the likes of her." Amethyst's nose wrinkled ever so slightly. "She's a bit of a show-off, that one. Always boasting about things like visiting speakeasies and going to jazz clubs, as though that's impressive. Daddy was dragging me out of speakeasies when I was thirteen!" She hiccuped a laugh, before adding with a frown, "If only he hadn't decided to be a Scrooge. That's the reason I was working with Katie in the first place. A little bit of fun money until he comes to his senses."

It seemed to Penelope Amethyst had more in common with Katie than she thought.

"At any rate, she and that little friend of hers seemed to think I knew people in the movie business. Granted everyone knows I *do* know anyone who is anyone in this city. My face is a constant in all the magazines." She smiled self-indulgently. "I figured the daughter of one of the most notorious gangsters in New York would be an interesting addition to one of my little parties, so I invited her. She was dumb enough to bring that pretty friend of hers."

Pen didn't need to ask why she thought it was dumb. Moira was far prettier than Katie, who wasn't unattractive herself.

"Were you at this party?" Pen asked John, hoping to catch him in a lie.

He narrowed his eyes. "If I had been there, then I would have recognized Stacy or Katie or whatever her name is," he said with a sour note of sarcasm.

"John and I weren't exactly talking at the time. Honestly, he's been such a stick in the mud, not doing anything fun." She turned to face him. "I'm surprised you wanted to go with me to the speakeasy on Friday."

He looked uncomfortable under the scrutiny Pen once again gave him. When he answered it was mostly for her benefit.

"I just thought we should settle down after your father decided to cut you off is all. You were the one whining so much about it. It certainly wasn't going to help things by getting caught in a sting."

"A sting," Amethyst said, dismissing it with a wave of the hand. "Considering you were the one to introduce me to that place, I coulda just blamed you." The liquor was beginning to affect her, but it also kept her talking.

"I thought you told her father she was the one to tell you about that place?" Pen pressed.

"Well, of course I'd say that, wouldn't I?" He said throwing up his hands with exasperation. "It doesn't mean anything, I heard about it from a few friends at school, about how they weren't too strict on age requirements and all. I think Sam was the one to tell me."

"*Anyway,*" Amethyst said, inserting herself back onto center stage. "Dougie, my producer friend, was positively dizzy for Moira. Told her that she had a direct ticket to at least be a dancing girl in one of his movies as soon as she made it to Hollywood." A devilish smirk came to Amethyst's face. "That's when Katie decided she had to, *ahem,* be a bit more innovative and do things solo. I admire the girl. Leaving your best friend behind to make it big? Ambition is *positute-ly* everything out there in Hollywood. The only problem was funding it, I suppose. Tickets to California aren't cheap, and if it's going to take a while to make it, then she needed to live somehow. So, a week ago she comes to me with her idea, thinking I might know people who wanted her egg."

"Where did Tino fit into all of this?"

Amethyst rolled her eyes. "She was too scared to go on her own. The daughter of a gangster and she can't even ride a train by herself. Some girls are far too coddled. Of course, some of us break free of that nonsense early on. I know with Daddy all I have to do is make sure to attend church every Sunday and pretend to read the Bible like a good little girl. It's always worked...until recently." She frowned into her cup.

"That's when she had to start using me," John said with a note of resentment in his voice.

"Oh stop, it wasn't as though you didn't get something

out of it. Besides, perhaps Daddy's right, maybe I should start taking more of an interest in the company."

"So Katie came to you with the idea of selling the egg?"

Amethyst seemed put out at having been interrupted. She rolled her eyes and continued. "Yes, like I said. She wanted to hasten her move out to Los Angeles, and seemed to think I knew someone who could help her sell it. I suppose because Daddy is so obsessed with singlehandedly recreating the entire British Museum right here in New York. But he donates everything, he doesn't sell it. Still, I figured I could bluff her until I found someone."

"Did you?"

Amethyst seemed to realize she was saying far too much. "Wait a second, are you cops?"

"As I said, I'm a private investigator," Penelope answered, avoiding looking at Richard, which would give him away. "But you don't have to talk if you're worried you might say something incriminating."

"Maybe you should shut up, Amethyst. These two look like trouble," John said, jerking his chin in the direction of Tommy and Richard."

"Don't *you* tell me what to do!"

"I ain't no cop," Tommy said easily.

"And that one?" John asked, looking at Richard.

Richard paused before answering. "Yes, I am with the police. I'm not here to turn you in to your father, if that's what you're worried about. There can also be a deal on the table if you give more information. Our interests are far higher than your little plan with Katie. Since you have yet to even take possession of the egg, an argument could even be made for you having done nothing illegal so far." He nodded toward the drink in her hand. "Except for that, which is grounds enough to arrest you and take you in right now."

"What?"

"He's not going to do that," Pen said, giving Richard a scolding look, she turned to arch a brow at Amethyst. "But you should be more cooperative just in case."

The sides of her mouth were still turned down. She looked at her drink, then swallowed it fully. She boldly walked over to pour some more.

"I suppose I could tell you about what *Katie* did." She turned to give Richard a questioning look.

"Go on then."

"I have no idea how Katie got a hold of her egg, and the little minx wouldn't tell me a thing. I must admit, it was a little outside of my realm of experience, but it was too fascinating for me to be left out of the fun. So, I asked a friend who...may have known a thing or two about illegal importing. I mean, if they're selling illegal alcohol, surely they might know about selling other illegal things, no?"

Tommy snorted in amusement. Next to Amethyst John rolled his eyes.

Amethyst glared at him, then cooled her look into something sly. "As it turned out, he did in fact know someone."

"Who is this person?" Richard demanded.

"Which one?"

"Both."

"I don't know who the end person was. That was part of the whole espionage bit," she said with a pert smile.

Penelope controlled her irritation at how glib she was becoming again. "And the person you talked to?"

"I don't know if I should say. Isn't there some kind of right to silence, or privilege I have, or something of that sort?"

THE GIRLS AND THE GOLDEN EGG

"Yes, if you're arrested, which I can easily arrange," Richard hinted.

Amethyst pursed her lips. "What if I didn't know his real name?"

"Is he worth going to jail for?"

"Just tell us who it is," Penelope said, curbing her impatience. Amethyst held the key to an entire criminal enterprise on the tip of her tongue.

"No," she retorted with a frown. "In fact, I think—"

"Oh for heaven's sake, it's Christos," John spat.

"How the hell did you know?" Amethyst asked.

"In retrospect it's obvious. You and he have been thick as thieves for weeks now."

"Only because you've been ignoring me!" she spat with a sneer. "I know you only used me to look good for Daddy."

John coughed out a laugh. "And you used me for exactly the same reason. You probably couldn't wait to ask Christos about something so scandalous. And he was probably more than happy to try and accommodate you. A bunch of peacocks all of you, including Katie...or is it Stacy?" John said with a bit of added venom. "And I was the sucker playing the fool, thinking it was just another night out at a speakeasy. Even stupider of me to play your delivery boy today. Now, the police think I'm involved in all this business. Honestly, I'll be glad to be done with you."

"You were paid," she snapped.

He coughed out a laugh. "Almost as stingy as your father is."

"Now you listen here, Bub—"

"Both of you stop, now! You're acting like children. Have you forgotten that there's at least one dead person?"

"At least?" John asked.

Pen figured that was an appropriate segue. "Do either of

you know a customs agent by the name of Connor
Davidson?"

Both of them returned blank looks.

"Now is not the time to be coy. He was seriously
injured and then murdered on Sunday night."

"I was here all night. Just as I was last night," Amethyst
said.

"So no alibi." Pen turned to John with a questioning
look.

"I was in my room in bed all night. I don't make it a
habit of going around town killing people, you know?"

"So neither of you have alibis for either murder.
Grand."

"We aren't the only ones who are involved in all of this.
You don't even know where Katie and Tino are. Maybe it
was them?" Amethyst suggested.

"We at least have Christos," Richard said. "He can tell
us everything, especially if he was working with this illegal
smuggling business we're looking at."

"Or maybe he was just humoring Amethyst, claiming
he knew someone, and planned on stealing the egg for
himself."

"No," Amethyst said in a needling tone. "He showed
me some biblical relic the man he was working with had
imported. It was in the papers this week."

Tommy whistled quietly. Katherine hummed in excitement. Richard exhaled. They had him...all they had to do
was arrest Christos and get him to confess.

"Swell! Just swell! You had me deliver an invitation to a
guy involved in some criminal organization?" John cried in
protest.

"Oh stop, like the officer here said, it's only a crime if

we...actively do something, right?" Amethyst turned to Richard for confirmation.

"There's no crime in delivering an invitation," he said in a droll voice.

"Did you tell Christos about Katie?" Pen asked.

"Gosh no, she wanted to stay completely out of it." Her eyes widened with some sudden thought. "Oh my gosh, that's why Anastasia was killed!"

CHAPTER TWENTY-SIX

"You know why Anastasia was murdered?" Penelope was the first to ask after Amethyst's outburst.

"Yes, it explains everything, don't you see?"

"Explains *what?*" Katherine asked in impatient frustration.

Penelope turned, along with Richard and Tommy, sporting similar looks of irritation. She just returned a look that said she knew they had the same question.

"Katie was really worried about being recognized and connected to her father. That's why we met at the speakeasy on Friday. She thought it might be safe as Christos's place isn't in her father's territory or something like that. She wanted to come and see if he recognized her at all. Thankfully, he didn't."

"Or so he made it seem," John said, his mouth twisted in a way that expressed exactly how gullible he thought Amethyst was. Pen had to agree.

"Why would he lie, silly?" Amethyst retorted.

"Please go on, Miss Easton," Richard urged.

"Anyway," Amethyst crooned, giving John the stink eye.

"The only problem was, I'd already said the egg would be delivered by a Katie. I didn't realize she would be so skittish about it, and I certainly wasn't going to do it myself! So we had this idea of talking about hiring someone else to do it, just in case Christos's friend might recognize her.

"I knew Anastasia because of Dougie, the producer she'd met at the party. She was there too—they're quite cozy with one another. She'd just won this beauty contest but had to give up the prize because she was older than the age limit of twenty-three, they discovered, and so she needed money, he said. She'd already cut and dyed her hair blonde, like us." Amethyst smiled and patted her own short tresses. "I gave her Katie's necklace and ring and her coat, and we got a similar dress to what she was wearing Friday. That way Christos's friend would know what to look for, you see? Katie was the one who set everything up from there."

"So that's why Anastasia was in Battery Park last night?"

"I suppose that's where Katie might have handed off the egg, like an attaché," she said loftily before her face fell again. "Only she would know for sure. And I don't know where she is." Amethyst's eyes widened. "Jeez, she was getting paid twice what she would have won at the beauty pageant. Two hundred dollars and now she's dead."

"I'd just like to reiterate that I knew nothing about this plan, so how would I have even known this Anastasia would be there last night!" John asserted, rather tactlessly.

"Yes, *John*," Amethyst said in a whiny voice. "We all know you're Mr. Innocent. So am I!" She added, eyes wide as she stared at the four others in the room. "That's why I was throwing the party. My part in all of this was done. I thought Christos's was as well. But...maybe *he* killed her?"

And suddenly the finger-pointing had begun.

Pen was still focused on playing everything back in her head and something struck her. Amethyst had mentioned the speakeasy being safe enough because it wasn't in Sweeney's territory. It was on 4th street, specifically the south side of 4th, which meant it was Messina territory.

Suddenly Tino's involvement didn't seem so coincidental.

Was it the Messina family that was Christos's contact? They would have been the ones supplying the speakeasy under his father's barbershop. No wonder he had been so willing to meet with Tommy and Penelope.

"Do I get to leave now?" John asked. "Amethyst confirmed I knew nothing about this."

"No one is going anywhere," Richard replied, sounding appalled that he would even ask. "The last thing we need is you two telling anyone, even inadvertently."

"Who am I going to tell? You think I want people to know I got duped into this nonsense?"

"Well, I'd hate for you to get duped into inadvertently telling someone," Richard replied, causing John to shoot a look so dark Pen was surprised it didn't do physical damage.

Amethyst snickered, which only made him angrier. He stormed over to the bar and grabbed a bottle to get a drink. He stared right at Richard, defiant as he poured far too much into a glass.

Katherine laughed, as did Amethyst. Pen had other concerns.

"Someone has to go get Christos," she pointed out. "Also, I suppose we should tell Mr. Easton his daughter is alive and well."

"We should probably hold off on that."

"What? Why?" Pen asked, then figured it out. "Surely you don't think that Mr. Easton is involved in all of this?"

"Daddy?" Amethyst coughed out a laugh. "Never."

"Perhaps not him, but someone associated with him. No one is above suspicion at this point. And he certainly has the resources."

"That would be an absolute hoot!"

"Amethyst, someone died," Penelope reminded her.

"Now you see why I had considered moving on," John said, flapping a hand her way. "The girl is just plain silly."

"And yet you went with her on Friday?" Pen said giving him an accusatory stare.

"Someone had to pay for drinks," he said in a droll voice.

"Consider it payback for all the times I paid your way!" Amethyst snapped.

Pen felt both her weariness and a headache set in. "I'm not staying to play nanny to these two while you arrest Christos. I need to continue searching for Katie and Tino, who are still missing. And don't tell me it's a police matter, as I already have some insight into the case."

Penelope could see the hint of reluctance on his face at her continuing her search, but he knew better than to argue.

"I certainly can't stay. I have to begin the search for Christos. He may have been our murderer, perhaps in both cases. He, or whoever his associate is, could be going after them next, as he still doesn't have the egg."

The two of them turned to Katherine and Tommy. The former was grinning. The latter wasn't.

"No," Tommy said sounding more blunt than usual.

"I'll happily stay," Katherine agreed.

Richard didn't like it, but it would have to do for the moment. "You stay and keep these two here. Period. No asking questions. No prodding or inquiring. This is an open criminal case, not a news story."

"Aye, captain," Katherine said with a smirk.

"If either leave, you call the police. Tell them Detective Richard Prescott had them sequestered as material witnesses, and suspects in at least two murders—"

John and Amethyst protested at the same time.

"Hey now!"

"*What?*"

"—and they should be arrested on sight," he finished, ignoring them.

"Of course, detective," Katherine said putting on a facade of extreme importance.

Back on the street, there was a short impasse as the three remaining people debated who would drive Penelope.

"Tommy's perfectly fine to drive me, Richard," Pen protested. "You have a suspect to find and time is of the essence. No need to waste it chauffeuring me around."

She could see Richard didn't like it. He gave Tommy a dark look. "Straight to the office. If I find you've done otherwise, I'll have you included in my business of arresting people for today."

Tommy just smiled. "Aye captain," he said, mimicking Katherine.

"Let's go," Pen said pushing Tommy away and toward his car. She turned to give Richard a smile that was half apologetic, half reassuring. "We'll be fine. It's just a car ride."

CHAPTER TWENTY-SEVEN

Tommy drove Penelope back to her office, where she planned on telling Jane the updates, or as much as she could. At the very least, she could send her home. After all, she had a wedding to continue planning, as small as she intended it to be.

Pen marveled over Christos being involved in this nasty business, which wasn't too much of a surprise in retrospect. He had seemed like a slippery character. It would be a sad day for all the young women who had been patronizing that speakeasy just to get a glimpse of him.

Pen wondered who it was he'd been working with. The Messina family seemed like the most obvious candidate, as the illegal drinking establishment was already their territory. Perhaps she would focus her efforts on those ties as she looked for Katie and Tino.

A thought was nagging at the back of her mind. Something about connections...

Tommy let her get out in front of the building where her office was, and went to find a place to park his car. Penelope waited for him, watching as the white car turned the corner at the block. It gave her a chance to think before she had to tell Jane everything.

As soon as he disappeared another car flew in, coming to a sudden stop right in front of her. Pen started in surprise, blinking at the rather large, shiny black vehicle. The man sitting in the front passenger exited and gave her a grim look.

Penelope recognized him instantly. He was one of Mr. Messina's goons. Before she could ask what the meaning of all this was, he spoke.

"Miss Banks, please get into the car." He opened the back passenger door for her.

"I most certainly will not! If Mr. Messina wants to talk to me, he can come to my office, or call and ask me to come and see him."

"I think you should get into the car," the man said, pulling aside his coat to reveal a gun.

"That doesn't scare me. Are you going to shoot me in broad daylight? Right here on Madison Avenue?"

"If I have to," he said, trying to seem menacing, though he didn't make a move for his gun.

"I've been kidnapped enough during this case, I won't be taken against my will yet again. Tell me what he wants and then perhaps I'll speak with him...on my own terms."

"Now, now, and here I thought we were friends, Miss Banks." Mr. Messina leaned out of the back passenger door to give her an ingratiating smile. "Please get into the car."

"What is this about?" Pen asked, feeling a certain sense of dread overcome her.

"I'd like to know as well."

All of them spun their heads to see Tommy approaching. His white suit jacket was already opened to reveal his own gun. He met Mr. Messina's gaze with a steely-eyed look.

Rather than seem upset, Mr. Messina sported a broader smile. "Ah, Tommy, I'm glad you're here. Perhaps you can persuade Miss Banks to have a small conference with me in my vehicle?"

"Perhaps you can tell me what this is about," he replied.

Mr. Messina sighed. "I had hoped I wouldn't have to resort to this, but..."

He sat back, disappearing from view. Pen waited, wrinkling her brow. Then she heard a voice.

"Pen, please get into the car." The voice was curt, as though the speaker was reluctant to talk.

"Lulu?" Penelope exclaimed.

Tommy was quicker. His gun was drawn and he rushed forward. The goon standing also pulled out his gun and blocked his way. The driver's side door opened and the other of Messina's men stood up, his gun also pointed at Tommy.

It was a three-person draw, and Penelope had the horrible feeling someone would get shot right there on Madison Avenue. The New Yorkers nearby reacted at once, exclaiming and running away. A woman screamed. A man shouted for someone to call the police.

"Stop this! For heaven's sake, put your guns away!" Penelope ordered.

None of them budged. Tommy honestly looked as though he would pull the trigger on all of them, Messina included. Consequences be damned.

Even amid that chaos, her heart swelled, that pathetically romantic part of her reeling at such a robust display of chivalry, as foolish as it was. He really did care about Lulu.

"I'll go with Mr. Messina," she said, gently resting a

restraining hand on the arm that held Tommy's gun. "I'll make sure she's safe."

Tommy continued to stare at both men, also holding guns. His jaw was taut enough to bounce a quarter off.

"Tommy," Pen urged, slightly squeezing his bicep. "I'm going. It's done."

Gradually he lowered the weapon. The other men followed suit. Pen waited until all weapons were re-holstered before she focused on Tommy.

"I'll make sure nothing happens to her. Don't do anything reckless."

"Listen to the lady, Tommy. You wouldn't want anything to happen to *Lulu*," the goon sneered in such a taunting way, Pen suspected he knew about Tommy and Lulu.

Tommy wasn't about to take that tone without payback. Before Pen could stop him, he gave him a good ringer right in the eye. The man fell back into the car, but came back up swinging. Tommy easily evaded it. He would have gone for another but Mr. Messina stopped him.

"Marco, no." That was all it took to bring him to heel, glaring at Tommy like an angry bull.

Tommy only had eyes for the passengers in the back seat. Pen quickly entered before things got even more out of hand. Mr. Messina promptly closed the door behind her.

While the two men entered the front seat, Penelope pulled down the seat facing Lulu and Mr. Messina in the back. She sat and studied Lulu. Her friend returned a sardonic smile, but didn't seem harmed in any way. In fact, she looked rather cozy in the large space that could probably accommodate three more people.

"There now, that was not so terrible was it?" Mr. Messina said pleasantly.

"I think you are going to be very lucky if the police don't make an appearance."

"I don't worry about such things," he said with a dismissive chuckle, which told Penelope all she needed to know about his relationship with the police. He probably also understood that Tommy would be the last person to call them for aid. The Sweeney gang had alternate methods of handling such things.

"You didn't have to resort to kidnapping. I would have gladly talked to you. After all, I'm also trying to find your son, who I believe may be in danger. Did you at least bring a sample of his handwriting with you?"

He seemed reluctant to start with that, but then exhaled and reached into his inner pocket. He pulled out a folded piece of paper.

"An essay for school." Mr. Messina sounded slightly dismissive about it, as though such tasks were beneath a real man.

Penelope unfolded the paper and studied the writing. Her eyes rolled up to meet Mr. Messina, who managed to look mildly curious.

"This is the same writing as the message I got."

He pierced her with his dark eyes. "And what message would that be?"

Pen paused, wondering what to tell him.

"No need to hesitate, Miss Banks. I already know about the egg you have in your possession. A Fabergé I understand?"

Now that they knew who was involved with the smuggling trade, she saw no reason to maintain that bit of subterfuge, especially with Lulu also at stake. "Is that what this is about? If it is, I regret to inform you that the egg is actually with the authorities—not the New York Police Department, so don't go searching there."

"That is a shame," he said lifting both hands in the air in resignation. "If you had the egg, this could all be over with."

"Well, I don't." She pierced him with a hard look.

Mr. Messina met her gaze with a sharp look of his own. "And yet my sources tell me otherwise."

"Your sources need to update their information. There *was* a rumor that I had the egg, so we could flush out the people responsible for the very thing your son has gotten himself tangled up in. A son who may be in serious danger, Mr. Messina. I assume you've heard of the murder in Battery Park by now?"

Something flickered in his dark eyes, a brief flash of actual concern for Tino. "My son knows how to take care of himself."

"Does he?"

"I think you have bigger things to worry about, Miss Banks. Like telling me everything that is happening with this case." He turned to Lulu. "Or we can go back to my favorite restaurant and I can get the information from your friend over another glass of Primitivo. I doubt it will be as enjoyable for you this time."

Penelope glared at him. "I suppose in your own territory it's easier to—"

She stopped suddenly. They were heading south, presumably back to Mulberry Street. That had sparked something in her head.

"What is it, Miss Banks? Did you have a change of heart?"

"I suppose you own multiple properties in the south part of Manhattan, as part of the territory you control. Do you own any buildings near Jeanette Park?"

He studied her with wary regard before answering. "Yes, I do. Why?"

"Any that have a direct view of it?" Pen asked, feeling a surge of excitement.

Again he paused. "Yes. Why, what does that have to do with anything?"

"I think Katie and your son have been hiding out there."

CHAPTER TWENTY-EIGHT

Mr. Messina's two men were driving Mr. Messina, Lulu, and Penelope down to the building he owned that overlooked Jeanette Park. She had earlier suspected the young runaways would be housed in a building owned by one of their fathers, but she hadn't considered Mr. Messina.

She wouldn't make that mistake again.

"How do you import the alcohol for your, *ahem*, establishments?"

"I believe *I'm* asking the questions, Miss Banks."

"Alright, what are your questions?"

"Who is running all of this and where?

"We don't know yet."

He studied her with more scrutiny. "If you're lying—"

"What reason would I have to lie? If I knew who was in charge, then so would the authorities, I'd have no reason to keep it from you, even without the kidnapping."

His inquiry did make her question her assumption that his family was the one working with Christos. Then again, perhaps he was testing her, if only to find out how much the police knew. She quickly dismissed that idea. It was a risky move to kidnap someone, let alone waste his time on this.

Mr. Messina's mouth and jaw tightened with displeasure. "So the egg is gone and you have no idea who is in charge of this business?"

"The speakeasy on 4th underneath the Barbershop, that's yours?"

He paused, working his jaw before answering. "It is. I own the building."

"Mr. Papadopoulos, I assume he knows what goes on beneath his business after hours. Are he or his son involved in it at all?"

"Why?"

Penelope waited patiently.

"They know to look the other way and become mute should the police come knocking."

"So no."

"Again, why?"

"I'm working it out. I won't know anything for sure until we find Katie and Tino." Penelope was stalling. Lulu knew her well enough to see that much, but her poker face was even better than Penelope's. Still, Pen knew her friend almost as well and could see the mixture of irritation, incredulity, and just a hint of amusement in those cat-like eyes.

The fact was, Penelope wasn't sure how Mr. Messina would react to learning Christos was involved in all of this. Until Richard had him in custody, he was a liability. He was also the only connection to the person in charge. Better for the police to find out first before he did. She could already picture Mr. Messina detouring up to 4th Street to kidnap Mr. Papadopoulos while he was in the middle of a haircut.

"And you import your alcohol by ship? I assume that's

how you know about the mysterious shipments you assumed were for Mr. Sweeney?"

He didn't answer.

"Everything I'm asking will help figure out who is responsible," she lied.

He exhaled slowly and settled back into his seat. "Yes, by ship. A method which we are strongly reconsidering," he said in a disgruntled tone.

"Why?"

A flash of irritation crossed his face. "We had a recent... loss. Interestingly enough, it was related to your little friend's importing, exporting business."

"Wait, was it that shipment of two-hundred and fifty thousand dollars worth of alcohol that was recently captured?"

"Yes," he said tersely.

"That was you?" Lulu asked, eyes wide at the prospect.

He glowered at them both. "We are exploring other avenues. A French connection, if you will." A cryptic smile came to his face.

He wasn't as clever as he thought he was. Penelope assumed he'd be importing through French Canada, which was less likely to be monitored by the federal authorities, for obvious reasons.

"*Basta!*" Mr. Messina exclaimed. Pen assumed he had reached his limit of indulgence. "If my son and Jack's daughter are not here, I expect information, Miss Banks. I know you are withholding something."

Pen swallowed hard, hoping her hunch was correct.

The apartment building they parked in front of was a small, insignificant thing. Pen had no idea why it was included as a part of his real estate holdings and certainly wasn't about to ask incriminating questions at that point.

Penelope exited the door that was held open by Marco. She felt a trickle of satisfaction noting the way his eye had already started to blacken. It served him right.

Mr. Messina came out after her.

"It's important that I talk to them alone. They're already terrified, and you'll just make things worse."

He simply stared back, not even bothering to reply. She realized how futile her plea was. She supposed a father had every right, even one who seemed as unconcerned as Mr. Messina was.

Pen looked back at Lulu, sitting calmly and comfortably in the car. Marco caught her looking and grinned.

"Don't worry, I'll see that she's taken care of."

Without thinking, Pen rushed to him until she was only inches away from his towering build. "If you lay a finger on her I'll do something to you that makes what Tommy did seem like a flick of the ear."

She was pleased to see how stunned he was. No doubt it was more from her bold act than her threat, but it still gave her a dose of satisfaction. His expression quickly turned into something dark and nasty.

"They aren't going to do anything to your friend. Unless, of course, I find you're holding out on me, Miss Banks," Mr. Messina said in a warning tone.

"I'm not. Let's go," she said, giving Marco one last warning look. She cast a reassuring smile down to Lulu, who looked positively tickled by her display of boldness. Pen felt reassured that should Marco disobey his boss, Lulu could also handle herself.

Penelope followed Mr. Messina into the building. She was chagrined to see his method of flushing out his son and Katie was to bang on every door until someone answered. A series of sad, terrified faces of mostly immigrants who barely spoke English—but were certainly able to converse with him in perfect Italian—met them on every floor.

Until they got to a door on the top floor of the apartment that had a perfect view of the Great War Memorial. As though he knew that his son and Mr. Sweeney's daughter were behind that door, his knocking was more insistent.

At first, there was no response. He banged again, this time shouting. "Tino! I know you're in there! Open this door or so help me God!"

That was followed by a string of Italian that Penelope couldn't have hoped to understand. But anyone listening could interpret that tone.

Pen winced, and they both waited. When there was still no response, Penelope intervened. By now, she was sure two terrified young people were behind that door. Any satisfaction she had from finding Tino and Katie, or at least one of them, was presently overshadowed by making sure they weren't catatonic with fear by the time the door was finally opened.

"May I?"

He frowned but stepped aside.

Pen knocked more softly. "Katie? Tino? My name is Miss Banks, I know you're both scared but we're only here to make sure you're safe. Your father isn't mad, Tino, just worried. I'll make sure he doesn't go too hard on you."

She gave Mr. Messina a pointed look, and he simply returned one of his own. But her method had an effect. The door cracked open and the handsome face of someone who shared some resemblance to Carlo Messina peered out. Tino's features were softer, more like those of modern film stars with their stage makeup that sometimes made them seem effeminate. Tino's eyelashes were full, his skin flawless, his mouth lush. It would be perfect for the screen, not so much for the son of a hardened gangster.

"Hello, Tino?" Pen said with an encouraging smile. "Is Katie there with you? Can I come in?"

"Enough of this," Mr. Messina said, stepping back into view.

Tino quickly swung the door open for his father. Mr. Messina strutted in, brushing right past him. Penelope quickly followed.

The apartment was sparse, filled with shabby furniture and not much in the way of heating. Pen found Katie on a sagging sofa bundled in an incongruently luxurious fur coat. Her wide blue eyes stared up at the terrifying Carlo like a rabbit caught by a wolf.

"Katie?" Pen said before Mr. Messina could ruin everything with his blustering.

It took her a moment to acknowledge Pen. After repeating her name, Katie's eyes flashed to her.

"My name is Penelope Banks. I'm glad to see that you and Tino are okay. You *are* okay, aren't you?"

She numbly nodded.

"Enough of this coddling. I want an explanation...now!"

Tino, to his credit, rushed over to sit next to Katie, who had started crying. He placed an arm around her. It looked more like brotherly protectiveness than romantic love. Tino had more gumption than his father gave him credit for.

"I just wanted to go to Hollywood, that's all!" Katie sobbed. "I didn't think anyone would get killed, I swear!"

Penelope and Mr. Messina cast a furtive look at one another. Penelope spoke before he could.

"Who was murdered?" Pen asked, hoping they would explain how they knew Anastasia had been murdered. Had they witnessed it? The apartment didn't offer a view of Battery Park, but perhaps they had still seen something.

"That customs agent, Connor Davidson. Tino and me, we read about it in the paper Monday morning."

Penelope hadn't been expecting that answer. It seemed there was a connection between the customs agent and this Fabergé Egg business after all.

"Are you saying Jack killed him?" Mr. Messina asked, a hint of a smile tugging at his mouth.

"I dunno," Katie blubbered with a shrug, then began crying again.

Tino squeezed her shoulders reassuringly, then stared back at his father and Penelope, putting up a braver front. "We decided it wasn't worth it anymore, not after he was murdered. It had to be related."

"Why do you think that?" Pen asked.

"Because he's the man Daddy got the egg from," Katie said, throwing up her hands. "Why do you think we got so scared? We were certain to be next."

Penelope exhaled sharply at that information. Suddenly all her suppositions about who had killed the man were obliterated. Jack Sweeney would have no compulsion about beating up a man and then killing him, tossing his body into the East River to permanently silence him. Better yet, he'd get his number one henchman Tommy Callahan to do it.

She almost admired his ability to bluff. He'd seemed quite convincing back in her office when he told her that wasn't Mr. Sweeney's doing.

"Why don't you tell us everything from the beginning?" Pen asked. "Start with how you learned about the egg. But first, do you know anything about any other murder?"

They both shook their heads and gave her curious looks, which meant they didn't know about Anastasia.

"Okay, go on. From the beginning."

Having Mr. Messina there wasn't ideal. But Penelope's nose for detection demanded the information. Besides, there was only so much he could do in response.

Katie was hesitant. One look at the stern face of Mr. Messina was all it took to get her talking. Pen supposed he did have his uses.

"It was in Daddy's office. I overheard him and Mr. Davidson discussing the egg. I think Mr. Davidson had a lot of gambling debt. He wanted to use the egg to pay them off. He was talking about how much it was worth. Daddy didn't believe him at first, but Mr. Davidson said he should look into it. But I knew. I knew as soon as Daddy learned how valuable it was, he would take it. So I had a plan to take it when he did and use it to go to Hollywood."

"Before you were eighteen?" Pen asked.

"I thought that was my only opportunity to escape. Selling it would have been enough to not only go there but live. I know it will take time to become famous. The egg was exactly the thing I needed. But, I didn't know how or to whom to sell it."

"That's when you approached Amethyst?"

"Yes, ma'am. I knew her father was in importing and exporting and he had done so much with getting important artifacts into the museums and things like that. I thought for sure he might pay for something as important as the egg. He's so wealthy, after all. At first I just wanted to inquire, you see."

Katie scowled. "She laughed at me, said she wasn't a criminal." The way she said it seemed to mimic Amethyst.

"That was a couple of weeks ago. Still, I figured I could find someone even if she wouldn't do it. Then, all of a sudden she changed her mind. She told me she had someone who could sell it for me, buy it even!"

"So I approached Tino, who I knew also wanted to go to Hollywood." She turned to smile at him.

"But not Moira?" Pen asked, remembering how Katie's friend had assumed they would go together.

Katie looked guilty, averting her gaze and blushing.

"You didn't want to go with her," Pen confirmed.

"I knew I shouldn't have brought her to that party! I suppose that's what I get for being a good friend." Pen didn't think Katie was such a good friend, but she understood her ambitions. "Anyway, I thought if I went out to Hollywood on my own without her, then he'd have to notice me! Even if I wasn't eighteen yet. I know it's wrong, leaving Moira behind after we made a pact to go together, but nobody makes it out there by playing nice.

"Anyway, I admit, the idea of going alone scared me. I'd met Tino before during one of those dumb—" She suddenly darted her eyes to Mr. Messina with alarm and cleared her throat. "One of the meetings between our fathers. I got in touch with him and we planned it out. I already had clothes for the trip set aside at a secret location."

"The old carriage house at your school?"

Katie looked appalled that Pen would know that. "I suppose Moira told you that," She sniffed.

"She was worried about you, Katie. She, like everyone else, including your mother, I might add, thought maybe you'd been kidnapped."

Katie's curled lip softened. "Yes, I suppose that wasn't very kind of me. But I did plan on writing them when I got to Hollywood, both Mama and Moira."

Pen reminded herself that she was just a seventeen year old who had been sheltered most of her life, despite who her father was. This experience would hopefully be a valuable education for the girl.

"Go on."

"When I found out Amethyst's connection was someone in one of, um, Mr. Messina's businesses," she gave him a wary look, then quickly averted her gaze, not liking what she saw on his face. "I was worried someone would recognize me. For the same reason, Tino obviously couldn't get involved. Amethyst was the one to suggest hiring an actress and making things so...complicated, what with the... atta—ata-something."

"Attaché," Pen said.

Katie nodded, rolled her eyes, and wrinkled her features as though still confounded about it all. "She wanted it to be so much more dramatic and exciting than it really was."

"Cloak and dagger," Pen said in a sardonic voice.

"I thought she knew what she was doing so I went along with it. She assured me he was trustworthy. Anyway, Friday night we worked it all out at the speakeasy."

"So Christos knew about the plan, but did John?"

She hiccuped a laugh. "Amethyst said he was too bluenosed, he'd positute-ly tell her father. Thankfully, Christos didn't recognize me, so we tried to make it seem like all we were talking about was clothes and makeup and actresses. You know, so they'd think it was silly girl talk?"

That lined up with what Amethyst had said.

Katie swallowed and continued. "Amethyst thought of the idea of code names. She was really excited about the whole Romanov part of it, and what with the actress being named Anastasia. I didn't care, I was fine being called Stacy that night, so long as it happened."

"Why did you even bring Moira if you didn't want her to be a part of it all?"

Katie looked sheepish once again.

Tino gave her a mild look of admonishment, then answered for her. "She wanted to show off. I told her it was cruel and dangerous. What if she learned about what we were planning and told Katie's father?"

"She didn't though! She was over by the bar, she was too far away to have heard anything!"

Pen remembered being seventeen, back when outdoing her peers seemed like the most important thing in the world. Being the prettiest, smartest, richest, and most fashionable; they were the ultimate goals. It all seemed so silly now, especially after she'd fallen the hardest when her father cut her off. In retrospect, it had given her the kind of education she never would have had otherwise, and she regretted nothing about it.

Still, Pen was close enough to that time of her life not to entirely dismiss Katie's sensibilities. Besides, Pen also had some experience watching another woman be chosen over her. Granted, *that* woman had been chosen on the night prior to Penelope's wedding.

"So Christos knew the details, but didn't know who you were?"

"Correct."

"And what exactly was Anastasia's role?"

"She was supposed to meet the person Christos was working with last night. We were going to hand over the egg at Battery Park just before midnight. We figured she would realize that the plan was off when we didn't show up to hand over the egg. After all, she already received her two hundred dollars, so perhaps she's not too mad. Have you talked to her? I can offer her some money to compensate for having to come out so late for nothing."

Penelope and Mr. Messina glanced at each other. Pen

subtly shook her head, instructing him not to reveal the fact that she was dead.

"After Mr. Davidson's murder on Sunday, we knew we had to put an end to all of this. At first, we were just going to secretly return the egg to my father and drop it off at my house. But he had so many of his men surrounding the place. Then, we saw you with Tommy leaving my house and I had a better idea. I've seen you at the Peacock Club before, sitting with Lulu. I knew who you were, and I figured I'd go through you instead. I knew where you lived because I'd read about that murder in your building last month, and how you solved it. I thought you would be the perfect...well, attaché, I suppose."

Despite the circumstances, Penelope felt a ripple of pride that her efforts had been acknowledged by someone. Technically, that murder had happened outside of her apartment building, but it *had* been that of a resident, so her building had made the papers.

"Why haven't you gone home yet?" She asked, turning her attention to Katie specifically. Tino's fate was already sealed.

"We were just working up the nerve to do it," Tino answered for her, his eyes toward the floor. He took a moment, then brought his gaze up to his father. "We knew everyone would be angry and, we just needed a day or two to prepare to face the wrath."

"Well it came to you didn't it," Mr. Messina growled. "Still, I can't say I don't admire your gumption, my son. Stealing Jack's Fabergé egg." He guffawed with delight.

Tino seemed relieved, but still slightly embarrassed.

Katie looked miserable. "Does my father know we're here?"

"No, but he will soon enough." Pen wondered if

Tommy had managed to catch up with the ostentatious limousine and follow them to their current location.

"Honestly, I just want to go home. I don't even care if he does send me to a convent like he's been threatening to do," Katie said, looking morose. "As for that damn egg, send it right back from where it came, I say."

"So, Christos Papadopoulos is the connection?" Mr. Messina said. "How fortuitous!"

Pen had almost forgotten he was there, and was rudely reminded by that ominous announcement.

"Yes...quite fortuitous." Pen looked off to the side in thought.

"Do you have something to say, Miss Banks?" he asked, half-amused, as though he suspected she might be attempting some ploy to thwart his attempt to go straight to the young man to get more information about this, apparently very profitable illegal importing business.

"It is all quite fortuitous, isn't it? The Fabergé Egg, Katie, Christos, Amethyst..."

She gasped in sudden horror. "Oh no!"

Everyone in the small apartment, including Mr. Messina flinched at her outburst.

"What is it?" He snapped, slightly embarrassed that he had reacted.

Penelope turned to face him. "We need to go. Now!"

CHAPTER TWENTY-NINE

PENELOPE WAS GRATEFUL THAT CARLO MESSINA'S Curiosity was the leading horse in the race that was going on in his head at the moment. It was well ahead of Boss of a Criminal Family and Masculine Stubbornness as his men drove them.

"I can't say anything yet," Penelope insisted. She couldn't tell him the truth, and she was too preoccupied to think of a lie.

"Need I remind you that your friend is still under my temporary guardianship?"

"No, I can see her sitting right next to you." Penelope probably shouldn't have been so short with him, but she was counting on that leading horse of Curiosity to get her to the finish line.

Where a third murder would be avoided.

Katie and Tino were in the car with them. Leaving them in that poorly insulated apartment was out of the question. They were probably glad Mr. Messina's attention (and irritation) was focused entirely on Penelope Banks at the moment. Tino maintained a stoic front. Katie seemed resigned more than anything.

Lulu looked slightly worried. Pen shot her a reassuring smile.

Penelope had figured it out.

At least, she hoped so.

"My patience is wearing thin, Miss Banks."

"And you'll have answers when we get there. I'm not bluffing." She almost added "this time" but caught herself.

When the car came to a stop in front of the address she had given, Pen shot out, opening the door for herself before they could even turn off the engine.

"You wait just a moment, Miss Banks!" Mr. Messina called out after her. Penelope didn't stop, figuring he was perfectly free to follow her.

She rushed up the stairs and knocked, banged really, on the door marked 3B.

"Katherine? Are you in there? Open the door please!"

Pen once again pressed her ear to the door when it wasn't immediately opened. She was just about to resume banging when it opened and the puzzled face of Katherine stared out.

"If you've come to check up on me, don't worry, I haven't been scheming on ways to get my story into tomorrow's paper." She lifted the glass in her hand. "I've been showing these two kiddies how to make a proper—"

"You're alive!"

Once again her face wrinkled in confusion. "Is there a reason I shouldn't be?"

Pen squeezed in past her to find John and Amethyst staring back at her with nothing more than piqued curiosity. She stormed over to John, who blinked rapidly in startled surprise.

"Who really told you about the speakeasy you went to on Friday?"

It took John a moment to comprehend what she was asking, as though he had expected a completely different reason for the censuring look on her face.

"Answer the question, boy." Mr. Messina had finally caught up to Pen and walked over to stand in front of him.

John flinched in surprise again, before composing himself and answering. "I told you, it was my friend Sam."

"Really? So, if I ask him, he'll say the same? And trust me, I will ask him."

"Yes, why would I lie about something as silly as that?"

"Because this connection to a speakeasy where Christos just happens to know someone who imports rare and precious artifacts from around the world is too coincidental. You've spent time with your father, working for Mr. Easton, who also imports such things, legally or at least openly. It's one coincidence too many, John. I've learned not to believe in coincidences."

"Well, that's what this is! Go ahead and ask Sam. Hell, he probably won't remember, but that won't be my fault, will it? I was rather annoyed to be the last to know about it. In fact, he seemed rather reluctant to—"

"What is it?" Pen asked when he suddenly paused.

"Oliver Dennis. He was the first one to know about it. I remember being sore he didn't tell me before everyone else, as he always seemed closest to me."

"In what way did he seem closest?" Pen asked. She thought about the boy with blond curly hair. Could he be the one in charge of all this smuggling?

"He was always trying to make nice with me," John shot up from the couch in outrage. "That's why Sam was so reluctant to tell me about the speakeasy. I wasn't supposed to know! That dirty rat, Oliver, had told everyone but me!"

"Oliver Dennis, go-to man for any of your needs. The one who always made sure that he got himself invited when Amethyst—conveniently enough, the daughter of a shipping tycoon who liked to scour the earth for rare artifacts to bring home—was hosting a party," Penelope mused aloud.

Everyone's eyes turned to Amethyst. She had a carefully constructed, wide-eyed look of innocence on her face. "I don't see what that has to do with me at all. I have no control over who he decides to bring to my parties. I barely even know this Oliver."

"Nonsense! You were the one to always insist on getting some of his muggle—a stupider name for it I can't even imagine. He always insisted on an invite for a steep discount when I asked him for some. I can't believe I was such a fool! Was this all a setup? You were going to have me take the fall! My connections to your father. To you. To that stupid speakeasy!"

"Shut your trap, you dummy! They have nothing."

"We have Oliver Dennis. I wonder how quickly he'll turn on you, Amethyst."

"Maybe we can suggest you were the one to give him up?" Mr. Messina said with a grin. "I know enough dirty crooks to know how well that goes over. No one likes a rat, sweetheart."

Pen wasn't a fan of terrorizing the girl, but she had to admit it was effective.

The color drained from Amethyst's face. "You can't! He'll kill me."

"What's this about murder?"

Everyone turned to see Tommy at the front door. Next to him were Lulu and Katie. Presumably, Tino had opted to stay in the car with his father's men. It was probably safer there than in the loft with Carlo.

"How the hell...?" Mr. Messina began in surprise. He exhaled in anger when Tommy gave him a deadly look. Pen could only imagine what he'd done to his men to get them to release Mr. Sweeney's daughter and Lulu. She hadn't heard a gunshot, so hopefully it was something short of murder, though she wouldn't have put it past him.

Amethyst paid no heed to their new visitors. She was still caught in the throes of terror at the prospect that Oliver might be informed she was a rat.

"John was the one to give up his name! Tell Oliver it was him," she stabbed her finger his way.

"Oh no you don't!" John leaped for her. Carlo was quicker. He took hold of his shoulder and shoved him back down onto the couch. That didn't put an end to his tirade. "You were going to set me up! All you did was use me to learn more about your father's business. I should have known better. A pathetic spoiled brat like you wanting to know the details of shipping and customs and filings? Your father was just as dumb as I was, believing you were finally starting to show an interest in the company."

"Shut up! Shut up!" Amethyst cried. "If you'd just kept your dumb mouth shut, they wouldn't have known anything. I wasn't setting you up to take the fall. *You're* the one who wanted to come Friday! Now Oliver is going to kill me just like he did that man. You have no idea how dangerous he is."

"Killed who?"

That was a new voice, coming from the doorway. Everyone turned to see Detective Prescott entering. He stared at everyone in the room, looking just as surprised at the faces he saw as they were to see him.

Penelope momentarily dismissed what Amethyst had said in favor of his appearance.

"What are you doing back so soon, Richard?"

"I could ask the same of more than a few people here. I came back because I couldn't find Christos, who seems to have disappeared. I wanted to question Amethyst again." His eyes landed on Katie. "I assume this is Katie Sweeney?"

"We found Tino and her only a while ago."

"What's going on, Amethyst?" Katie asked, turning her attention to Amethyst. "Who is Oliver? Why is he going to kill you? Who did he kill?"

"That's what I'd like to know as well," Richard said.

"I can't! You have no idea what he's capable of. The people he's associated with. They make Katie's father seem like a group of nuns. But he's bad enough all on his own."

"You said he killed someone?" Pen urged.

"That customs agent, Connor Davidson."

That sent a shock through the room.

"Tell me everything," Richard said. "It's the only way I can provide protection."

Amethyst held firm for a moment, then seemed to unravel.

"I met him when John brought him to one of my parties. I didn't think much of him, except he was the one who had brought," a guilty look came to her face before she continued, "the muggle."

She quickly moved on. "But then Daddy cut me off, and I'd run out of my mother's money. He approached me with the idea that there was a way I could make my own money, a lot of it. He just wanted information about the shipments Daddy brings in, the ones that carry the old stuff he sends to museums. I guess there are people in the world who pay a lot of money for some of those things. The thing is, a lot of countries are starting to get possessive about it, so a good portion has to be under the table or outright stolen, you see? That's where Oliver and his...friends, come in."

"Who are these friends?"

"He wouldn't tell me, and I didn't want to know. I didn't think much of his role in everything...until Sunday."

"What happened Sunday?" Pen asked, her gentle voice a better prompt than Richard's more authoritative version.

"Oliver was livid when he heard about the egg going missing. It was one of the most priceless things he and his people had managed to get their hands on. All he knew was that Mr. Sweeney had it, someone that would be difficult to, um, recapture it from. What he really wanted to know was who had originally stolen it."

"That's why you started being so nice to me at dance class!" Katie accused, a hurt expression coming to her face.

"It was easy enough," Amethyst said with a shrug. "You were so desperate to make it to Hollywood. All I had to do was dangle a producer in front of you and you couldn't come to my party fast enough. I made sure John wasn't at that party, which meant Oliver didn't come either. Then I dropped hints about having connections to international black market exports, people who'd pay a nice penny for something priceless."

"You had no intention of selling it, did you?"

"You should talk, you stole it!"

"So did you, or at least this Oliver did!"

"Ladies!" Richard said. He nodded at Amethyst to continue.

With one final frown at Katie, she did. "Unfortunately, Katie was so tight-lipped about everything! She wouldn't say a word about where it had originally come from. I almost let it slip that I knew she had stolen it from her father, if only to get her to reveal what she knew. Oliver was getting angrier and angrier.

"Thankfully, he learned from some source in the federal government that they were looking at Connor Davidson, who was the customs agent Oliver's people worked with. He'd been found out because of some chase they had done of a huge shipment of liquor. One of the small boats carrying artifacts from the warehouses had been discovered."

Pen avoided looking at Mr. Messina, who she was certain was scowling about that, knowing it was his liquor that had been nabbed.

"Connor was going to cooperate with the authorities. So, Sunday, Oliver took care of him, but first, he wanted to find out how much he had already told the feds."

There was a somber silence on the heels of that confession.

"There you have it. It was all her and Oliver, I had nothing to do with anything," John said in a sullen voice. "He's probably already gotten to Christos, which is why you can't find him."

"He was the one you really planned to set up, wasn't he?" Penelope asked Amethyst.

Amethyst's mouth fell open, and she had the tact to blush with self-reproach. "He was a nobody, is all. Oliver said he would make an easy target. John was too close a connection. Besides, Christos was already involved in that speakeasy business."

"Ha!" John spat, giving her a look of disdain.

"But, he's somewhere safe," Amethyst quickly added. "The invitation I had John deliver to him told him he needed to get away or hide for a while; that things might be dangerous for him. That was a good thing, no? The police will take that into account, won't they? That I saved him?"

"And you couldn't do the same with me?"

"He wasn't going to do anything to you, silly," Amethyst said with a sneer. "As I said, you're too close to him."

Something about that struck Penelope, but Richard continued to interrogate her before she could put her finger on it.

"What was the point of throwing a party? Did that have something to do with all of this?"

"Anastasia was supposed to bring the egg after getting it from Katie and Tino. It was my idea for a party. I thought if there were a lot of people there, Oliver couldn't do anything to me. He still doesn't know the jig is up, and I'm certainly not going to tell him!"

"Then who killed her last night?" Katie asked.

"I thought you and Tino had, considering who your fathers are," Amethyst said. "I figured you had discovered that Oliver didn't plan on paying you, so you—"

"We're not murderers!" Katie exclaimed. "You're the one involved with a crook."

They were set to go at it again, two reckless, silly girls who had gotten in over their heads, squabbling like—

"Freckles."

That shut everyone up, and had them turning to her.

"What is it, Penelope," Richard said, knowing that she was on the cusp of something.

Instead of answering, she turned to Katie. "How much did you tell Moira?"

"What?"

"Moira, your friend. How much did you tell her about your plan."

Katie lifted her chin, ready to deny everything. "I didn't tell her about the Fabergé Egg, I'm not stupid. But..."

"Go on," Richard urged when the pause ran long.

"I may have hinted that I had big plans for something, a way to make some money."

"And you brought her Friday to rub it in, keep her wondering what it was you were up to. All because you were jealous?"

"I wasn't jealous!" Katie snapped, the resentment on her face belying that statement. "I'm a better actress, everyone says so. Who cares if she's prettier? That producer only wanted one thing, and she didn't even see it."

"Where are you going with this, Penelope?" Richard asked, just as confounded as everyone else.

"You think Moira killed her?" Katie asked. "But...how? She didn't know anything."

"She knew enough," Penelope said, turning her attention to another person in the room. "And she knew the right person to fill in the blanks for her."

Everyone's eyes followed where hers landed...on John Foster.

"Me? I didn't even know her! We'd never even met before."

"How did you know about her freckles? They're only noticeable if you're right next to her."

"I...I must have walked past her close enough to notice."

"No, you didn't!" Amethyst said.

"He didn't! He didn't!" Katie added.

That's when John foolishly tried to run, which only cemented his guilt. Mr. Messina wasn't quick enough to stop him. Richard was on the other side of the loft, near Amethyst. Tommy was by Lulu, too far from the door.

Fortunately, their newest arrival had just reached the

threshold. John ran right smack into Agent Kent Simpson, both of them falling to the floor in a jumbled, surprised pile of arms and legs.

Tommy and Richard rushed over to pull John up and hold onto him, dragging him back into the loft. A rather embarrassed Agent Simpson pulled himself up, dusted himself off, and strutted inside.

"Anyone care to tell me what the heck is going on?"

"John here was just about to explain how he and Moira Mahoney committed murder."

"No! She had nothing to do with it. You leave her alone." He looked morose. "She just wanted to go to Hollywood is all."

Pen caught Richard's eye, and he looked just as incredulous as she felt.

"*Moira?* You killed Anastasia because of Moira?" Amethyst protested, looking perfectly offended.

"She's worth ten of you!"

"Why don't you explain everything?" Pen said, using the voice she knew encouraged people to speak.

John seemed lost in his own head, staring down at the ground as though no one else was there.

"Or we'll have to arrest her right now," Richard said, using the voice *he* knew got people to speak.

John's head popped up. "Like I said, she just wanted to go to Hollywood. That producer had all but said she could be a star."

"Ha!" Katie scoffed. A censuring look from Lulu had her backing down with a sheepish expression.

"Moira knew Katie was up to something. She kept hinting at things, but wouldn't say what. Moira decided to go around her, straight to Amethyst, who actually knew the producer. She figured Amethyst could put in a good word for her, maybe even pay for her move to Hollywood. She secretly followed her around to learn more about her, that's how I first met her. She approached me after I'd gone out with Amethyst one night.

"When Amethyst first met with Anastasia to hire her, Moira didn't understand why. She dismissed it...until Friday at the speakeasy. That's why I insisted on going with Amethyst that night. Moira had told me Katie was going and Amethyst would be there.

"When I told her what the two of them discussed, she figured it out right away. Anna and Stacy? Obviously, it was code for Anastasia, and she put it together with Amethyst meeting her. We went to meet with her and ask what it was about. All she told us was that she'd been paid $200 to pick up something and deliver it. She didn't know what it was.

"We knew that had to be it, the big thing that Katie wouldn't stop talking about. Only when we got there last night she tried giving us the brush off, said no one had shown up. That's when...the gun came out. We just wanted to make sure she wasn't hiding anything. We ordered her to take the coat off. We checked the pockets, not even sure what we were looking for. That's when she tried to make a run for it. We caught up to her and...the gun went off." He shrugged, looking despondent. His eyes widened as he stared at Penelope, then Richard. "But it was me! I had the gun. Don't arrest Moira. She had nothing to do with this. I'll testify to it!"

"John, this is serious. It's a life sentence," Penelope said, amazed that after everything, he would still protect Moira. It couldn't have just been her beauty, which was substantial. No, she had beguiled the poor boy.

She was a better actress than Katie gave her credit for.

"I don't care, if it means she gets to Hollywood then it's worth it."

There would be no Hollywood for Moira Mahoney. At best, she was an accomplice. At worst, John's attorney would persuade him to give up taking the fall for her. Either way, Penelope had solved both cases she'd originally been hired for.

And all before Friday.

Agent Simpson put his hands up, trying to settle the room, which was already quite settled. "Alright, no one is leaving. I need a detailed report about what just happened. I leave to get the address to this place, only to get the runaround by that damn newspaper. As though the law means nothing to them. They lawyered up quick and dirty. I had to wait for them to finally go to press before I got the address."

Katherine, who had been deceptively quiet during all of this, laughed.

Agent Simpson glared at her, then gave the same look to Richard. "I do you the favor of going back to the office to try and find you, Richard, only to find your little helper," he glowered at Penelope, "is there by herself, on the phone making sweet talk to some man named Alfie. Then I hear you've all decided to go off on your own? I repeat, what in the darned hell is going on?"

Penelope was the one to answer him. "Well, I suppose, as with most things in life, it began with an egg."

EPILOGUE

"THE FABERGE EGG IS GONE!"

It was late morning on Friday and Richard had just entered Penelope's office. Jane, Lulu, Kitty (Katherine had insisted she was off-duty so her favored pet name could be used), and she were...not exactly celebrating. More like commiserating. The only one truly satisfied with how things in her most recent case had turned out was Kitty. She'd had front-row seats to the scoop of the year, decade perhaps. Even she felt a little terrible about so much youth wasted.

Of course, the particular youth at issue mostly came from money, enough to obtain the best legal defense that money could buy. Still, none of their legal and police department connections could save any of them from arrest, not for such a high-profile case. Which was all they deserved.

It seemed that for all his vices, New York's newest mayor, Mickey Driver was incorruptible when it came to more serious crimes. He had been quite vocal about making sure justice was served, earning him quite a bit of favor from the common folk that had gotten him elected.

Moira had been arrested as an accomplice to murder. A gun that several witnesses could attest her father owned was nowhere to be found. The make and model matched what Anastasia had been shot with. Thus far, John had yet to name her as the one who had pulled the trigger. Who knew what would happen by the time they went to trial, but both faced some serious time in prison.

Katie and Tino had been arrested as coconspirators to theft and possession of stolen goods. So far, neither of them had ratted on their fathers, which probably made both dads quite proud. The public at large was less thrilled. If they served any time at all, it wouldn't be much.

Amethyst had been similarly arrested, though she had been all too happy to tattle on her coconspirator for a plea deal. Her father had gone on public record stating that he would provide legal defense "as any American deserved according to the Constitution," but he otherwise had washed his hands of her. She had already begun using her fame (now, infamy) to her advantage, becoming even more of a celebrity. It wouldn't make her rich, but it would make her popular, for a while at least. The *New York Tattle* had already labeled her the "Felonious Flapper."

Christos, at the insistence of his father, had agreed to testify to what little he knew. After all, he'd been set up as the fall guy. The speakeasy below the barbershop had mysteriously disappeared overnight, conveniently enough. As was often the case with young, attractive people involved in a bit of scandal, he'd become a minor celebrity in his own right. Once his photo hit the tattle pages, the girls of New York couldn't get enough of that bona fide sheik.

Oliver was in federal custody, facing the heaviest charges, and rightfully so. His "partners" had turned out to be a criminal sect that had come from the Black Hand Camorra, notorious for operating out of New Orleans.

But all four women forgot about the excitement of the earlier part of the week at the announcement of Richard's news.

He was momentarily taken aback by the four of them in her office, but he recovered quickly. More so when they all reacted at once.

"Oh no!" Jane cried.

"I coulda seen that coming a mile away," Lulu said, pursing her lips.

"Who was it? The Agent? Was he dirty? I knew something was wrong about that one."

"What happened, Richard?" Pen asked, giving Kitty a look of admonishment.

"Three agents, including Simpson, were in charge of transporting it to D.C. It was taken down via automobile, top secret. Even I didn't know where and when they'd leave or by what route. But someone did. Four masked men and... now it's gone. Thankfully, Agent Simpson and the others were unscathed, though I think his career might suffer a dent."

"Zounds," Penelope said, shaking her head in wonder.

"On top of that, my captain isn't pleased about being kept out of the loop. I've been placed on administrative leave."

"What? That's hardly fair!" Pen was outraged.

Richard tilted his head conceding a bit. "Technically, I should have informed him, but I erred on the side of precaution. Too many of both Sweeney's and, frankly, Mr. Easton's men on the force. He understands, but...rules are rules."

"If it makes you feel better, I've been placed on my own

version of administrative leave from the Peacock Club," Lulu said.

"What?" Pen swiveled her attention to her. "Why?"

Lulu just gave her a look as though she should know. "Mr. Sweeney's not happy. He really wanted that egg. Tommy's getting it worse."

"Well, he can forget about me going back until you're brought back." Lulu smiled in appreciation, but there was a subtle suggestion in her gaze that told Pen she would no longer receive VIP status should she try to patronize her old haunt. She frowned. "And after I found his daughter, which is exactly what he hired me to do!"

"Maybe my wedding will cheer you up. April is such a nice time of year. The tulips will be in bloom here in New York."

"Yes! Your wedding!" It did cheer Penelope up. "That will be a nice distraction. Frankly, I'm tempted to take my own honeymoon away from this city and all its murder cases."

"Here, here!" Lulu said with a laugh.

"Oh, that would be nice, all of us going to Paris," Jane said with honest enthusiasm.

"Don't be silly, Jane. Of course we aren't going to intrude on your honeymoon. I don't think Alfie would be quite as excited at the prospect."

Still, it was something to consider. Pen hadn't been back to Europe since her father had cut her off over three years earlier. Now that she was flush with kale again, more than enough to treat her closest friends, it was something to consider.

Richard caught her eye and a wry look of amusement came to his face, as though he could read her mind.

Before it could be discussed further, there was a knock at the door.

"If it's another case, I absolutely refuse! I don't care how minor it is," Pen said as Jane jumped up to answer it. "The same if it's any reporters," she called after her. They had been relentless the past day or so, even calling or stopping by Penelope's apartment for a statement.

Jane came back in with a case, but it wasn't that of the mystery-solving type. Instead, she was followed by a young man rolling in a square, wood case. He picked it up, grunting with the effort, and placed it on Penelope's desk. She signed for it, staring at the box with curiosity.

Before he could leave, she begged a lever to open the lid, offering a generous tip. When he left, everyone in the office crowded around the box as she fully removed the lid and dug through the straw that covered the top.

They all gasped at what lay beneath: twelve bottles of red wine. Pen grabbed one by the neck and pulled it out. She wasn't surprised to see the D'amico Vineyards label on the side.

"From Mr. Messina," Pen muttered aloud.

"I'll pretend I haven't seen this," Richard said. Still, he arched a brow. "Though I wouldn't mind sharing a glass over a private dinner at some point."

Pen laughed.

"The least he could do was send me some. I was the one kidnapped," Lulu groused.

"How about the usual ten percent? Though in this case, you probably deserve more."

Lulu laughed and slapped her on the shoulder. "I'm teasing, though I wouldn't mind one of those."

Pen pulled two out and handed them to her.

"What about my efforts?" Kitty protested.

"Oh, fine," Pen said, offering her one. She pulled one for Jane as well. "I know you aren't a big drinker, but every newlywed couple deserves to enjoy a fine meal with real wine. I suspect your new husband will appreciate it, especially after you come back from Paris where it flows so freely."

She flashed a smile to Richard. "You can always come to my apartment if you want a taste."

The women all crooned teasingly at that. Richard couldn't deny a begrudging smile.

"Why do you think it was sent to you?" Jane finally asked.

"I assume it's an apology for his interference."

"Or a thank you for finding his son?" Kitty suggested.

"Perhaps for something else," Richard said, suddenly alert.

He and Penelope stared at one another, the same disturbing thought coming to both of them.

Was Carlo Messina presently in possession of a stolen Fabergé Egg? They knew they would probably never know.

AUTHOR'S NOTE

FABERGÉ EGG

I've always been fascinated by the Fabergé Egg collection and the Romanov family. When I started this series, I fully intended to incorporate them into one of my stories.

It isn't difficult to believe that in the chaos following the Russian Revolution and the assassination of the Romanov family, some of the wealth would find its way into the clutches of a few profiteers.

The Fabergé Eggs and most of the imperial wealth were taken to the Kremlin Armory when the Bolsheviks took over Russia. However, the egg mentioned in this story, the Third Imperial Fabergé Easter Egg, was one of a handful that were in fact lost in the fray, perhaps due to its small size. It made a brief reappearance in 1964 by Parke-Bernet in New York, in the catalogue for their auction of the 7th March 1964. Without provenance, it sold for $2,450.

The most fascinating (re)discovery of it was in 2004 when a man bought the egg at a jumble sale in the American midwest and failed at his attempts to sell it for scrap metal. Years later, in desperation, he tried to discover if it had any value and...well you know the rest of the story.

MUGGLE

Yes, this was indeed a slang term for wacky tobacky in the 1920s, mostly down in New Orleans. Sometimes I include these things in my books just because I find them fascinating. Thank you for indulging me. But yes, the 1920s did seem to be a decade rife with banning various substances that might leave one under the influence. Along with alcohol, cocaine, marijuana, and absinthe were among the substances that had finally received their official seal of disapproval from the government.

SHEIK AND SHEBA

I was absolutely tickled to learn this bit of slang for hotties in the 1920s. I definitely think it should make a comeback. Far preferable to the current nomenclature for teenage crushes. But I suppose I'm just an old fart in that respect.

THE NAME STACY (STACEY, STACIE)

Speaking of labels, I did a bit of research on this name and was surprised at the results. I figured it was a rather modern name, but prior to the mid-1950s the name was positively nonexistent in the United States, and even then it was mostly given to boys!

GET YOUR FREE BOOK!

Mischief at the Peacock Club

A bold theft at the infamous Peacock Club.
Can Penelope solve it to save her own neck?

1924 New York
Penelope "Pen" Banks has spent the past two years making
ends meet by playing cards. It's another Saturday night at
the Peacock Club, one of her favorite haunts, and she has

her sights set on a big fish, who just happens to be the special guest of the infamous Jack Sweeney.

After inducing Rupert Cartland, into a game of cards, Pen thinks it just might be her lucky night. Unfortunately, before the night ends, Rupert has been robbed—his diamond cuff links, ruby pinky ring, gold watch, and wallet...all gone!

With the Peacock Club's reputation on the line, Mr. Sweeney, aided by the heavy hand of his chief underling Tommy Callahan, is holding everyone captive until the culprit is found.

For the promise of a nice payoff, not to mention escaping the club in one piece, Penelope Banks is willing to put her unique mind to work to find out just who stole the goods.

This is a prequel novella to the *Penelope Banks Murder Mysteries* series, taking place at The Peacock Club before Penelope Banks became a private investigator.

Access your book at the link below:
https://dl.bookfunnel.com/4sv9fir4h3

ALSO BY COLETTE CLARK

ABOUT THE AUTHOR

Colette Clark lives in New York and has always enjoyed learning more about the history of her amazing city. She decided to combine that curiosity and love of learning with her addiction to reading and watching mysteries. Her first series, **Penelope Banks Murder Mysteries** is the result of those passions. When she's not writing she can be found doing Sudoku puzzles, drawing, eating tacos, visiting museums dedicated to unusual/weird/wacky things, and, of course, reading mysteries by other great authors.

Join my Newsletter to receive news about New Releases and Sales!
https://dashboard.mailerlite.com/forms/148684/726783564877673 18/share

Printed in Great Britain
by Amazon